ROSAMUNDE BOTT

Out of Time

Third edition

This book was professionally typeset on Reedsy.
Find out more at reedsy.com

To Clara, for always being there

PROLOGUE

May 1833

The heady scent of May blossom filled the air, but William Days barely noticed. He looked down at the man lying still at his feet. His neck was broken; that much was obvious.

William stood for a while, the significance of what he had done filtering through his befuddled brain. He was a murderer. He could be hanged for what he had done, no matter what.

The man's horse seemed unconcerned, and was now calmly nibbling on the fresh grass and clover that was growing fast in the spring sun.

William looked around him, towards the big house where his gaze lingered for a few moments, and back towards the village from whence he had stumbled only a few minutes ago, yet a lifetime ago. No-one else was near. He looked back down at the man.

Without any further thought he turned and walked away through the fields, away from the house and the village, and away from the life he had once known.

Chapter 1

October 2010

I first met Will Days when he came freewheeling down the church footpath on a bicycle, got tangled up in my dog's lead, and ended up in a heap of metal in front of me while Charlie (a Jack Russell and Westie cross), ran round him in hysterical circles.

It was partly my fault. I had not been paying attention as I had been staring dreamily at the old manor house by the church and not looking at what was happening in front of me. Charlie had leapt forward to scare off an unsuspecting blackbird just at the moment that Will came hurtling out of the gate.

'Fuck!' he said, as he got himself into a sitting position.

The first thing I noticed as I crouched down beside him was that he had a guitar strapped to his back.

Charlie, now over his initial shock, crept up slowly to sniff at the man's hair, which was thick, long and dark brown.

'Bloody Hell!' he said, as Charlie tried to lick his chin.

'I'm so sorry,' I said, pulling Charlie away, 'Are you OK? I – I just didn't see you coming. Are you all right?'

'Jesus!' he said, looking at his bike, which was a crumpled mess of metal, its front wheel upright and still spinning.

'Can I help you at all?'

He managed to disentangle himself from his bicycle and looked up me for the first time.

It was then that a look of utter amazement came over his face, and at the same time I had a sense of total recognition, although I had never seen him before in my life. His pale blue eyes had an intensity that almost knocked me backwards.

'Grace...' he said.

I was not sure whether this was another exclamation, a statement or a question, or whether he was now talking gibberish due to concussion. The word did not seem to belong to the so far rather stilted conversation, and had no meaning to me, as far as I could tell.

'Um... you've grazed your face,' I remarked. His hand went to touch his cheek, and as he did so, he frowned and looked at me again. He appeared to be looking at my clothes, jeans, sweat-shirt and trainers, with some surprise. He then looked around him at his bicycle, at Charlie, and at the cars parked on the street.

He ran both hands through his hair and then rubbed his hair vigorously the way some men do just after getting out of bed.

'Is your guitar all right?' I asked.

He looked at me again, this time he looked at little less dazed, and then stood up, lifting the guitar strap over his head. He looked over the woodwork; his hands – which I noticed were long and sensitive – running over the surface for scratches, while his eyes totally focused on the instrument, like a lover's eyes for his mistress. He was wearing faded jeans, a maroon cotton shirt and over that a waistcoat with a tapestry of dark flowers on the front. He looked as though he should be on stage at some folk festival.

Having satisfied himself that his guitar was unharmed, his eyes returned to me.

'It's fine,' he said, smiling for the first time and strumming each string in turn.

I looked down at the bicycle.

'Do you think your bike will be OK?'

Still looking at me in a slightly curious way that was making me feel self conscious, and wishing that I had spent more time on my hair that morning, he returned the guitar back over his shoulder and then bent to lift up the bike.

'The chain's gone,' he said.

'I'm really sorry. It's all my fault,' I said, 'If only I could stop Charlie chasing birds. He's a rescue dog, you see, and... Look, I only live around the corner. Why don't you come back with me? I'll have a look at that graze, and you can see to your bike in the front garden. I'll make some tea as well.'

He looked at me with those intense eyes, and the corners of his mouth lifted slightly. I could have sworn his eyes flicked away and behind me towards the manor house behind us, as if he thought for a moment that it was where I lived. But it could have been my imagination.

'All right. Thanks,' he said.

The manor house was certainly not where I lived – though it was probably what I would call my dream house – and it had been that house that had first attracted me to the village about five months ago. In fact, it wasn't just that it was a lovely olde worlde setting, with its old ivy clad walls and wobbly 17th century roof; the sight of it had actually made the hairs stand up on the back of my neck.

But the house I had bought on a total whim was something

far more modest, and this was where I now led the cyclist.

We walked back past the church, the manor house, the village green and its duck pond without speaking. It was a quiet, still day, with bursts of sunlight that still had warmth in it, though the air was autumnally cool. The trees were shedding their leaves, and as we passed the great, ancient chestnut tree on the green, he bent down to pick up a smooth, glossy brown conker which had fallen out of its case.

He grinned at me and said, 'Takes me back...'

'I know,' I said, 'me too.'

I resisted the urge to make any further small talk, and the silence between us had none of the awkwardness that it might usually have done in a situation like this. And he seemed to be a man of few words anyway – not the kind of person to make small talk with.

When we turned into Mill Lane, I felt him turn to look at me, and he seemed to hesitate, and walked slowly behind me pushing his bicycle. As I approached my own front gate and reached out to push it open, he stopped completely. When I turned back, he was staring at me with eyes that seemed to have strayed from bemusement to bewilderment.

'You live here?' he asked.

'Yes,' I answered, ignoring the now familiar tingling sensation as I touched the iron gate, 'it's my house. I own it.' Although it was a modest little cottage, I could not help looking up at it with pride as I said this, and a spark of happiness went through me.

'You own it,' he said in a way that was somewhere between a statement and a question.

'Yes. Come on in.'

We stepped through into the front garden and he wheeled his bike to the front to lean it against the wall. Then he looked around him, his eyes exploring the garden, the small cherry tree, the front of the house, the windows and the front door.

'How long have you lived here?' he asked.

'Just two months. I moved up here from London.' I paused. 'It's a long story.'

'Sure.'

We entered the house, and I suddenly saw it with new eyes, as if I was seeing it again for the first time, the way that you do when you first invite someone round. The first time I had seen it it had been empty, when the estate agent had shown me around on that dreary, wet and weird day back in May, and I had seen my new life with all the clarity and confidence that I had struggled to remember until now. Looking at it today, it seemed more homely, with my few bits of furniture and my lovely old red and gold rug on the floor.

The front door opened onto the front room. On the left was a large open fireplace with stone surrounds and a wooden beam across the top. A door opposite the front entrance led into a short hallway with stairs rising up to the left, and forwards into the kitchen.

The stone flags in the kitchen revealed the cottage's age, and as we entered the kitchen the house seemed to sigh and settle around us.

I looked at the stranger and noticed that slightly bewildered look again as he looked around. There was definitely something odd about his behaviour and the way he kept looking at me and this house. He walked across the room to the sink and stood there for a while looking out at the secluded and rather wild garden at the back. Then he turned and looked at me, a strange smile on his face.

'This is really your house?' he asked.

Perhaps he was slightly concussed from the fall – or perhaps he wasn't quite the full ticket. For a moment I wondered whether I was completely insane to invite a complete stranger into my house. It was certainly something I would never have done in London. But I somehow could not believe he was going to turn out to be an axe murderer. However, it would be best to humour him.

'Yes, it really is my house.'

To be honest, I still felt a sense of surprise when I said it, and I still wondered after all this time whether it had been the right decision. I had been a city girl for twelve years, but in one momentous decision I had left the city, left my job, my tiny flat, my boyfriend Jake and thrown everything up in the air to live a life of solitude in the country and to try and write my first novel. Sometimes I felt I had been a bit silly.

He was staring at the flagstone floor.

'Lovely, isn't it?' I said, rubbing the toe of my trainers along its dark, smooth and uneven surface, 'one of the original features...'

'That wall's new,' he said, looking at the wall dividing the kitchen and the small utility room that housed my washing machine and pantry.

'Well... I don't know. It's certainly not original...'

'No. It would have been all one room once.'

I invited him to sit down at the table, while Charlie, excited at having a visitor, brought him a squeaky banana, and then teased him by running away with it when he tried to take it. I put the kettle on and found some cotton wool and TCP to attend to his face.

'Are you interested in old houses?' I asked.

'I...suppose you could say that. I lived... I lived in one for a long time. Ow! That stings!'

'Sorry.'

'No... it's OK.'

Then he said, almost to himself:

'It's like being a child again.'

I made the tea, opened a packet of digestives, and sat down at the table with him.

'Do you take sugar... um... sorry, I didn't ask your name.'

'Will. Will Days.'

'Will. OK, do you take sugar?'

'No. What about you?'

'I don't take sugar either. Oh – I see what you mean. I'm Catherine.'

'Catherine...'

'Burns. Like the poet. Only, not Scottish. So, do you live round here, Will? I haven't seen you around before.'

'No... I... come here every so often. I... had relatives here, and I like to...'

'...visit?'

'...their graves. Yes. That's why I was at the church.'

'Oh. Oh, I see. I am sorry. You must have been very close if you come here so often...'

'Yes. You could say that.'

There was an awkward pause, and I wasn't sure what to say next. Thankfully, he changed the subject.

'Catherine, do you mind me asking why you moved here – I mean to this house in particular?'

He seemed to have some kind of fascination with my house, and if the question hadn't hit me like a cold slap in the face I would probably have asked him why he was so interested, but his question was exactly the same question I had been asking myself ever since I moved in and I just stopped and stared at him instead. Could he read my mind and sense my doubts?

I suppose when you meet anyone for the first time, there comes a point where you decide whether to trust that person or not. Usually it takes a bit longer than the twenty minutes or so I had known Will, but in this case I knew that moment had come. With anyone else I would probably have trotted out some half truth about needing a break from the city and a change of career, and needing some peace and quiet to write my book. I would have said that I wanted some lovely little 18th century cottage in a rural setting that would give me inspiration and allow them to think that I could actually afford it. But when I looked at Will I decided just to tell him the simple truth.

'You know, Will, I have absolutely no idea why I bought this house.'

He said nothing, and looked neither surprised nor judgmental, but continued to look at me steadily.

'I love it, though. I really do. It's just that, I'd been looking for something else; something more affordable. Really, I should be living in an ex-council house on the outskirts of a town, but...'

I stopped, wondering how far I should go.

'Go on,' he said, quietly.

So I did.

Chapter 2

My life in London had become empty. I disliked my job, and I hated the daily commute to it even more. Some days just the thought of yet another morning squashed intimately against complete strangers in an invasion of space that you would normally go out of your way to avoid, listening to the overspill from their MP3 players, staring at the blank, pale faces and breathing in halitosis and stale clothing was almost too much to bear.

And at the end of the commute, when I was ejected like a cork out through the electric doors onto another crowded station, all I had to look forward to was teaching English to bored teenagers, who resented the necessity to conjugate verbs on a Friday afternoon, and whose main understanding of punctuation was how to use it to make smileys on their mobile phone texts. Their main topic of conversation who should win the X Factor. They were rude, spoke back in insolent and frankly, sometimes threatening, ways and there was very little one could do, given the state of discipline in the present day educational system.

Every night I arrived home feeling like I had spent the entire day trying to teach English to a ferocious and stubborn pit bull terrier. Every night I poured myself a red wine, thought about writing my novel, and then would decide I was too exhausted and end up with my feet up in front of the television and a glass at my elbow. I ate badly because I had no energy to cook properly.

I lived in a small but adequate flat on the High Street of Balham, just above a charity shop.

My boyfriend, Jake, was a David Bowie look-a-like and on some Saturday nights he put on a very creditable tribute act in pubs in the area around Clapham and Lavender Hill. We had met at some smoke-filled, slightly sordid, party and he had taken an interest in me initially because I had the same surname as Bowie's mother, like it was some kind of sign we should be together. I was attracted to him because he did actually look a bit like David Bowie and could sing pretty well. I know they're not great reasons for any two people to get together, but we kind of grew into each other, or perhaps we just became a habit. He had some wacky friends, and we went to some wild parties, smoked illegal substances and drank too much. It was an escape from the dreariness of the rest of the week, and we had a lot of fun, but inside I knew that I was just treading water, going nowhere. On the inside I knew I was a writer, but on the outside, I was just another work-tied commuter, stumbling from day to day as best as I could, trying to ignore the deep inner gnawing of dissatisfaction. As for Jake, he worked as an accountant for a company in Lambeth who sold chair lifts, and he seemed content to keep things the way they were, working by day, and breaking out only at the weekend – or so I was to find out.

As so often in life, it took a bit of a thunderbolt to make me sit up and take notice. I had a small win on the lottery, which brought me in around £25,000. Normally it takes the jackpot wins to really change people's lives, but in this case this modest but not insignificant windfall was going to change mine for good.

But it was Jake's reaction to my win which really started me thinking.

We were both overjoyed, of course, and we celebrated with champagne and an expensive meal in a top class restaurant in Covent Garden, and it was then that things began to go wrong.

'So what are we going to do with it? We could go on a Caribbean cruise. You could get a new car and buy me a new guitar...'

It was in that moment that I saw what an opportunity had just fallen into my lap, and if I wasn't careful, it would just disappear in a big spending spree, leaving me back in the same old routine. I couldn't let that happen. This had to be a way of breaking that routine, of starting something new. I sat there, picking at my pan-fried sea bass, doing sums and making plans in my head while Jake went on chewing steak while he lectured on the best makes of cars for driving in the city. A Mazda perhaps, or a top of the range Peugeot..

After a while I interrupted him.

'I don't want to live in the city,' I said.

He stared at me as if I had just spoken in Chinese, his fork in mid-air.

'Eh?'

'I don't want to live in London any more. I want to live in the country, and I want to write.' I continued to eat my fish.

'What are you talking about?'

I swallowed, and put my knife and fork down on my plate.

'Jake – you know what I'm talking about. How many times have I said to you that I want to write? Well, it's just not going to happen while I'm working full time in a job I hate and spending two hours of every day commuting.'

'Yeah – but, what's this got to do with the money?' He waved his fork in the air as I watched, hoping that the piece of fillet steak was not going to fly off and land in someone's lap, 'twenty five grand isn't going to buy you a country cottage.'

'No. But with my current salary I could buy something modest, and the money will let me live for a year while I write my book. I could give up my job and...'

'That's crazy! That's completely unrealistic!' He put his fork down with a clatter. 'Come on, Cath, you're living in dream land. Have you noticed in the middle of the worst recession for decades? You can't just give up a perfectly good job for some stupid romantic idea of living in some rural fantasy land and becoming some kind of Barbara Cartland!'

It was in that moment that I realised I had never really known Jake at all.

'I have no wish to become Barbara Cartland,' I said. I was vaguely aware that other diners were turning their heads and I was speaking too loudly, but I didn't care. 'I want to be me! And if you don't understand that, then you don't understand me at all!'

'And where would I fit into all this?'

'Nothing has to change, Jake,' (although I was beginning to see that it would have to), 'we only see each other at weekends anyway. We could still do that. You could come to see me, and I could come to see you...'

'Babe – you're not thinking straight. You know I've got commitments here at the weekends. And what happens when the money runs out and you find that you're not a best-selling novelist?'

'Then I will have to get a job. I can teach again. The kids will be nicer in the country.'

There was a long and uncomfortable silence. We both picked up our knives and forks and continued eating, but I could no longer taste the food. Jake finished his plate and took a large swig of Pinot Noir.

'It's a ridiculous idea.'

And that was the beginning of a long, drawn out, painful argument where both of us came to the brutal realisation that we did not know each other at all. The main thrust of his argument seemed to be that I was being completely selfish and living in cloud cuckoo land (or something really unoriginal like that) and the main point of my argument was that he was a boring old fart (which was also unoriginal but entirely accurate). He said that he'd always thought I was intelligent and sensible, and I said I'd always thought he had guts, imagination and passion, and obviously I was wrong. Then he became soft and gentle, and oh so understanding, and tried to persuade me to stay, saying if I wanted a place of my own why didn't I buy a little flat in town. That was when I lost my temper because he really obviously had no idea what it was I really wanted, and I found myself shouting in this very posh restaurant with people staring at us and the waiters beginning to look uncomfortable.

'How will that change anything? I'll still be in a job I hate and I'll be paying a huge mortgage that I can't afford for some poky little flat and everything will just be the same!'

There was a long silence. Other diners went back to focusing on their food.

Then he said, 'Now I know you're an idiot. Well, if it's change you want, then you can have it.'

And he got up and left.

Right there in the restaurant, leaving me with the bill to pay and no dessert.

Bastard.

So on a wet, cold, grey day in May I had driven out to an area of the Midlands, not too far from the Cotswolds, but not too near to be over expensive, and had spent the day viewing houses that I had seen on the internet.

It was one of those days where you feel cheated of the promise of spring, and thrown mercilessly back into winter. I was tired, in a foul mood, and my cagoule was allowing rainwater to drip down my spine. House-hunting was no fun on days like this, especially when all the houses you've seen are just wrong.

Some fool on the radio was playing 'Beautiful Day' by U2, rather cynically, I thought, because it certainly wasn't. It was a song I usually liked to hear, but on this day it just made me feel even grumpier.

This was probably not the DJ's fault, nor even the rain's, but partly due to the fact that I was beginning to think that Jake had been right. I had already handed my notice in at work, and now wondered whether I had made the worst decision of my lifetime. It was crazy to give up a secure job in the current financial climate to follow some pipe dream. I must be out of my mind. Wasn't it better to suffer a job you hate than to step into an unforeseeable future without guarantee of success? What the hell was I thinking?

But I knew that I'd had to make a change, it's just that now the change seemed harder than I had thought. I was stuck half way between a life I no longer wanted, and a life I needed but couldn't afford and I while I didn't want to take a step backwards, I couldn't see where to take the next step forward. It was making me cranky.

But as I had come round that bend into the village, the clouds had broken and a shaft of sunlight hit Little Dipping church spire, and I then saw the village green, its wet grass glistening in the new ray of sun and the chestnut tree coming into bud, the duck pond shaded by willows, and behind it, the manor house, sitting smugly in its rightful place by the church. It was that house that made my skin tingle with an emotion that I could not fathom.

It was a typical kind of village manor house, tucked in snugly beside the old vicarage and conjuring up images of BBC costume dramas and Jane Austen novels. Half-timbered, ivy-covered, with mullioned windows and original roof tiles, it sat back proudly over a gravelled path, only partly concealed by a thick stone wall which was covered in climbing honeysuckle and green lichen. Beside the curving drive was a blue spruce of giant proportions.

My eyes stung with sudden emotion. What a lovely place it would be to live. Of course, even if it had been for sale it would have been way out of my league. Judging by what I'd seen so far, the only way I would get to live in a nice village like this was to buy something on a modern estate or something derelict. Each property I looked had felt like I'd attached a weight onto my heart, so by now it felt like it was somewhere around my knees. Disillusion was setting in, and all my plans felt doomed. I would have to return to London in defeat. There was no way I could find somewhere decent to live. I wondered whether they would let me have my job back...

It was difficult to think such thoughts in such a pretty village. I needed to stretch my legs. I had been under a cloud all day –

and now I wanted to breathe and enjoy this patch of sunlight.

As I got out of the car I noticed a little lane on the other side of the green, wandering off out of the village. With a slight jump in my stomach I also spotted a For Sale sign about three houses down.

Well of course I had to look even though it was obviously going to be outside of my budget otherwise I would have seen it on the internet; but like any house-hunter knows, one is drawn to any For Sale sign like a bear to a honey trap.

It was really quite delightful; a small, eighteenth century cottage, set back slightly from the road and surrounded by its own garden. Above the front door was a stone plaque with the words Carter's Cottage. When I got to the tall iron gate set into the Victorian red-bricked wall which fronted the property, I stopped. Shards of electricity prickled my skin.

I reached out and touched the rusty gate and my fingers caressed the wrought ironwork as if they had found an old friend. For one moment I felt that I had stood here before with my hand on the gate, about to push it open and enter.

Behind the gate a stone flagged path overgrown with weeds and unkempt grass and edged with overgrown bushes of lavender, led to the front door of the house, where wisteria curled its way around the entrance and crept along the front, its purple blossoms just beginning to open to drip and droop against the whitewashed wall.

It was empty. The windows, bare of curtains, stared blindly back at me. Almost without thought I pushed against the gate. It was padlocked.

For a moment I felt a wrenching pain. It was as if the house had rejected me, and the feeling was much worse than when Jake had walked away two weeks ago. I shook my head to try to rid myself of that feeling, and looked up.

The For Sale sign proclaimed the company of Woods Estate Agents to be handling the property. Looking at my watch, I thought they might just be willing to do a bit of overtime if a possible sale was in the offing.

Another voice in my head was asking me whether I was completely barking mad. This was a period cottage in the centre of a quiet village. OK, it was small, but there was no way it would be in my price range. With some kind of mad instinct, I chose to ignore this voice, got out my mobile phone and dialled the sign's number.

As I drove home that day, Jake's words, 'crazy', and 'unrealistic' kept echoing through my head as I wondered why I had just committed myself to a mortgage that was far more than I had intended to pay. Yet, having seen that cottage, I somehow knew that I had no choice. Something had pulled me towards it, and something had made me fall in love with it.

I had plenty of doubt of course. At times, I very nearly picked up the phone to my solicitor and pulled out of the whole deal. But then, I thought about the alternatives: to carry on with my dreary life, or to partially follow the plan and live in some soulless modern flat on a housing estate. Then I would take out the estate agent details and look at that little house with its very English cottage garden, its two charming beamed bedrooms and the stone floored kitchen, and an overwhelming sense of wellbeing would descend upon me, and I knew that no matter what the outcome of all this would be, that house was a part of me, and I had no option but to follow the course of action I had chosen. I just knew this cottage was for me, even if it was going to eat up the money I had left.

If the only way out of my present rut was to take a huge risk, then a huge risk I must take.

As I explained all this to Will, he listened without interruption, and did not look at me as if I was crazy. He just listened. I left out the bit about my strange feelings about the manor house, but when I came to the bit about my first views of the cottage, his eyes became quite intense, and a little smile came to his lips.

When I finished I felt slightly embarrassed, like I'd been caught with my skirt in my knickers, or had dropped the contents of my handbag on the floor.

I got up and briskly started clearing away the tea things.

'Well, I know it sounds stupid, but it's a lovely house – and it's a wonderful place to write...' I laughed. '... that's if I can get down to it... There's been so much to do, I haven't really done much to be honest. And I needed some company, so I went to a rescue centre, and that was where Charlie found me.'

He said nothing, but continued to look at me. It was beginning to get disconcerting, and slightly irritating.

'I suppose you'll be wanting to get your bike fixed. It looks like it might rain again soon so you'd better be quick...'

It was then that he said something that nearly made me drop the teapot I was carrying to the sink.

'And the old manor house, did that mean anything to you?'

I carefully put the teapot down on the sink. It was a pretty, Victorian one with yellow honeysuckle pattern which had been a present from my aunt, and I did not want to have it smashed on the floor.

'Why do you say that?' I asked, trying to keep my voice steady. I did not turn round, but turned the tap on, and poured out the contents of the teapot, trying to act and sound normal.

'I just wondered whether – oh, nothing. I just thought you might have noticed it.'

OK. Who was this guy? He was beginning to freak me out. He'd been giving me funny looks ever since he'd fallen off his bike. We'd only met less than an hour ago, and now he was talking to me as if he... as if he *knew* me for crying out loud. It was a bit of a damned cheek...

I turned round and tried to talk steadily, without emotion. But I knew there was an edge to my voice. An edge you could cut yourself on.

'I'm sorry. Do I know you? Have we met before? I'm sorry, but I don't normally discuss my feelings with complete strangers. Don't you want to get your bike fixed?'

He held my gaze for a few seconds, and then looked down, nodding to himself. Then he stood up.

'Yes,' he said, 'I'm sorry. I didn't mean to be... I just wanted to... Never mind. I'll see to my bike.'

'Do you need any help?' I asked, feeling slightly guilty now for my little outburst. After all, I had just told him some fairly personal details about my life. I suppose I was feeling a little vulnerable.

'No. I've got a repair kit. It won't take long.'

He was right. He was finished in twenty minutes. He popped his head through the door and said 'I'm off now.'

'Oh,' I said, suddenly feeling it was too soon, 'would – would you like another cup of tea?'

'No,' he said, smiling, 'it's time I went.'

I walked out to see him off, with Charlie at my side who looked slightly crestfallen that his new friend was leaving so soon.

'Well – take care,' I said, feeling slightly at a loss, 'don't run into any more odd females.'

He laughed.

'I won't. Not for the time being anyway.'

'Do you know your way back?' I asked, mentally kicking myself as I said it. Of course he knew his way – he'd had relatives here, hadn't he?

'Oh, yes,' he said, 'I know the place very well. I was born here.'

'What, in this village?'

He looked behind me and nodded towards my house.

'Yes. In this house. Cheerio.'

Then, before I could completely take in what he had said, he was gone, pedalling speedily down towards the church and disappearing round the corner, while I stared, gaping, after him.

Chapter 3

I felt very embarrassed.

Every day after the day I had met Will I went over our strange meeting in my head, and when I remembered the way I'd spoken to him, I could not help but cringe.

It had been a purely defensive knee-jerk reaction. I had made myself feel vulnerable by talking about my personal feelings about the house, so when he had asked about the manor house, everything went a little too weird for me.

It wasn't just because I had got a little bit weepy the first time I had seen that place. The question Will had asked me had hit a nerve because ever since I had moved to the village, the manor house had taken on some sort of significance in my head. It was as if, in a bizarre switch to the way hauntings normally work, the house was haunting me.

It had started the day I moved into Carter's Cottage.

It had been a hot, muggy day in August, and once the removal van had disappeared round the corner I had sat in my new living room, barely able to move due to the amount of packing boxes there were around me, and in the profound silence left after the bustle and flurry of the moving in, I contemplated my new position.

I had left London.

I had left my job.

I was newly unattached.

I knew no-one in the near vicinity.

I was completely alone.

Except for the cottage, which felt, strangely, like an old friend. And now I was here, all the panic and stress, the butterflies, and nail-biting, and the sheer physical effort of all the packing, trips to recycling centres, the last minute madness of getting the final little bits of packing done, the old flat cleaned and then the long and seemingly endless and surreal journey from one home to another, it all now faded away, leaving me in a state of almost paralysed serenity.

After a while I began to think about food and drink – and unpacking a few essentials. It was round five in the evening, still plenty of time to explore the village a little.

But – first things first. I wanted to explore the house. Of course I'd been in every room since getting here, showing the men where to put my rather meagre collection of furniture, watching them, with my knuckles in my mouth as they navigated the rather steep and curving staircase with my double bed. But now I was alone I needed to make contact with every room, and actually try and tell myself that this was indeed my house.

Firstly, I went into the kitchen and stepped out through the back door to feel the stone slabs of the patio beneath my bare feet, still warm from the August sun.

I looked back at the house.

Was this really mine?

Indoors again, I peeked into the utility room, jammed solid with cardboard boxes – and the small downstairs loo – and then climbed the stairs, enjoying the intimate and personal feel of the carpet on my feet.

Curving round to the left, the stairs brought me to a small landing. Pushing open the latched wooden door on my left I walked into the main bedroom where the ceiling sloped down towards the front of the house and a small window with a window seat overlooked the lane. I opened the small casement and stuck my head out. To the left I could just see the church and the big manor house beside it.

I felt dizzy for a moment, and took some deep breaths of the warm air, scented with next door's rose blossoms. A dream-like longing overcame me and time stood still.

The sound of a passing car brought me back to reality and I drew my head in. The stress of the move must be affecting me, and I probably needed to eat. The duvet and sheets lay on the bed, ready to be made up, but they could wait.

Before going out I went across the landing and looked into the small second bedroom that I was going to use as my study. My computer already sat ready on my desk in the corner of the room, waiting to be plugged in and brought to life. Through the window on the left I looked down into the little bit of garden on the side and then across a few more gardens to the fields at the back of the village. It was a perfect place to write.

Later, as I ate fish and chips washed down with a bottle of Merlot from the village shop, I began my plan of action. The next few days I would spend the mornings unpacking, and the afternoons writing. After all, there was no point in waiting. Time was limited and I had a novel to write.

It hit me in that moment how ridiculous my plan was. The chances of my plan working were minimal. Even if I could get a book written within a year, and get it published, it would take a lot longer than a year before I would make any money from it, and even if people bought it, the amount of money I would make would be very unlikely to cover the mortgage on this house, not to mention the hefty local council tax.

The odds were totally me. I knew that Jake had been right in many ways. I had done a mad and reckless thing.

Why?

Why had I given up everything to come and live in a place where I knew no-one? And why had I chosen this particular house, with its crippling mortgage repayments and council tax? Why did I still get a tingling sensation down my spine when I approached the front gate?

And why, oh why, had I very nearly walked through the gates of the manor house without thinking on my way back from the chippy?

Over the next few days I was busy looking for new bits of furniture in the nearby town of Clayford, a pretty little market town with an old corn exchange in the middle of the high street and an old stone bridge crossing the River Clee. By the end of my first week there, the furniture had been delivered, I had unpacked half of the boxes and I had not written one word.

The nights felt too quiet. I was used to the hum of traffic continually moving up and down Balham High Street along with the occasional yells and brawls of late night drinkers.

At Carter's Cottage I lay awake listening to the silence, made even more profound and eerie by the little creaks and tapping noises that every old house makes at night, but still convinces you that there is someone creeping around downstairs. And now and then, the hoot of an owl or bark of a fox would have me jumping awake just as I was beginning to get drowsy.

The answer was to find a canine companion who would keep me company and let me know if and when there was any real threat.

That was how I came to choose Charlie from a nearby rescue centre, or rather, I should say he chose me. If it had been at all possible I would have taken every single one of those sad, lost dogs home with me, but in the end it could only ever have been Charlie. The moment I appeared in front of his pen, he leapt up to greet me with his tail wagging so fast it was almost a blur, his patchy brown and white whiskery face with its huge brown eyes trying to push through the bars, as if I were someone he had known all of his two-year life.

Every morning Charlie and I went for a walk. Sometimes we walked down the lane if it hadn't been raining, and find a field where Charlie could use up some of his endless energy. The hedgerows were covered with thick clusters of elderberries, drooping with heaviness and fighting for space with dark, luscious blackberries. Sometimes I picked a few to eat, and once I had even brought a bowl home and made the most delicious crumble I had ever tasted. It made me feel very much like a country girl again. I could not regret leaving the city.

There was one morning when the lane was muddy with pools of rainwater from an overnight storm that had kept us both awake for some of the night, Charlie pressing up close to me at each thunderclap, his ears back and twitching, staring at the window as lightening lit up the room. To save having to wash Charlie's paws later, I took him into the village, keeping to the relatively dry pavements, and keeping him well away from the duck pond where his fascination for ducks could have led to a major washing and drying job.

Passing the manor house, my eyes were drawn to its walls and windows, and again I had that strange sense that time was standing still, and I had the need to take large breaths as the air seemed to fracture and swim around me.

A tug from Charlie brought me to my senses.

There were several mornings like this when I would take a walk past the duck pond, the old chestnut tree and the manor house, and it had been such a morning when I had been once again entranced by the sight of the manor house when Charlie had suddenly decided that blackbird would make a good lunch, taken a lunge and Will Days had suddenly landed in front of me, his bicycle wheels spinning like my head.

Now I felt bad about the way I had spoken to him. After all, he was probably just politely asking what I thought about the manor house – architecturally, or historically, or something like that. Unwittingly he had touched on something that was personal to me, but which I did not understand, and it had scared me. I had over-reacted in a most horrible way.

And he had been so nice about it, and when I thought about it, he was the kind of person I could have made friends with. OK, he was a little odd, but I kind of liked him, and I had been rude to him – in his childhood home too.

And that was odd too – the way he suddenly told me he had been born in my house and then cycling off like that. Why had he waited until then? Most people would have said straight away, amazed at the coincidence that the person responsible for knocking them off their bike happened to live in the house of their birth. It certainly explained some of the funny looks he had given me though when I had led him home.

If only I had some way of contacting him – apologising. But

I had no way of finding him – I had no surname, no number, and he hadn't even told me where he lived.

It was then that I thought of Maureen.

Maureen was my opposite neighbour, and I had met her a week after I moved in to Carter's Cottage. That week had been a long flurry of unpacking, phone calls and general sorting all the things out that went with moving into a new house. I had to spend a whole day looking for a bookcase for the living room that would accommodate my large collection of books. There was the telephone to get connected and utilities to be set up. I had intended to start writing within the first few days, but as sod's law would have it, the essential attachments for my computer – its leads, mouse and keyboard – had been packed in a box which the removal men had put in the corner of the study and then piled more boxes on top and around it, none of which I could lift or move without unpacking them first.

However, on the seventh day after the move I decided that that was a very feeble excuse for not writing. Paper and pens were still readily available, and it also occurred to me that with paper and pen I could write anywhere. In the garden, in the churchyard, the pub...

So I sat down at the kitchen table on that day, and as soon as my pen touched the paper, the front doorbell rang.

It was the woman who lived in the thatched half-timbered house opposite, asking if I needed anything and if I was settling in all right.

I was tempted to politely tell her I was perfectly fine, thanks for asking, and send her away. I admit I've never really been into all that neighbourly, community sort of life, and I had decided to keep myself to myself, but there was something about Maureen that made me want to be friends and I warmed to her as she was speaking. She was in her sixties, with permed blond hair, wearing cotton slacks and a powder blue short-sleeved blouse. Her expression and tone of voice were genuinely friendly and I liked her. It was partly because she added 'Of course you can tell me to go away if you like – I really will understand', that made me do the opposite, so I invited her in for tea, and that was the end of my writing that day.

Maureen had been widowed a few years ago when her husband died only two months after being diagnosed with cancer of the liver. She had three daughters, and seven grandchildren, and I heard about all them that afternoon. She had stayed in the house although it was too big for her because her family could come and stay any time they wanted – though that was not as often as she would have liked. But the option was there for them, and that's what it's all about isn't it? And anyway, she'd been there now for 40 years – ever since they'd been married, and she didn't feel she could leave it now.

She asked me about my own family.

I told her that my parents lived in my old home town in Oxfordshire, and I related, with a laugh, how surprised they had been when I had told them I was coming to live in a small village on the edge of the Cotswolds.

The conversation I had had with my mother on the telephone had been less of a laugh. I remembered that horrible sinking feeling at the sound of her voice, the slightly squeaky, wavering tone it took whenever she was worried or hurt.

'But I thought you were happy in London, love,' she said with still an old hint of her scouse accent.

'Not really, Mum. I need to get away. And I'll be much closer to you now...'

'And have you got work there? A local school or something?'

'No, mum. I... I don't want a job for a while.'

'Oh, Catherine...'

There it was. The dreaded sound of disapproval, making me feel about five years old.

'I don't understand, love. How are you going to manage?'

'I told you, mum. I've got some money put aside – enough to live on for a year, while I write my book.'

A long silence. Then the next dreaded question.

'And how does Jake feel about all this?'

'He... we split up.'

'Oh Catherine...'

It had taken some very aggressive packing, followed by half a bottle of red wine and a third of a tub of Ben & Jerry's chocolate fudge brownie ice cream before I felt my proper age again.

Maureen did not even flinch when I told her my plans, and I warmed to her even more. By now, we were sitting on the patio with our second cup of tea and a plate of chocolate digestives, looking at the untidy garden.

She reached and touched my arm.

'My dear, I think you are frightfully brave and totally marvellous. In fact, I feel rather envious, you know. If only... Well, I did have a wonderful marriage, and bringing up a family leaves you very little time for... Oh well, I suppose it's too late for me now, but you're young, and you should do the thing you want to do. Now...what do you plan to do with the garden, I can help in any way you like...'

But I wasn't going to let her get away with changing the subject. I had seen the brief flash of sadness in her eyes.

'What was it that you wanted to do, Maureen?'

She laughed nervously and touched her hair.

'Oh, well...it's very silly really. I don't want to bore you...'

'Try me.'

'Well... I used to dabble a bit with a paintbrush – oh a long time ago. Pen and ink and watercolours. Once thought I could make a go of it – you know how it is though – the years go by and you have a family, and it's too late now.'

'Why? Why is it too late?'

Another nervous laugh.

'Oh, well... starting something like that. At my age. But you get on with it my dear. I hope you do very well with it and I shall look forward to reading it when it comes out. What is it, a juicy romance, that kind of thing?'

'Er...no. It's more like a thriller – set in a rough school in London. A sort of murder mystery I suppose.'

'Oh, well...how wonderful! I love Agatha Christie and Ruth Rendell and all those authors. How fascinating. I'm, sure you'll do well... but I really must go now – I have the church flowers to do for tomorrow's wedding. It's been so lovely – and do let me come and help you with the garden, I really don't mind. And drop in any time. And anything you need, you know, don't hesitate to ask...'

I thanked her and watched her cross the road.

Well, I thought, walking back up my garden path. I at least have a friend and ally now. She wasn't exactly someone to paint the nearest town scarlet with, but at least I felt I had someone on my side. And a help with the garden wouldn't come amiss.

It was while I was thinking about Will and what he had said about having been born in this house as I was weeding the front garden one day, a couple of days after I had met him, when it hit me.

Maureen was having her thatch done. I had been watching the men, on and off, whilst doing battle with dandelions and nettles, and remembered that Maureen had mentioned it to me the other day.

'Oh, having a thatched cottage is all very well, and looks very pretty – having it repaired every ten years or so may not sound like much – but it's frightening how quickly the time goes by. You think yourself lucky with your slate roof – but we've had to have it done four times now since we came here...' I remembered then that she had told me she'd lived there for 40 years.

I pulled off my gardening gloves, shut Charlie in the house, and went and knocked on Maureen's door.

'Hello, dear! Do come in, won't you? I was just putting the kettle on – those workmen love their cup of tea – move the cat off there and sit down. Lovely day, isn't it? Is there anything you need?'

'Well,' I said, picking up a rather large tabby who mewed in protest, and sitting at her large kitchen table, half of which was covered with pieces of brightly coloured fabric, 'I was hoping you might be able to give me some information about someone who used to live here.' I sat the cat on my knee and stroked its head, while it kneaded my knees and started to purr. I leaned forward to look at the fabric on the table.

'Oh? Well, I might, dear. I know just about everyone – oh don't mind those; I've been making the costumes for the local school Christmas play. I always help them out every year. They're doing Aladdin this year – so I'm getting a head start, there's so much to do. Now, who was it you were asking about?'

'The people who used to live in my house – not recently, but back in the sixties, probably. You were here then, weren't you?'

Maureen put a tray on the table with matching teapot and china cups, a lemon drizzle cake and a plate of flapjacks – all homemade.

'Just help yourself while I take the tea out to the men...'

She came back and sat down, pouring herself a cup.

'Well, now, the sixties. That is a long time ago. It was 1962 when we moved here. I was a young bride of 21. The village has changed a lot since then – and not always for the better. Now...'

She looked into the distance, trying to remember.

'Yes, I remember. There was an old couple living there then. Very nice they were, but quiet. Never went out much and kept themselves to themselves.'

'Did...did they have any children?'

'Oh, no. Well, at least, if they did they would have been adults with families of their own by then. They were quite old these two – in their eighties at least.'

I frowned. 'So... this probably sounds like a silly question... but was there anyone born in that house – or a child living there at all in the sixties – or even the seventies perhaps?' I had assumed Will was about my age, but perhaps he was younger than he looked.

'Oh, goodness, no. There were no children in that house at that time. This couple were far too old... and then they died, one soon after the other, in the late seventies. A family came then – but they moved here from Yorkshire – none of them were born here. Perhaps it was one of those children you were thinking of?'

'No...no, I don't think so. Never mind. I must have been mistaken – someone told me they lived here as a child, and I thought you might know. I was trying to get in touch... but I must have got it wrong. This is lovely cake, Maureen...'

Had he lied to me to make me feel bad? Somehow, he did not seem to be the kind of person who would do that. Was he, perhaps, much older than he looked? Even so, it sounded as though this old couple who lived there in the sixties had been there for some time, and their children would have probably been in their sixties or seventies at least by now.

The mental arithmetic was doing my head in. But there was no way that Will could be much older than 40 or so.

Eventually I came to the conclusion that either he was a liar or mad and the whole thing was best forgotten about.

All the same, a week later I was still thinking about the way he'd looked at me the first moment he set eyes on me. I could only describe it as recognition combined with deep surprise. I had racked my brain over and over again, but I was absolutely sure I had not met him before...and yet, there was a feeling of familiarity...

By seven pm on the following Saturday evening I was feeling pretty damn miserable. I had no-one to see and nowhere to go, and it seemed that an evening of Saturday night reality shows yawned in front of me. God, I was sad.

I tried to stop myself from thinking what I might have been doing if I'd still been in London. But it was no good; my mind was mentally drawn there. Probably, at some lively night club watching Jake play, and then on to a bar or restaurant with our friends, getting hammered, smoking the occasional spliff, and then waking up in Jake's bed with the luxurious feeling of having the whole Sunday to relax in and enjoy.

I missed Jake. Or at least, I missed having the companionship of someone to go out with and to share a bed with. I missed our friends, but the more I thought about it the more I realised they had mainly been Jake's friends. I had never really made any close friends in London, but because I had Jake I hadn't thought about it much. It alarmed me – but of all the girlfriends and women I had ever known, I had never met anyone that I particularly wanted to share secrets and shopping sprees with. I realised with a hollow feeling that most of my so-called friends in London were all pretty shallow. What did that say about me?

Not wanting to follow this chain of thought, I turned on the television. A barrage of screams hit my ears and I instantly hit the mute button.

'Oh my God,' I said, as a wave of depression and loneliness hit me, 'I'm watching The X Factor with the sound turned off and my best friend is a woman who bakes cakes for the W.I. I've turned middle-aged overnight. My life is over, and I can't even write one chapter of one bloody novel. Oh, Charlie, what is to become of us?'

Charlie looked up at me and wagged his tail, just happy to be talked to. I rubbed his ears and said, 'well, at least I know I can rely on you little friend.'

The doorbell rang. Charlie barked frantically, while I quickly turned off the TV, and tried to flatten my hair which I knew would be a mess because I'd been running my hands through it. Who on earth could be calling on me now?

When I opened the door I could not see who it was because of the bunch of flowers that were in front of the person's face, and the autumn evening was already darkening.

But Charlie seemed delighted. He was excitedly sniffing at the person's legs and jumping up, his tail wagging furiously.

'Hello, Charlie,' said a calm, steady voice I knew straight away, despite the fact that I had only heard it once before.

'Will?' I said.

He appeared from behind the flowers.

'The very same,' he said, 'I've...er...brought you these...but if you're in the middle of something just say so – I'll go away. Sorry it's a sudden visit – but I had no number and...'

'Oh... no... it's fine. Come in, please.' Oh god, did I sound too desperate for company?

'Wow – these are lovely – you really didn't have to. Come through to the kitchen while I put them in something.'

Will followed me into the kitchen with Charlie panting at his heels.

'There's this as well,' he said, producing a bottle of red wine and putting it on the table, 'I thought we could either share it, or you could keep it and tell me to get on my bike again...'

I smiled sheepishly.

'I'm sorry about that. I really didn't mean to sound rude, but I...'

'Oh, please,' he said, 'don't – there's no need.'

He looked at the wine.

'It's claret. I hope that's OK. I've always been rather fond of it, and this is a particularly good one – so I would rather share it than leave it behind...'

I handed him the corkscrew and put the flowers in a vase while he opened the bottle. I turned round as the cork popped.

'I can't tell you what a welcome sound that is. I was having a bad attack of the Saturday night, no friends and nowhere to go blues – so your timing is excellent.'

He nodded.

'I could play the accompaniment to those blues – but I didn't bring my guitar.' He smiled, and I decided that all my London friends could go to Hell.

I put down two large glasses for him to fill, and watched him pour the deep red liquid into them, my spirits rising as the glasses filled.

'Are you hungry, Will? I've got a pizza I could throw in the oven – and some bagged salad.'

He smiled. 'I was hoping you were going to mention food. Yes, I would like that.'

'Of course, if I'd known you were coming I would have cooked something...'

He looked at me over his wine glass.

'But you didn't. So it's fine.'

This was almost normal. And it felt so easy, as if we'd been friends for years. We ate our pizza at the table while Charlie lay at Will's feet.

I asked him where he lived and what he did. He told me that for now he had a small flat in Crayford – tiny, but overlooking the river, so it was a nice location. He was a musician and played with a band at the moment, but did casual work during the day to pay the rent. He did not seem to want to talk much about himself.

'Married?' I asked, cursing myself for asking.

'No.'

Immediately he started to ask me about myself.

'Tell me about your writing.'

'There's not much to tell at the moment. I came here to give myself time and space to write a book, but nothing's ever that simple, is it? I mean, life always seems to get in the way. There's this huge pressure from other people to have a proper job and be earning lots of money – you know, pensions and all that. All my 'sensible' friends think you're mad if you give up a perfectly good job and try to do something – well, real. So, for a start, you're doubting yourself. And that's a huge hurdle to get over. Everyone seems to want to tell you the terrible odds that are against you being successful...'

'Everyone?'

'Well...OK, that's a slight exaggeration. But it only takes two or three people who you're close to and it can feel like everyone. And then, it's not just that – it's just... all the things you have to do just to get through each day, like housework and shopping and dealing with stuff – it all gets in the way...'

I stopped. Listening to myself I knew I sounded like a whiny old misery, and hearing the echo of my words it all sounded horribly thin and ridiculous – like I was making up excuses for my inability to write. And perhaps I was. Perhaps I actually couldn't write – perhaps I just wasn't good enough. Perhaps I was just completely kidding myself.

There. I'd said it to myself. The horrible thing that had been growing beneath my consciousness that I had not been allowing myself to bring forward into the light; the dreaded, terrible fear that actually I wasn't a writer after all and I had made a huge mistake...

'Catherine...?'

I blinked at him. I had been staring into space like some petrified rodent under the shadow of an owl. But when I looked at Will, the fear subsided.

How was it I could ramble on like this? I never spoke to anyone about my feelings. I was hugely defensive – I especially did not go round telling strangers about my writer's block. But there was something about the way Will listened – as if he was really interested – that made you want to tell everything that was on your mind.

'I'm sorry,' I said, 'I sound so pathetic. It's not what I intended... I wanted to get on and prove everyone wrong. It seemed like a good idea at the time, as they say...'

'What about your parents? What do they think?'

'That I'm crazy. Oh... that's not really fair. They try to be nice about it, but I can tell they don't really understand – they really wish I was back in my job, my 'respectable' teaching job, and that I would settle down and have some security. That seems to be what life is all about to a lot of people – security. Dad's not too bad, I suppose, but Mum was - Disappointed In Me - without really saying it. I could just tell.'

There was a silence. I thought to myself that he must be thinking what a complete loser I am. Pity. The evening had started off so well.

He poured me another glass of wine, and then one for himself.

Well – at least he wasn't running out of the door. Not yet.

'Shall we go and sit down?' he said.

We moved into the front room, and I switched on the electric heater. The nights were getting chilly, but it was too soon for the central heating.

'You could do with a real fire in there,' he said, looking at the fireplace, 'I could help you... if you'd like. Sometime...'

'Thanks,' I said, and then felt slightly awkward. It reminded me about what he had said about the house. I started to say something, but he started first.

'What do your parents do?' he said as he sat down in the one armchair. I sat on the sofa.

'My dad was in Sales in British Telecom. He's retired now

– left before it all went privatised. He'd kill me if he knew I was using a different service. Terribly loyal, my dad – his generation were always loyal to their jobs, I think.'

'Your mother?'

'A housewife. She never had a job – as far as I know. It wasn't expected then, I suppose. And she had the three of us to bring up, me and my two younger brothers.'

He said nothing. He seemed suddenly to be miles away, staring into the middle distance.

'Will,' I said, before he could interrupt me again, 'did...did you say that you were born in this house?'

He looked at me with those piercing eyes for a few seconds.

'Yes,' he said, eventually, 'Yes, I did say that.'

'It's just that... my neighbour opposite – she's been here forty years and I thought she might remember you, but I just mentioned that I'd met you in passing – and she couldn't remember any children living here then. It just seemed...'

'Odd,' he said, smiling gently.

'Well... yes.'

'She wouldn't remember me.'

'But...'

Will got up suddenly and stood in front of the fireplace, resting his land lightly on the wooden beam above it.

'Catherine,' he started, and began to speak rather quickly, as if he wasn't looking forward to saying something but had to get on and say it anyway, 'Catherine, I have to tell you something. Something I've never told anyone before. In my life. And you're not going to believe me – which is why I've never told anyone – because no-one would – but, for some reason, I don't know why, you have turned up here, of all places, in this house of all houses...'

'Will – what on earth is it? Sit down, won't you?'

It was the first time I had seen him ruffled.

He sat back on the armchair, leaning forward with his elbows on his knees, and held his glass with both hands, turning it round and round.

Everything was about to go weird again, I could feel it.

'I'm going to explain something to you, but I'm not going to tell you the whole story all in one go. It would be too much. I'm going to tell you one thing, and that will be difficult enough to believe. But I just would like you to listen. And then, if you like, you can throw me out and never see me again. I know you'll want to. But I have a feeling you won't.'

There didn't seem to be anything for me to say to this, so I just got up and got another bottle of wine from the kitchen.

'Sounds like we might need this. Sorry it's not Claret.'

'All the same, that's a very good idea,' he said.

He waited for me to pour the wine and sit down. In the silence, my mind was racing. What was he going to tell me? Why should it be so unbelievable? And, why me? We'd only met each other twice now – not long enough to be telling each other our darkest secrets. Yet, I had myself been doing just that, hadn't I? And was this really only the second time we had met? It felt like years. As if we were old friends.

I had no idea what he was about to tell me, but I supposed it was going to be something about himself – something he'd done, perhaps, and this was a sort of confession. I felt a little nervous, and I prepared myself for something shocking, and hoped I'd be able to cope with it.

It was then that he said the thing that was so outside what I was expecting that I did not quite understand it at first.

'I knew your mother before you were born.'

It would not have been a startling statement from someone who looked at least 20 years older than me. A surprise and a coincidence, perhaps, but it would have been quite real.

Coming from someone who looked no older than 35 – about the same age as me – it took some thinking about. I stared at him for a while before I realised that what he had just said was pretty well impossible.

'You must have been very young,' I said.

He looked at me in his steady, calm way.

'No,' he said, 'no...not very young. I was an adult.'

'That's impossible.'

'I told you you wouldn't believe me.'

It was true. He had. But that didn't make it any easier to believe now.

Unless...

'Oh, for crap's sake. You're not going to try and tell me you're my father, are you? Because, if you do, then you can leave right now...'

He smiled.

'No,' he said, 'I am not your father. That would be too weird.'

'It's weird enough already. I mean, I know that they can do wonders with cosmetic surgery these days – but even so, you'd be a miracle. Come on, Will – you're just having a joke on me aren't you? A pretty naf joke, I think. It's not even remotely funny...'

'Catherine,' he said, his voice still calm, and without emotion. It was his stillness that stopped me.

'Catherine, I know it sounds ridiculous. But, whether you believe me or not, I would like to you to hear me – and then you can decide whether or not to believe me when I've finished. It's not a joke, and I have never had cosmetic surgery. But I did know your mother back in the sixties...'

'Well, then,' I said, feeling strangely close to tears, 'you'd better prove it. Tell me something you know about her.'

'OK,' he said, 'I'll tell you some things you probably know about her and some things you possibly don't know. Her name was... is Joy. And before she met your father, her name was Joy McEwen.'

'Yes,' I said, that's true. But you could have found that out.'

'...and she was among the first people who saw the Beatles live before they had their first recording contract.'

I stared at him. It was one of those things my mother had always boasted about. Nearly every time they played the Beatles on the radio, she would say: 'I was there, you know, before they were famous. Saw them at the Cavern...' and then we would all shout: 'Yes, mum, we know...!' It was a kind of family joke. My two brothers and I, at first impressed by this snippet of our mother's previous life, had quickly got bored with the story and shouted her down every time she said it. But it was a family thing – not something I thought many people knew about. Mum didn't talk much about herself in company.

'How did you know that?' I asked.

'I told you,' he said quietly, 'I was there.'

His eyes didn't flicker. He looked as though he was telling the truth.

'You'd better tell me, then,' I said.

'Thank you,' he said, I will.'

'It was 1962. I was known as Billy then. Billy Days – though some of the billboards advertised me as Billy Daze. I didn't mind – it was all part of the scene.

'I was in Liverpool for a few months – booked in at the Cavern every Saturday night with a jazz band I'd been playing with on and off for years. Jazz was becoming less popular then – most of the youngsters were more interested in what was happening there during the week: the beat groups that were emerging out of skiffle. In particular, everyone in Liverpool seemed to be talking about a band called the Beatles.

My band members were furious about it – they hated the fact that the music was amplified and thought it sounded dreadful. They were a bit 'old school' – but I'd always been fascinated by changes in music fashions. I have found it's best to move with the times. There was a real buzz going round about the lunchtime sessions during the week, and it sounded quite exciting, so I went along to see what the fuss was about.

'It was August in the day time; the kind of day when most people should be outside, in the parks or hanging round on street corners or in cafes listening to Elvis on juke boxes. But the Cavern was packed. Half the youth of Liverpool seemed to be there, in that hot, stuffy little underground place that seemed like it had been hewn out of the ground.

'They were playing when I walked in. The minute I heard that sound I knew something special was happening. I actually felt the hairs on the back of my neck rise. They were four young lads dressed in suits with three guitars and a set of drums. Their drummer, Pete Best, had just been sacked and a young lad called Ringo Starr was playing with them. Funny – most of the people there were complaining because Best wasn't with them – but it was a historic moment. Somebody happened to record that session: the first time the Beatles were recorded playing together in the form in which they would become the phenomenon that they did. They were playing an upbeat version of the old Ray Charles number, *Some Other Guy*.

'It was then that I saw your mother for the first time...'

Chapter 4 - Joy's Story

August 1962

She was leaning on the wall by one of the arches, mouthing the words and tapping her feet, unsmiling; a cigarette held in her hand, just by her left hip. She wore a lemon yellow knee-length sleeveless dress, belted at the waist, but narrower in the skirt than the last decade had seen, and white stilettos. Her hair was mid-brown, cut in a Jacquie Kennedy style bob.

Billy looked back at the stage, a quiet smile on his face. He had recognised the line of her jaw and the dreamy look in her eyes. He knew he didn't need to go over to her just yet. If she was who he thought she was he would meet her sooner or later. He knew from experience it was inevitable. At the moment he just wanted to get close to the stage and see what was happening. There really was something about this group; you could feel it in the air. They had an edge; a rawness and a kind of quirky style that was exciting and new. They also had talent; the music and harmonies were good, and all around him were bobbing heads, winkle pickers tapping the floor, people moving to the beat because they couldn't help themselves.

There was a crowd squeezed together around the tiny, semicircular stage, close enough to reach out and touch the players. Billy managed to get himself to the front, enjoying the buzz of raw energy that was coming from these youngsters.

As they finished *Some Other Guy*, the crowd cheered, a few girls screamed, and a couple of people shouted: 'We want Pete!', and John Lennon, one of the lead singers, said, 'Yes... but we have here the marvellous Ringo Starr, who we borrowed from Rory Storm and the Hurricanes...' Some of the crowd cheered, and as Lennon began to introduce the next song, Billy heard a familiar voice behind him, shouting over the commotion.

'Hey, Billy! Billy Days!'

He turned around reluctantly. Beside him was a shortish man with short dark hair, thick rimmed glasses and a Teddy boy jacket.

It was Mike Wallis, one of the sound technicians who worked at the Cavern. Billy knew him from his Saturday night gigs. He'd never liked him much, but he couldn't put his finger on why. He just felt that he didn't want to trust him, and he'd been in the music business long enough to know his instincts were usually right.

'Hi Mike,' he shouted, barely audible above the amplified music.

'What do you think?' Mike shouted, nodding towards the stage, 'Good, aren't they? Few more people down here than on your Saturdays, eh?'

Billy smiled, ignoring the dig, and turned back to listen to the group, who were now playing *Hello Little Girl*. They both listened to the rest of the set, and when they finished, Mike said, 'Hey Billy, come on over here where we can talk, I want you to meet someone.'

She was still leaning against the arch, oblivious to the condensation that ran down the walls, a dreamy, far-away look in her eyes, watching the group clear up, and still swaying as if she was listening to the music in her head.

Mike sidled up to her, offered her a cigarette, and lit it for her. Then he lit one for himself.

'Billy – this is Joy McEwen. Joy, this is Billy. He plays with one of our Saturday night bands.'

Joy turned her eyes to Billy and gave a quick smile, blowing smoke into the air above.

'Hi Billy. What do you play?'

'Oh, it's mainly trad jazz. I play guitar and banjo, but I like this sound.' he gestured towards the stage. 'I think I might try electric guitar...'

'They're so cool, the Beatles. I've been coming here at lunch times since they started, when they were the Quarrymen.'

'Joy wants to sing, don't you baby?'

'Oh, Mike, give over. I can't sing. Don't be daft.'

But Billy noticed that she was smiling for the first time since he'd seen her.

'Oh, she can sing all right. I'm trying to help her out – you know, get her in here maybe. She's got a lovely voice – lovely and soft, like.'

'Oh, Mikey – do stop.' She stubbed out her cigarette on the damp wall and flicked it to the ground, 'I've gotta go anyway – I'll be late for work. See you round, Billy.'

'Yeah, see you.' He smiled. He knew he would.

Mike and Billy sat down at a table. Mike had a bottle of coke that he was drinking out of, and he lit a cigarette.

'Pity they don't sell beer here; this stuff makes me belch.' He nodded towards the exit. 'Isn't she a bit of something? I think I might be in there, you know. If I can get her a job here – just get her on the stage, you know.. I think she'd be eternally grateful, if you know what I mean...' He blew out a cloud of smoke and winked.

Billy knew exactly what he meant and mentally winced, but he chose not to respond to this.

'What kind of stuff does she sing?'

'She's a bit of a crooner, you know? Kind o' Connie Francis – but softer. Really good with the old tear-jerker ballad stuff. The girls all like that kind o' thing – and the boys'll just love the way she looks. She could be big round here. If we could just get someone interested in giving her a chance – like some band that needs a singer. If you know of anyone... I'd be grateful – and so will she...'

He grinned and winked again. Billy's stomach churned.

'Yeah. Sure. I'll keep a look out.'

'Thanks Billy. I gotta go now...'

Billy walked out into the street, blinking in the sunshine after the darkness of the Cavern, and headed down towards the docks where his band had a rehearsal room. The music from the Cavern was still going round in his head, and he felt the familiar lurch of excitement in his guts. Another change was in the air, he could feel it, and now that he had seen Joy McKewen he knew his life had moved on to another stage. He had made the right choice when he came to Liverpool – and somehow, no matter where he chose to go, it always did seem to be the right place...

He was a few minutes early for rehearsals so he took a quick detour down a side street to a music shop that he knew. In the window was a Gibson Les Paul SG electric guitar. It was a deep cherry red with a mahogany neck and it cost a lot more than he could afford right now. He'd have to get some extra work to save up and pay for it – perhaps working on the docks. In the past, he'd got casual work as a builder, but the new tower blocks that had gone up in the central areas of Liverpool that had been bombed during the war made him feel sick to the stomach and he did not want to be part of that. They were terrible, soul-less metal boxes that had nothing to do with real human needs. No, if he was going to stay in this city for a while – and it seemed as though he was, the docks were the best option.

It was Saturday night, a few weeks later. His band was playing their usual set at the Cavern – some Kenny Ball covers and some of their own stuff. Billy had written a few numbers for them, and he'd also written words to some of them – but Robbie, the band leader said he wasn't interested in vocals. He wanted to stay strictly instrumental.

The audience were sparse. A few of the loyal fans were there, but Billy sensed that there wasn't the same buzz as there was with the lunch time crowd. While it was still essentially a jazz club, there was no doubt that the tide was turning in favour of bands like the Beatles. Billy felt that same old restless need to move on, to do something different. He had always moved with the times. It had been essential for him all his life.

The evening crowd were noticeably older and quieter but Billy noticed one person who wasn't so old. She was leaning on the wall, over by one of the arches, smoking a cigarette with the same far-away look in her eyes he'd noticed before.

After their set he went over to her.

'Hi Billy.'

'Hi, Joy. Good to see you here – you with Mike?'

'No... not really. But he's around somewhere, I suppose. Hey, you're really good, you know?'

'Thanks. How's the singing going?'

She smiled again.

'Oh...I don't know. It's Mike's idea really – me dad wouldn't like it if I started singing in public. He doesn't even know I come here. Don't know what he'd do if he knew...'

Billy was quiet for a moment, watching the smoke curl up from her fingers, a slight frown on his face.

'But – you like singing?'

'Oh yeah. There's nothing like it. When you're singing, the world just goes away, you know what I mean? And you just feel so good afterwards, like you've really said something – I don't know. Sounds daft really. Don't know why I'm telling you this, I mean, I don't really know you do I? But – you're kind of easy to talk to.'

Billy half smiled and looked down at the floor, and then back up at her. 'Would you like to come over to our rehearsals some time? I know it's not quite your thing – and we don't do vocals usually – but I might just get Rob to let you sing one of my numbers. I'd like to hear your voice.'

She took a drag on her cigarette and blew the smoke away sideways, so it wasn't in his face.

'Yeah? All right, then. If you like.'

It took Billy more than a little effort to persuade Robbie to allow a totally unknown girl to sing at rehearsals. But he bought him a couple of beers and explained that it wasn't for the show. He just wanted to hear her sing and try one of his songs. It could just be a bit of fun.

'I don't know what it is about you, Billy, but you have a way about you. I don't think there's anyone in this city who could change my mind about this – except you. But – just this once, OK?'

Her voice had something very special about it. It was soft with a strength behind it that could easily carry a long note – but also had a fragility at times that hit you in the gut. It reminded Billy of Marilyn Monroe, with those soft, warm lower notes and strong head notes. Mike had been right – she could be big, if she had the determination to see it through and committed herself to some practice and training. Sheer talent wasn't enough in this business and competition was high.

Even Robbie was impressed.

Later on in the Mitre pub, where the band always had a post-show beer or two, he came up to Billy and bought him a pint.

'That girl's got something hasn't she?'

Billy nodded.

'Look – I know I've said I don't want any singers, but I've been thinking. I suppose it would be quite nice to have a song like that to close the set with – might even get the numbers up, you never know...'

'...Wait a minute,' I said, interrupting Will's story, 'are you telling me that my mother sang at the Cavern?'

Will smiled broadly.

'She did. And very good she was too. For a while we had our own singer, and it brought the punters in too...'

'But – she's never told me! Or any of us for that matter, as far as I know. I don't believe it...'

'I did say I would probably tell you some things that you

didn't know.'

'Yes, but... hang on, I've got to get my head round this – my mother, Mrs Average Housewife, mother of two - was a singer – in the Cavern – in public...'

I had forgotten, for the moment, all my doubts and confusion over Will's age and the impossibility of any of this. I was just trying to deal with this new bit of information. I tried to remember anything my mother had told me about her life before she had a family, but I realised, with not a small sense of shock, that I knew virtually nothing about her – except that she had been born in Liverpool to an Irish father and a Manchester-born mother, and had seen the Beatles at the Cavern.

'How come she never said anything?'

'She never was very good at self-promotion,' said Will, 'she lacked confidence in herself. I'm not surprised she's not spoken about it. It's not her style.'

What he said had the ring of truth in it. My mother had never talked about herself as if she mattered; would trivialise her abilities as if they were nothing; and if anyone ever praised her would say something like, 'Oh, well, it's just what anyone would do,' or 'Oh, don't be daft, it's nothing really.'

I had to admit that everything Will had told me so far sounded as though he really had known her.

'So – what happened?' I asked, 'I mean she didn't become Cilla Black, did she? I think I might have noticed that.'

Will sighed.

'No – she never did make it really big. But she was popular at the Cavern for a while. Some of the local papers said things like: "Marilyn lives!" or "Joy to our ears at the Cavern..." and most of the reviews were great, but – things turned out differently.'

'Why? What happened?'

'Partly her low self esteem, and partly Mike Wallis. He was bad news. I could see what was happening, but there was nothing I could do. Of course, Mike was furious with me. He'd wanted to give her the break himself, and get all the kudos, so she'd be grateful and fall into bed with him.'

Something entered my mind then that I found deeply disturbing. It was so disturbing that it made me feel nauseous and I didn't want to put a voice to it – but I had to.

'And – was she grateful to you...?'

He looked straight at me with his candid eyes, and without any judgment about what I had just suggested, said,

'It wasn't about that. Of course she was glad I'd given her this opportunity, but I never expected anything for it. I saw a girl who could sing, and wanted to sing, and I did something about it, that's all.'

Though he had accused me of nothing, I felt ashamed, and rather small.

'I'm sorry,' I said, '...it's just all so – difficult. I don't know how to trust you...yet. You must admit this is all a bit weird for me.'

'I know,' he said, 'it's weird for me too, even after all these years.'

I poured out another glass of wine for us both while we listened to the church clock strike ten.

'She allowed Mike to flatter her,' he continued, 'he could really charm the women somehow. When he opened his own little night club – God knows where he got the money from – he put her under a contract that tied her to him. He promised her he could eventually get her a recording contract and make her a star, but all he really wanted was to take control and keep her to himself. He did nothing to promote her, and she was too inexperienced to know any better.'

'Were they – an item?' I asked, the words almost sticking in my throat.

'They... were dating. I don't know – I really don't know, Catherine, whether it went any further than that. Women were, well they were more careful then. The whole liberation thing hadn't quite exploded in the way it did later. Many women still waited until they got married...

'OK. So, what happened with my father, then? Did you know him?'

He smiled. 'Jim Burns – Yes, I did.'

I took a large swig of wine.

'You'd better tell me, then.'

Billy turned the corner into the dark little side street where MIKE'S BAR flashed in neon down near the end. A wind blew down the street, and he turned up the collar on his jacket. It was February 1964 and one of the coldest winters he'd ever known.

A voice behind him made him turn round.

'Hi, Billy. Where you off to with that suspicious looking parcel under your arm?'

It was Jim Burns, the base player who played in a small supporting group at the Cavern now and then. Billy had met him a few times and played alongside him. He was no longer with the jazz band. They didn't play the Cavern any more and were now playing the social and golf club circuit. The Cavern had for a while become the Mecca for Beatles fans and the new beat groups that were playing the club in their wake. Bands like Gerry and the Pacemakers, the Swinging Blue Jeans and the Searchers had found their own success there, and now it had begun to be taken over by bands that were playing the new R&B. Billy had made himself available as a stand-in for band members who were off sick or dropped out for whatever reason. He didn't want to get on a permanent basis with any of them. It was too dangerous. There would come a time when he would have to move on again. The Cavern was beginning to look shabby now – and he wondered how long the bubble would last.

'This suspicious looking parcel is a bottle of very good claret, actually. The place I'm going sells only beer and cheap wine, so I always take my own. You're not playing tonight?'

'No – the Hermits are on tonight, with the Roadrunners. The place was packed – you could hardly get in. Thought I'd take an early night.'

'You could come with me if you like. There's a girl I know who sings here – she used to be at the Cavern for a while. Great voice. You'd like her.'

'All right. Might as well. Be warmer in there anyway.'

The place was drab, sleazy and choked with cigarette smoke. Most of the punters were middle-aged business men, out to have a few drinks and see a bit of skirt before going home to their wives.

Joy was already on stage when they walked in, singing *Moon River* to an audience who mostly seemed more concerned with discussing business matters between themselves. Those who were listening grinned in a leering kind of way. She was wearing a neat little black dress, cut just above the knee, and her hair was cut in a bob, the top backcombed to give it height, her eyes black with eyeliner. She looked a little like the new singer that had hit the charts the year before, Dusty Springfield.

Billy looked at Jim and saw that he was instantly transfixed.

They sat at a small round table that still had the beer spillage and cigarette ends from the previous occupants. Billy went to get a couple of glasses from the bar and came and sat down.

'She's gorgeous,' said Jim.

He was hypnotised. All the way through her set he could not take his eyes off her.

Mike Wallis passed their table and nodded without smiling as he saw Billy, but did not stop to say hello.

After she'd finished to appreciative applause, and a few wolf whistles, she came straight over to their table.

'Billy! It's lovely to see you. You are good coming out in this freezing weather. Hey, have you heard our Cilla on the radio? She's only in the charts now, isn't she?'

Billy nodded. 'She's done well.'

'When you think she was only checking me coat at the door not so long ago.'

'Joy, this is Jim – he's been playing at the Cavern.'

'Hi, Jim.' She smiled and shook his hand. Billy noticed that her eyes lingered on Jim's for a moment longer than was usual at a first introduction, and that Jim held her hand a little longer than was necessary. He grinned at their mutual attraction.

'Hello, Joy. Look, don't think I'm being funny, like, but you have got the most gorgeous voice.'

'Oh, give over,' she said, blushing.

'No – really. Why don't you sing at the Cavern any more?'

'Long story. Me dad found out didn't he? Thought I was hanging out with a bunch of layabouts down there. Would you believe that Mikey sweet-talked him into me singing here instead? He thinks this is a more respectable place because it's full of business men – he'd have a heart attack if he saw what it's really like.'

'Hasn't he been to see you?'

'Nah – he doesn't get out much. He was injured in the war – only got one leg; well, one and a half really. But he just sits around the house all day, while me mam does everything for him.'

'What does she think?'

'Me mam? Oh – I don't know. Not sure she thinks for herself at all...'

Billy felt a stab of pain, and turned away. He didn't like to hear her describing her mother in that way, but there was nothing he could say.

He was glad that Joy and Jim were getting on, and it didn't seem to matter if he was there or not, so he looked around the room, trying not to think about the past.

Over in the far corner he could see Mike talking to some men and occasionally glancing over to Billy's table. After a while he made his way over. He did not look pleased.

'Hey, you,' he said, flicking the back of Joy's neck, 'no hogging the punters, love, the others will be jealous.'

He shot Jim what could only be described as a warning look, and turned back to Joy.

'Why don't you go and talk nicely to my friends over there.'

'All right, Mikey.'

'Mind you talk nice, now,' he said as she got up. He slapped her behind, gave another look at Billy and Jim and walked away.

Billy grabbed Jim's arm as Jim tried to leap up from his chair. A bar room brawl wasn't going to help anyone.

'Not now, Jim. Another time.'

'Who the hell does that guy think he is, talking to her like that? I'd like to give him a piece of my...' Jim's hands had automatically made fists.

'Yes – we all would. But not now.'

Reluctantly, Jim sat down again, his eyes still eyeing Mike as he smugly mingled with his clientele.

Billy leaned in towards him, keeping his voice low. 'Joy's a great kid, and that guy's got her completely under his thumb – but if you really like her, you've got to give it some time. Between us, we can think of something – but it's going to take some patience.'

It all happened fairly quickly all the same.

Over the next few weeks Jim was a frequent customer at Mike's Bar, much to Mike's obvious displeasure. But there was very little he could do about the way things were going. Billy could see that Joy and Jim were made for each other. They began to meet away from the bar, though Joy was scared that if Mike found out he might get nasty.

One night, Mike came over to the table in a particularly bad mood. The bad weather was keeping customers away (even though the Cavern was still packing them in every night), and he had made a loss that week.

He mussed Joy's hair as he came up behind her and then pulled her out of her chair.

'Isn't it time you got ready for the next set? And go and do something about your hair. It's a right mess.'

This time, Jim stood up and Billy didn't try to stop him.

'Get your grubby hands off her, you filthy bugger...'

Mike smirked.

'That's right,' he said, his voice oily and self-satisfied, his right hand still gripping Joy's arm, 'you go right ahead and call me what you want. That'll get you just where I want you – out of here. You're barred from coming inside these doors again, right? Now – Joy – go and get ready.'

He let go of Joy's arm, but she made no move to go.

'Well, go on you silly cow, what are you gawking at?'

Jim moved closer to Joy.

'I told you not to talk to her like that...'

'And I told you to get out of here...'

'Oh – I will. But she's coming with me. Aren't you pet?'

Joy looked sheepishly at Mike.

'I'm sorry, Mike...'

Mike's face was ugly as he looked at her through narrowed eyes.

'You will be. Don't forget you're under a contract here. You leave here now and I'll sue you for breach of contract, plus you'll never work again. I'll make sure of that. You're not going anywhere, love...'

Billy stood up and nodded to Jim. Jim put his arm round Joy and they turned towards the door.

Mike went to grab Joy's arm, but Billy stopped him.

'You'd best let them go, Mike. There's nothing you can do.'

Mike turned on him, the hatred raw on his face.

'What the fuck has it got to do with you, you interfering bastard? You always did get in my way – I should have barred you from here weeks ago...'

Billy spoke calmly and quickly.

'Jim's brother works in a solicitor's office. He had his boss take a quick look at Joy's contract. It's not worth the paper it's written on and you know it. You've been conning her for months. Now, just let her go and say nothing about it, and we'll not say anything either. Otherwise, this place could be closed within a fortnight.'

Mike stared at him with utter loathing for several moments, but with the look of a man who knows he is defeated. But just as Billy made a move to leave, Mike's arm shot back so fast that Billy had no time to see what was happening before Mike had given him a right hook that had Billy sprawling across the beer-stained table.

Chapter 5

Will stroked his chin.

'He was quite strong considering his size.'

I was curled up on the sofa, holding an empty glass.

'I never knew my parents had such an exciting time. That is, of course, if everything you've told me is true.'

'It's true.'

'So how come I was brought up in the suburbs of Oxford instead of, well, wherever it is the children of rock stars get brought up. I'm sure it would have been a lot more fun, anyway.'

Will leaned back in his chair. Charlie woke from his doggy dreams, scratched his ear, and slumped back on the floor.

'They had plans. They were going to put their own band together. They did a few gigs, got married and then Joy got pregnant and Jim got a temporary job as a sales rep. I kind of lost touch with them after that, but I suppose when the family started growing they chose the security of full-time work and a family home life. Many people do.'

There was a long silence. Charlie twitched in his sleep. The church clock struck eleven.

Quietly, I said, 'So I was the reason they gave up their music careers?'

Will flicked me a look.

'Don't sweat it. It was always their choice.'

There was another silence. Of course, he was right. It wasn't exactly my fault that mum got pregnant, but it was still an uncomfortable thought that my existence should have had such a drastic effect.

'I should go,' said Will.

Again, it seemed too soon. But it was late, and I felt woozy from so much wine.

'So – what now? You said this was only part of the story; the thing you had to tell me. What about the rest of it? When does it all start to make sense?'

Will got up and Charlie leapt to his feet, shaking off the remnants of sleep.

'If you want it to make sense, you'll be waiting a very long time,' said Will, 'it's never made much sense to me, so I don't expect you to understand. If anything, the more I tell you, the less sense it will make. Look, if it really is too weird for you, we can stop here. It's completely up to you. I could just go, and leave it at that...'

'No,' I jumped in quickly, '...no. No, I would like to hear the rest – really. But I suppose I need to think about this for a while. Will – would it be OK if I asked my mother about you?'

He went into the kitchen to get his jacket from the back of a chair and pulled it on.

'I don't suppose it would do any harm – except – she would expect...'

'...an older man. How old?'

Will stood in the door frame, the light from the kitchen creating a silhouette. He was in good shape; very fit, young looking and full of life.

'She would expect someone in his seventies.'

I shut my eyes. Perhaps it was the wine, but the air around me seemed to distort and fracture.

'Are you all right?'

'Yeah... just a little queasy. Too much wine I guess. I'm fine.'

'Tell her you met his son.'

I looked at him, wondering why I hadn't thought of that before...

'Are you his son?'

He smiled his warm smile.

'No. Sorry. It was me. You think I would get that kind of detail from a parent?'

'...no...'

He put his hand inside his jacket and pulled out a small card.

'Here,' he said, holding it out to me, 'when you're ready, call me.'

I took the card. All it said was, William Days, Musician. And then a mobile number.

'OK,' I said. I was no longer able to make coherent conversation. I needed to go to bed.

I watched him open the door and collect his bike from the front gate. I stepped out into the cool night air.

'I suppose I should thank you,' I said.

He looked sideways at me, his foot ready on the pedal.

'Why?'

'If it wasn't for you – if it was you – then I wouldn't be here. My parents would never have met.'

He looked away, breathed in the night air, and then looked back at me. I could just detect his grin in the darkness.

'There's something to think about,' he said with his quiet,

still voice, and then he slipped off into the night, and Charlie and I wandered slowly back into the empty house.

It took me several days before I plucked up the courage to ring my mother. I'm not sure I could have explained why at the time. Half of me was desperate to find out whether everything Will had said had been true, but the other half of me wanted to keep it all to myself; as if something would be broken or spoiled by talking about it. What if she said she'd never heard of Billy Days? That she had never sung at the Cavern? It was the most likely, yet I did not want to hear that. Yet – if it turned out that Will's story was true, what then? How could I fit my idea of reality around a 75 year old man who looked 35? Perhaps, after all, it was possible. Perhaps...

'Hi mum.'

'Catherine, love, how lovely to hear from you. We were just talking about you – it's Catherine (this aside presumably to my father in another room) – we were just saying it's time we came to see you, weren't we Jim?'

'Yeah – that would be great mum...'

'It's so nice of you to ring – you are all right, aren't you?'

'Yes, I'm fine. I – er, wanted to ask you something. Something about your past – before you met dad, when you were in Liverpool.'

'Oh... yes?' she sounded surprised. She had every right to be. I never asked her anything about her past.

'Did you... do you remember a man called Billy Days?'

I held my breath.

'Good heavens. Billy Days? Yes ... yes of course I remember him – what's that love? (her voice became muffled as she spoke to my father again) Yes, your father says it was because of Billy Days that we met – do you know, I'd almost forgotten that. But how did you...?'

'I ...er ... I met his son; at a party at Clayford ... we worked out our parents were both in Liverpool at the same time and used to go to the Cavern, so he asked about you and...'

'Well, what an extraordinary coincidence. I'm so glad you're getting out and meeting people. But, well now, Billy Days – fancy that. He used to play at the Cavern, with some of the bands. I used to see the Beatles there, you know. In fact, I think the first time I saw Billy was when they were on. Heavens, that's a long time ago. Oh, makes me sad to think... poor old John Lennon. And George has gone too...'

'Yes. Mum?'

'Yes, love?'

'Is it true that you used to sing at the Cavern?'

There was a brief silence. When she spoke again there was a slight far-away sound in her voice. I could imagine the dreamy look she had when she was thinking hard or remembering something.

'Oh, well ... yes, just a little bit. In fact, now I think about it, it was Billy who helped get me into that. Him and that other guy - oh what was his name Jim?'

I heard my father say the name and I could tell that his teeth were gritted: 'Mike Wallis.'

'Yes, of course... but it was all a long time ago.'

Her voice sounded sad. I cleared my throat. For some reason my chest felt tight.

'I think it's amazing. I bet you had a great voice.'

'Oh, well ... I don't know about that. Jim always said that – but then he would wouldn't he, the silly date? Oh, everyone was doing something back then – it was very exciting.'

'I bet it was. And dad played guitar?'

'You have been finding out a lot, haven't you? He was pretty good, your father – pardon? Oh – he says he could have given Eric Clapton a run for his money – cloud cuckoo land as usual. Don't get him started – he's supposed to be putting up some curtains for me...'

I suddenly had a mental image of my father playing air guitar in our front room, a curtain hook as a plectrum. I shook my head. I had always thought of my parents as pretty conventional, middle-class people who had never done anything more exciting than a cruise-ship holiday to the Bahamas. Now, my whole world seemed to be shifting.

'How come you never told me?'

'Well – you know how it is love. Other things take over, and by the time you were old enough to talk, there were just so many other things – and you know I'm not one for blowing my own trumpet. It was just a bit of fun we had in the old days – but the family was always more important. But what a coincidence you meeting Billy's son like that. I suppose Billy's getting on now...'

'Mmm. How old was Billy when you knew him?'

'Oh, in his thirties, at least. I remember he seemed quite old to me. Very mature – he was nice though; had a way about him, like he knew more than he would tell, if you know what I mean.'

I nodded. I did know what she meant.

'Had nice eyes', she continued, 'and a kind of stillness. I don't know – perhaps he was much older than he looked. Come to think of it...'

Prickles went down my spine.

'What?'

'Well, I've just remembered something. Talking of coincidences; something Billy said once – it's just come to me. I thought it was odd at the time, but it's a little thing he said in passing, and you've just reminded me...'

'What was it?'

'Well, he once said that he'd known my mother.'

I felt my stomach do a kind of back flip, and I went cold all over.

'What? He said what?'

It was just in passing – I meant to ask him about it, but somehow I never got the chance. We lost touch after your dad got work down here. I think that's what he said, but he must have been very young if... I mean, mum never went out much that I knew. He must have been mistaken. Oh, well. Perhaps I didn't hear him right. It just stuck in my mind – and with you meeting his.... Are you still there Catherine?'

'Yes. Yes, I'm still here,' I said, though it came out a little hoarsely.

'Well, it's a small world, isn't it? Do tell your friend to send our love to Billy. Darling, when can we come and see you? We'd love to see the house, wouldn't we Jim, but I do wish you had a job...'

'I'm OK, mum, really. You can come when you like. You decide, and let me know, OK?'

We finished the conversation and I put the phone down and stared at it. I felt slightly light-headed. Will's card sat staring at me next to the phone.

I turned away.

I wasn't sure I want to continue along this road. I suddenly wasn't sure that I wanted mum and dad to be anything other than the mum and dad I had always known. I felt as though I had stepped into a world that was not the world I thought I knew, and it was scary.

Perhaps I wouldn't call him. I didn't have to – he'd said that. Perhaps I'd just forget the whole thing, and just let life be normal again.

Except that my life wasn't exactly normal any more. I had this house, and no job, and one chapter of a book that wasn't going to burn a hole in the bestsellers' lists as far as I could tell. I mean, I knew it lacked something, but I didn't know what.

And now mum and dad would be visiting and they would want to start reminiscing about the old days – now I had lifted the lid. Like Pandora's Box.

I stood there, in the middle of the room and for a moment I wished I could have turned the calendar back six months. I had been safe then. I had a job I hated and a life of compromising my creative needs, just like most people I knew. My life had been normal. No Will, no strange feelings about houses in villages, and no parents who had been the UK equivalent of Sonny and Cher.

It seemed I had wandered into strange new territory and I felt homesick.

I hardly went out for the next few days, except to walk Charlie. I slept in late, put on old clothes and avoided seeing anyone. I spent hours watching daytime television with Charlie curled up on my lap, and the curtains drawn. I ate little and drank too much. I didn't write.

The day before my parents came down, I roused myself and spent a whole day cleaning and shopping. They arrived, made the usual polite and helpful sounds about the house and the village, expressed their concern about how I was going to keep up this lifestyle, and then talked again about the old days – how exciting it had been seeing the Beatles, knowing Cilla Black and following all the bands and seeing some of them go on to further success and fame. They were animated and alive; they kept saying, 'Oh, do you remember...' and telling me anecdotes about John Lennon and Gene Vincent and others.

When they left, I felt exhausted. I felt old and dull. I'd always thought I'd led a far more interesting life than my parents, but I was a complete fake. Even the only serious boyfriend I'd ever had had spent his evenings copying someone else. But at least that was something. I had done nothing worthwhile, except tell a few kids how to use a comma. Big deal.

The next day I could hardly get out of bed, and when the doorbell rang at quarter past ten, I was still in my dressing gown.

I opened the door, thinking it was the postman, but it was Maureen, holding a plastic envelope.

'Hello, dear. I do hope I'm not disturbing you. I haven't seen you for several days, and I was wondering if you were all right...'

I could see her clocking the dressing gown and my unkempt hair.

'I've not been feeling too good,' I said, moving aside to let her in, 'I'm sorry – the place is a mess...'

'Oh, don't worry, dear, it's very difficult when you're poorly isn't it?' I won't keep you, but I just bought something round for you.'

We sat down and she pulled a piece of paper from the plastic envelope.

'It's nothing, really, but I'd just gone up in the attic the other day because I thought I had some buttons put away up there that would be just right for Aladdin, and I saw a box with some old drawings in and I thought of our conversation the other day, and I just thought I'd have a look, and I found this...'

She handed me the paper. It was a drawing in pen and ink, sensitively executed, of my house.

'...I thought you might like it, seeing as you live here and love it so much...'

'Oh, Maureen,' I said, genuinely touched, 'it's lovely – it really is. You really are talented.'

She was. The details of the house – the slope of the roof, the window frames and the front door with its little pedimented porch, the wisteria – not quite as established as it was now – just beginning to grow round the porch, were all very well observed, and the background was faded out in a kind of wash, which brought the house itself into focus.

'I did it years ago, before the children arrived. It's nothing, really, but...'

'Maureen, it's not nothing. Not at all...'

And, for some reason, the tears started rolling down my face and I couldn't stop them.

'I'm sorry,' I choked, 'I've just been feeling very low – and this is so lovely...'

'Oh, now, don't you worry, dear. I quite understand. You just sit there and I'll put the kettle on and make us a nice cup of tea.'

I smiled through a mist. She was so kind, and so very English that I wanted to cry and laugh at the same time. The cup of tea. The righter of all wrongs. I wondered, slightly hysterically, whether a nice cup of tea would make me a better writer, and then I burst into tears all over again.

'Here we are, dear,' she said a few minutes later, bustling in with a tray. She had found my teapot, the best mugs and a few biscuits, which she had put on a plate. She had even found a box of tissues that I'd forgotten I had.

'You're so kind,' I said, taking a tissue and applying it to my face and nose, 'thank you so much.'

'Oh – really, don't worry. I wasn't doing anything very much, and it's nice to have company, isn't it? Now, there you are – good and strong. Would you like to talk about it, dear, or rather not?'

I wondered what to tell her, but in the end I said that I was suffering from a bad case of writer's block and wasn't sure that I could write at all and that perhaps I had made a big mistake in moving here. It sounded really pathetic.

'Oh, but I'm sure that's not true, dear. I'm sure it will come right eventually. Everyone goes through rough patches, don't they? You know, you've taken a very big step, moving up from London, leaving all your friends behind and starting a new life. It takes time to settle down – I'm sure you'll be all right when you've been here a while and feel more settled. You've just got to give yourself a little time.'

It sounded completely logical and sensible. She was probably right. Except – time was a luxury I didn't have. All the same, perhaps I should stop beating myself up and give myself a bit of slack.

After Maureen left, I got dressed and took Charlie out for his belated morning walk.

Somehow, I found myself at the gates of the manor house. A silver Mercedes was parked in the drive. It looked incongruous to me, like it didn't belong there. I looked at the strap work along the lower walls of the house, the wood-framed mullioned windows and the slate-tiled, uneven roof, and felt I knew every detail. I looked away, past the village green, past the duck pond and the chestnut tree and down the lane to my house.

Will's house.

I felt empty and drained after the emotional morning, but the heaviness of the depression I had been in had lifted slightly, leaving me flat and slightly sleepy. Something about the day was missing. What would I do now? Go home? Have a bath? Go shopping? I should really have another stab at the book, I thought. But – no, it was too soon. I needed to let it lie; allow it to come together again in my head. But – what should I do?

Charlie pulled on his lead. He was sniffing the ground, catching the scent of something, pulling me towards the church gate. I remembered my first meeting with Will. I looked over the wall, almost expecting – hoping – to see him cycling down the path again. But the churchyard was empty. There was no-one about. The day was cold and grey and the trees in the churchyard bowed slightly in a gust of wind.

I sighed and mentally kicked myself. It was no use resisting it any more. The next piece of the puzzle was inevitable. The alternative seemed, at present, to be a bleak nothingness.

'Will?'

'Hello.'

'It's Catherine.'

'Yes.'

'I – er – it seems you were telling me the truth.'

'Yes.'

'My parents are now having a glorious trip down memory lane.'

He laughed, softly. 'That's good.'

'They send their love to your father.'

He laughed again. 'That's nice to hear.'

'Will?'

'Yes.'

I took a deep breath.

'Did you know my grandmother?'

'Yes.'

'I thought you might say that.'

Silence.

'I'm very low on red wine stocks.'

'I'll bring some.'

'Tonight?'

'If you like.'

'OK.'

He arrived on the doorstep with two bottles of claret and a bag of firewood.

He saw the drawing straight away. I had found a frame for it and hung it on the wall.

'That's good,' he said, studying it closely.

'Yes – my opposite neighbour did it – about 40 years ago.'

'Does she still paint...?'

'No. Life... family... same old same old...'

He made a fire while I put a casserole I'd made into bowls, sliced up some crusty bread and poured the wine. I felt whole again, and at peace. I kept telling myself that Will was the most surreal part of my life at the moment, but somehow I couldn't feel it. For the first time in days I felt... what was it? Content. That was it. Was it days, though? Or years?

When I came back in the room there was a glowing, crackling

fire. Charlie was approaching it cautiously, his ears pricking at the cracks and starting back each time a piece of wood shifted. Soon, however, the heat and glow hypnotised him, and he curled up in front of it, looking the very picture of a country dog who had slept by fires all his life.

We ate our food in silence, but it did not feel awkward. It was so nice to have the company, and the fire and the wine were making me feel relaxed. I did not want to start the subject of Will's knowledge of my family. I just wanted to stay like this for ever, in this cosy domesticity, without any weirdness.

It was not to be, of course.

'That was good,' said Will, putting down his plate and bowl on the floor and leaning back in the chair. He watched the fire for a while, the glow and movement of it reflecting on his face, sharpening his fine cheekbones and making his eyes sparkle as he appeared lost in thought. Finally he looked at me and smiled.

'Well?' he said.

I cleared away the bowls and poured more wine.

'Well, you'd better get on with it, I suppose.'

He looked back at the flames.

'Is she still alive?' he asked.

'No. She died five years ago. Pneumonia. She was in a home.'

He flinched slightly and nodded, still staring at the fire. I knew he was remembering a young woman; no doubt full of life and vitality. I had known her as a frail, tiny white-haired old woman, and had never thought of her as having a life before old age had crept up on her. I suddenly felt very sad that I had never bothered to really get to know her.

'She knew me as Bill,' he said, 'and I met her on December 10th, 1936. The day of the abdication of King Edward.'

'How old were you then?' I asked, not without a note of something edgy in my voice.

He didn't answer for a moment. Then he said, 'You'll probably guess that I looked the same age then as I do now.'

I had guessed, but all the same I wished I hadn't asked.

'OK,' I said, 'go on...'

Chapter 6 - Lizzie's Story

'He's only been and gone and done it.'

'Whose done what? Hey – Bill! Come and sit with us.'

Bill sat down at the table where some of the band members were talking to two couples who had been on the dance floor. One of the girls, a vibrant curly-haired blonde with bright red lipstick and a regular face at the jazz club, was waving a page from a newspaper. The girl sitting next to her had the light brown hair, dreamy eyes and features that he slightly recognised. He knew he would shortly be introduced.

'The king! He's abdicated – all because of that awful woman. Didn't you know?'

'No, Kitty – don't you know? We've been practising *all* day, just so you and your friends can come and dance here in the evenings. Haven't seen a paper or heard a wireless for a *lo-ong* time,' said Dave Baxter, who loved to drawl out his words in imitation of his favourite American jazz musicians.

'Well, it's all over the place. Everyone's talking about it – just think – giving up your throne and everything – for that!'

'She must be hot stuff,' said Dave, blowing a short toot on his trumpet, 'you know what I mean?'

Kitty's dance partner grinned, but Kitty gave him a look of

mock disgust.

'Well, I don't know how anyone could give up anything for her – I mean, look at the hats she wears.'

'Well, I think it's romantic,' said the girl sitting next to her in a small voice.

'Oh, Lizzie – you would, you're such a soppy date. Don't you think she's soft, Alan?'

'Oh, I don't know – she's not bad, you know – for a cousin. Say, Dave – aren't you going to introduce us to your new sax player, then?'

'Oh, yeah – sorry. Kitty and Lizzie, Ken and Alan – this is Bill Days, saxophonist and keyboard player extraordinaire. You should hear him playing *Star Dust* – there is nothing like it.'

'It's a great sound, the saxophone,' said Ken, 'does it take long to learn, Bill?'

'It takes a lot of practice,' said Bill.

'Hey, when are you fellers getting back? I want to dance some more.'

'Patience, Kitty, patience – we need a break – five minutes, OK? That's what Take Five means, right?'

'It's the longest five minutes I've ever known...'

Bill turned to Lizzie. Yes, he had seen those green eyes before – long before she was born.

'You enjoy this music?'

'Oh, yes. I just adore it. It's just like being in one of those movies – you know, with Fred Astaire. Not that I'm anything like Ginger Rogers of course...'

She laughed nervously, putting her hand over her nose.

'But you like dancing?'

'Oh, yes,' she said, her eyes widening again, 'I just love it – but, I like acting as well. I'm in an amateur company with

Kitty – that's where we met. It's such fun. We're doing Noel Coward's *Private Lives* at the moment. It's so funny – you should come and see it.'

'I might do that.'

She smiled shyly.

'This is my cousin, Alan. He works for the Ford Motor Company – got an office job too. He might even have his own car soon, then he says he'll be able to drive me home afterwards – imagine that!'

Alan nodded to Bill, then turned back to say something to Ken.

'Well – it will be better than the tram,' continued Lizzie, 'we'll have to go soon anyway. My step dad doesn't like me back too late - and I have to be at work tomorrow.'

'Where do you work?'

'Boring old cotton mill – my mother wanted me to go to college – study medicine - but someone had to bring in some money didn't they? Me dad – step-dad, that is – he couldn't get any work for ages – well, you know what it was like, so I've been working for years, doing what I can. I suppose things are better now, but you never know what will happen do you? Got to earn a living somehow. Anyway, I'd rather be an actress – if it wasn't for the Ardwick Players, I don't know what I'd do. Sorry – I don't usually talk so much.'

Bill smiled.

'It's quite all right.'

'Come on, Bill – we're on. Enjoy yourself, girls – don't hold her too tight in *Begin the Beguine* now Ken, I might get jealous...'

'Oh, go on, Dave Baxter, you're all hot air, you musicians.'

Over the next few years Bill met Lizzie and Kitty several times at the jazz club, and sometimes the whole crowd of them with Dave and Alan and whoever was around, would go out somewhere else for an evening, perhaps to see a Gracie Fields or George Formby film, or occasionally take a picnic out on Heaton Park. When Alan got his car, they took trips out of the city to have lunch at a pub.

Bill warmly remembered these years, but they were tinged with the feeling of a growing apprehension as the German and Italian leaders threatened world peace and plans for air-raid shelters were made.

In the early autumn of 1938 Bill sat in the café on Oxford Street, opposite the Palace Theatre, reading a newspaper. The news was disturbing. The piece of paper that Chamberlain was holding aloft on the front page, and on all the billboards he had passed that day, did not ring true to him.

He thought about the personal consequences of a war for him, and wondered how soon there would be conscription – papers to fill in, dates to be divulged...

As he was thinking about this, the door opened and shut, bringing with it a gust of autumn wind, and Lizzie came in with a young man with dark hair and deep set eyes. Lizzie was wearing a fitted suit and her hat was at an angle that almost covered her left eye.

'Bill! Hello! I'm so glad you're here. I want you to meet someone.'

They came and sat at his table.

'Have you been spending your money in Reno's Bill?'

'No,' he replied, smiling, 'I've been looking at all the nice shiny saxophones that I can't afford in their shop window.'

'Bill – this is Frank McEwen. He's playing at the Palace at

the moment, in The Follies.'

'Hello Frank.'

'Hello, yourself, Bill,' he replied in a broad Irish accent, 'It's nice to meet you. You play saxophone, is that right?'

'Bill plays with Ted Spiller's band at the Ritz. I've known him for two years now, haven't I Bill?'

She looked over at the paper he had been reading.

'"Peace for our Time" – oh, it's such a relief, isn't it? Frank was saying they might close the theatres if there's a war – but it wouldn't come to that would it? Even if there was a war, which there won't be now...'

'I don't know whether I would trust the signature of a man like Hitler...' Bill began.

'Oh, I think that's a pessimistic view,' said Frank, 'you're surely not saying that a man would go back on an agreement like that? Chamberlain has been wonderful – after all, we could have been catapulted into a war right now, but he's prevented it.'

'For the moment, perhaps – and at the expense of Czechoslovakia...' began Bill, but Lizzie interrupted.

'Oh please,' she said, putting a hand on Frank's arm, 'please let's not talk and argue over this. Can't we talk about the play, or music – or the weather – anything other than this terrible talk of war.'

'All right darlin'' he said, patting her hand, 'whatever you say.'

She turned to Bill, her face beaming.

'Frank is getting me an audition at the Palace. Isn't that wonderful?'

'That's great, Lizzie, I'm really pleased for you. I know it means a lot – I hope it goes well for you.' Billy smiled with genuine pleasure, but inside he knew that all of their lives would shortly be changed for good.

A year later, Lizzie was in the same café with Bill, wiping her eyes with a handkerchief. The low sun was shining through the coloured glass of the art deco windows, reflecting reds and greens on her face.

'It was going to be a wonderful wedding, Bill. Hundreds of guests and a big dress and cake – it was all arranged. Bloody Hitler – I'm sorry, but I can't tell you how disappointed I am, and now Frank's in France and God knows when I'll see him.'

'You can still get married, Liz,' said Bill, pouring her another cup of strong tea, 'that's the most important thing isn't it?'

'Oh, yes, of course it is. I just wanted it to be so special, you know? Now all we'll manage is whatever I can get on rationing, an eggless cake and a few close friends and family. You'll come, won't you Bill?'

'It's difficult to say...'

'Oh, of course, I suppose you'll be called up soon, won't you? Oh, it's just too bad. And they're closing the theatres, Bill, and I'm going to train to work a teleprinter. Everything is just upside down. Do you think it will last, the war? Do you think that perhaps it will all be over soon and we can get back to normal? Perhaps I can have my big wedding after all...'

'No, Liz. I'm sorry; I don't think it will be over soon. I know some people are saying that, but I just don't think it's going to be that easy. Hitler's troops have been preparing for a long time, and we were nearly caught on the hop. We're in for the long haul, I'm afraid.'

Liz sipped her tea in silence.

'Listen,' said Bill, 'it's unlikely I'll be called up. My job on the railway will be too important and I'll probably be exempt. I'll be volunteering as well for building shelters and filling sand bags – I'll do what I can – but I'll be around. So, if you need anything, you know where to find me. You know I'm in here most lunch times.'

'Oh Bill – you're such a good friend...'

By the end of 1940 the café no longer existed.

The theatre, like so many others, had re-opened soon after it had closed when the government realised that keeping up the morale of the country was of such importance, but by then Lizzie was working full time for the post office in the communications office.

Bill was there on the night the air raids began, playing piano in the orchestra pit of the Palace for the annual pantomime. At about 6.30pm the sirens sounded and everyone was evacuated to nearby shelters on Oxford Street. Some people, realising how crowded they were going to be, walked to Piccadilly Gardens shelters, or even walked home to their Anderson shelters.

Hundreds crowded into the brick shelters; many dressed for a night out in frock coats and evening dresses. Huddled together in the damp, dark and claustrophobic spaces, they sang songs to keep away the terror and the feelings of claustrophobia all through that long night.

When they emerged into daylight, they emerged into a city that was in flames. A city that, over the next few weeks, would be so devastated it would almost be unrecognisable.

Will stopped and stared into the fire.

'It must have been terrible,' I said, for want of something better to say. 'I mean, we always hear about the London blitz –

but so many other places were bombed just as badly...'

'It was an inferno,' he said, 'it was like the end of the world.'

We sat in silence. The fire hissed and crackled. Will sighed.

'Kitty was killed that night, walking home from a dance.'

'That's awful. That must have dreadful for my nan – to lose her best friend. I never knew...'

We sat in silence for a few minutes.

Then he said,

'It was only a few weeks after the raids had quietened down that Lizzie got the news about Frank.'

She met Bill one Saturday lunch time. He was no longer working at the theatre. It had taken a direct hit in the air raids of September 1941, and he now played at a night club that refused to close whatever Hitler chose to throw at them. Lizzie met him at the stage door. Her face was pale and she looked tired, though most people did at that time. The sleepless nights of the blitz had taken their toll.

'Bill – how good it is to see you. You're – you look better than anyone I know!'

He laughed. That did not say much for the other people. He was feeling the strain of working hard all day, repairing tracks, and then playing all night. He worried sometimes that his fingers would be too stiff to play the piano, but somehow they always seemed to loosen up, once he got going. He was tired, though. More tired than he had felt for a very long time.

'Will you take me for lunch, Bill? I've got to get back to work for one thirty, but I need to talk to someone or I will scream. I – I've just had some news, and I just don't know how... what...'

'All right, Liz,' said Bill, taking her arm, 'come on, we'll go next door and get something solid – you look as though you need some nourishment.

'It's so dreadful, Bill,' she said, as they emerged onto the ravaged streets where squads of salvage workers were clearing piles of rubble across the road, 'Baxendales has disappeared too – that great building, just gone. I just can't believe it.'

'Come on,' he said, opening the door of the restaurant, 'sit down by the window here. At least we can have at least one portion of eggs, or cheese – if you want, Liz – my treat. You do look all in – would you rather something stronger to drink?'

'No – no tea will be lovely, really.'

'So what is it you wanted to tell me?' he asked as soon as he'd ordered.

Liz lit a cigarette; her hands were shaking slightly.

'It's Frank. He's been wounded – badly. They're sending him home.'

Her voice was fragile, as if she was only just holding on.

'What happened?'

'He was hit by shell fire at point blank. His leg was severed at the knee. His other leg was pretty smashed, but they managed to save it.'

'Liz – I'm so sorry.'

'I know it could have been worse – and at least he'll see the war out at home now – but, oh Bill, he was going to – he always said, once the war's over, he was going to "sing and dance into Hollywood." Sing and dance to Hollywood – that was it. Silly, I know, but – he was so full of energy and life. I – I don't know how he'll manage. He so wanted to make a go of it – on the stage or film – I can't bear it...'

She broke down into sobs, tears falling unchecked into the brown liquid that passed as tea. People in the restaurant looked at her with sympathy but detachment. The war had affected them all and grief was a common enough sight.

Bill reached into his pocket and pulled out a clean handkerchief.

'Here. Keep it – I have plenty. They come in handy at the moment, I find.'

'Oh, Bill – I'm sorry – breaking down like that – and you're such a brick. I bet all the girls at the club just adore you.'

'We get along.'

Lizzie laughed, despite herself, and then looked serious again. She took a drag on her cigarette.

'There's something else.'

Bill waited.

'I haven't told anyone. You're the first to know. I would have told Kitty – but... oh dear – poor Kitty – so full of life too. Well, she's gone now, and you're the only friend left I can talk to – and I need to tell someone...'

'What is it?'

She leaned over the table towards him making sure that no-one else could hear.

'I'm going to have a baby.'

She looked up at his face, anxiously awaiting his reaction. A slow smile spread across Bill's face.

'Liz – that's wonderful. I'm very pleased for you.'

'Are you, Bill? Really? Thank you. That means so much. I couldn't bring myself to tell anyone, and my mother doesn't know either – she'd flay me alive. I was so scared you'd disapprove – but the war, you know – and Frank was home on leave for such a short time, and you never know when you'll see someone again...'

'It's all right, Liz. I understand. Does he know?'

'I wrote to him – just before he got wounded – I don't know

if he got the letter, but I'm hoping we can be married as quickly as possible now. It will be a very small, registry office do – just family and one or two friends. You'll come, won't you Bill?'

'I'll try,' he said, wishing that it was possible.

'I feel so much better now I've told you. I even think I might be able to manage this – oh, a real fried egg too...'

'You'd better,' he said, smiling, 'you've got to keep your strength up now...'

'They were married as soon as Frank was well enough, and lived at Liz's parents' house for a while. A few eyebrows were raised when the baby came early – but it was what happened at that time. People turned a blind eye. After the war, they moved to Liverpool. Liz said there were too many memories in Manchester. Too many friends and places had gone. Dave Baxter had been shot down and killed over Hamburg in '42, and her cousin Alan had not survived Dunkirk. The old days had gone for good.

'I helped them move, but it was the last time I saw them. I was on the move myself. But I know that she gave up her career to look after him, and supplemented his disability allowance by working at the post office.'

I was sitting on the sofa with Charlie's head on my lap, stroking his ears.

'I was always a bit scared of my grandfather,' I said, 'I remember him as a cantankerous, bitter old man in a wheelchair who used to snap at us children for the slightest thing. Gran would just fuss round him and never seemed to mind. He died before I ever got to know him. I do know that he was once offered a prosthetic limb – but he didn't want it. He'd just given up on life, I suppose. You just don't know, do you? The dreams people have. Had. It's so sad. I never knew... I never knew they were on the stage...'

Will said nothing, but stared at the fire that was now little more than dying embers. Then he said, quite slowly,

'It has always seemed to me that most people are very good at collaborating in the destruction of their dreams.'

'But – if you get your leg blown off and...'

'Yes – of course. It changes things. But it doesn't end things. Frank had another – what, 30? Years of life left. He did nothing with it. He wasted it. Just as Liz wasted hers.'

'That seems a little unfair. That's my grandparents you're talking about.'

'OK. I'm sorry.'

He got up.

'I must go.'

'Must you?'

'Yes.'

'But – isn't there – I mean – aren't you going to explain anything?'

'In time.'

'When?'

He looked at me for several moments.

'Come to my flat. I'll cook you dinner. Besides, it's getting too cold to cycle so much this late at night.'

'Don't you have a car?'

'No. I don't drive.'

'Oh,' I said, wondering why I was so surprised, when there were so many other things to be surprised at.

He turned at the door and said: 'How's your book going, anyway?'

'It's not. I've got writers' block.'

‘No such thing,’ he said, rather curtly, I thought, ’that’s just an excuse.’

‘That’s easy for you to say...’

‘Yes,’ he said, ‘it is. Because it’s true. The truth is easy. It’s resisting the truth that makes things difficult.’ Then he looked at me straight in the eye and said, ‘Your grandfather had his leg blown off. He could still have made a life for himself. What’s your excuse?’

I felt like I’d been slapped in the face. I must have shown it because he suddenly softened.

‘Look...I’ll call you, OK?’

Then he was gone again. This time I didn’t watch him go down the lane. I shut the door and leaned my back on it.

‘Bloody cheek!’ I said.

Charlie wagged his tail.

‘"I’ll call you." Huh! Who does he think he is? Well, perhaps I might just be busy next time...’

Chapter 7

Despite being furious with him and what he had said, I had a nagging feeling that what he had said was right. What was my excuse? People did all kinds of things against the greatest of odds, and here was I moaning about writer's block.

The following day I got out the meagre Chapter One I had written so far and read it.

I could see what was wrong with it. The characters I had introduced so far seemed thin and two-dimensional, like cardboard cut-out stereotypes. I had thought that my own experience of the people I had known as a teacher would be enough to provide a sense of realism, but the opening classroom scene with the difficult, rude teenagers and the murderous thoughts of the female teacher just sounded like a hard luck story told by a bitter and whining critic of the education system. It wasn't going to interest anyone beyond the first sentence.

I had thought, when I was writing it, that I had been writing the truth. But what I now saw was only a surface, superficial version of the truth. It was one-sided and bigoted. That was why it didn't work. I had made the mistake of making my main characters' views to be the right ones – perhaps if I explored the other characters a bit more...

'Coo-eee! Catherine?'

Blast and botheration.

'Catherine?! Are you home?'

I put down my writing folder and went out onto the landing.

'Hi, Maureen. You OK?'

'Oh, there you are dear. I'm sorry to bother you, but your front door was unlocked – I did knock but I don't think you heard me – and I thought I'd just pop my head round the door and see if you were all right.'

'Oh,' I said, coming down the stairs, 'thank you – that's kind of you. I'm feeling a little better thanks. Tea?'

'Oh no, dear, really – I don't want to take up your time. I was just concerned – you seemed so down yesterday.'

'Yes. I was. Stupid really - I mean, there could be so many more things to be down about. I got things out of perspective, I think. How are things with you?'

'Oh, busy as usual – I'm just off to a parish meeting right now, and then I'm seeing the local amateur operatic society tonight – they're doing *The Pirates of Penzance* – they really are very good. You should come – though I'm not sure if there are any tickets left...'

'It's OK, really. Maureen...'

'Yes, dear?'

'Have you done any drawing lately?'

'Oh, I don't think I have the time. And anyway, I'd be very rusty now. I probably couldn't draw a thing...'

'You could go to some night classes.'

She hesitated.

'That's an idea... But I don't think I'd like to go on my own...driving at night...'

'I'd go with you,' I said, surprising myself, 'not to drawing – but if they had some creative writing classes on the same night, we could go together. It would be fun.'

I had previously had no thoughts of doing any such thing. The suggestion had been totally spontaneous and out of the blue, similar to when I decided to buy the house. I rather liked this new side of me.

'Well, do you know, that might be rather nice. This year's courses will be just starting too – or already started, but we'd only miss one or two. Oh, I think I'd like that Catherine. Of course, it would depend on the evening – I do have commitments...' She suddenly looked doubtful.

'Maureen – do something for yourself for a change. You are very good at looking after other people, but this would be a special treat for yourself. I think you would really enjoy it.'

'You're quite right – I do forget myself sometimes. All right – why don't you look them up and we'll talk again later. How exciting! I really must go now – they'll be wondering where I've got to...'

I felt lighter and bursting with a sudden energy as I rushed up the stairs to log on and search the local council website. Everything suddenly felt easy again, as it had when I had put in my offer on the house.

Will's words came back to me. 'The truth is easy.' Was this what he meant? This feeling of running with my instinct and creating something new? Was this the real truth?

It took a while to find the two courses running on the same evening but eventually I managed to find what we wanted in the county town fifteen miles away. I was able to persuade Maureen, when I spoke to her later, to re-arrange a few of her plans so that she wouldn't upset too many people, and then I booked them, feeling for the first time since I had arrived in Little Dipping that I was doing something purposeful and interesting.

There might even be one or two eligible males too, I thought, which could be an added bonus.

I sang and did a little cha-cha step as I put the kettle on and made myself a coffee, and in this mood of enthusiasm, I sat down to re-work my first chapter. I began to think about the backgrounds and lives of my characters – even the 'bad' ones. As I was working on this my thoughts continually strayed to Will and the story he had told me about my grandparents. They had been brought to life for me – they were no longer just Gran and Grandpa, they were real people who had had terrible experiences, losses, hopes and dreams. I began to understand why my grandfather had been so difficult, and the terrible sacrifice that my grandmother had made.

Something – well, lots of things actually – but one thing in particular was bugging me and kept on niggling at the back of my mind. I wanted to know the answer, and I wanted to get to the bottom of Will's life and why he was so connected with my family. Not to mention the mega-coincidence of his having been born here. And not to mention a whole lot of other things that weren't remotely possible, but somehow were.

I wasn't going to call him, though. He'd said he would call me, and I was damned if I was going to give him the chance to think I was after him or desperate to see him in any way. He could make the effort this time, especially after what he'd said about my grandparents, as if it was up to him to have an opinion. Anyway, he'd seemed decidedly edgy the last time I saw him, and I wasn't sure I wanted someone who... who, well, who I'd only really met three times after all, telling me how to write my own book. How on earth did he get people to talk about themselves so easily anyway? It was almost creepy.

By the time three days had passed and he still hadn't rung, I was getting more than edgy myself. I kept catching myself looking at the phone, as if it would ring just by my looking at it.

I got on with the book, and I even managed to make forays into a second chapter, but I was still doubting myself, and my ability to write words, sentences, paragraphs that would be remotely interesting to anyone. So progress was still slow and every so often I asked myself why Will hadn't rung, and kicked myself for asking.

But at least I was writing.

When he did ring, he sounded just as calm and cool as usual. It was infuriating.

'Hello, Catherine.'

'Will? I thought you'd left the country.'

'No. I'm here. Can you come over tonight?'

Of all the nerve.

'You do give short notice, don't you? I might have plans tonight. Why didn't you...'

'OK. Tomorrow night then?'

Damn, damn, damn, damn, damn. Tomorrow night was the first night of evening classes.

'No. I'm busy tomorrow night. Tonight will be fine, as it happens...'

'That's all right then.'

'Yes.'

'It's Flat 16, Waterside. I'll see you at seven.'

I put the phone receiver down and stared at it for a few moments, called it a smarmy bastard and went off to wash my hair.

The flats where Will lived were converted from an old Victorian mill by the river. The building itself was large and imposing from the outside, but the river, with its little public footpath alongside it, and the trees on the banks offered a picturesque setting that off-set the grimness of the mill walls.

Inside, the place had been turned into small but modern and well-designed flats that had a feeling of spaciousness. Will's place had a lovely view across the river to open fields beyond.

Although it only had one living/dining room, a bedroom, a small kitchen and a shower room, it felt larger because of the way the rooms were laid out, with the kitchen opening out onto the dining area of the living room, which was L-shaped, giving the illusion of an extra room.

'This is lovely,' I said, taking in the flat and the view, 'is it yours? Do you own it?'

'No. It's rented.' He handed me a tonic water with lemon. 'I've never owned a property in my life.'

It figured, somehow, with what I knew of him, which was very little; but it figured anyway. He didn't want to put down roots or sign too many important documents.

I watched him lay the small table with cutlery, mats and a bottle of claret.

'There's something I want to ask you.'

'I'm sure there are lots of things you want to ask me,' he said, not looking up.

'Yes. There are. But there's one thing in particular.'

'Well?'

'Why didn't you go to my grandparents' wedding? I mean, you were a close friend. You were invited. But, you didn't go, right?'

'Right. I didn't go.'

'Why?'

His eyes flickered up at me briefly, and then he went into the kitchen where he began to stir something on a stove.

'I think you can probably guess,' he said.

I walked towards the kitchen and leaned against the wall where the two rooms met.

'Well,' I said, slowly, 'I suppose Liz's mother was there – presumably...'

'Yes, she was.'

'...and...'

He looked at me with the slightest hint of a twinkle in his eye.

'Go on.'

'...she would have recognised you...someone she used to know years earlier...?'

He smiled, still stirring.

'You know,' he said, with more than a hint of amusement in his voice, 'you're a lot brighter than you give yourself credit for.'

I sat down at the table. He left the food simmering in the kitchen and came to sit opposite me, folding his hands together and resting his head on them to look at me.

'Olive?' he said, pushing a bowl of kalamatas in front of me. I bit into the succulent flesh of a reddish black olive. It was superb. The flavour of the olive rose above the dressing, and had none of the over-saltiness of olives I had tasted before. The taste made me think of sun-drenched Greek islands.

'You didn't buy those in Tescos,' I said.

'No. Farmers' market. Supermarkets give me a headache.'

I grinned. I had to admit that I liked his style, even if he was driving me nuts.

'Who are you, Will?'

He took an olive stone out of his mouth and put it onto a small glass dish he had provided for the purpose.

'I was wondering when you were going to ask me that.'

I waited.

'How do you want me to answer that question? I mean, if I asked you the same question, who are you, Catherine? What would you reply?'

I thought for a moment. Who was I? How did I define myself? I could not think of an answer. I had roles: writer (perhaps), house-owner, friend, daughter; I had definitions: English, female, mid-thirties, average build, light-brown hair, but did any of things really say anything about who I am? And if they didn't, then who the hell was I?

'I don't know,' I said, it's not that easy to answer...'

'No. Then perhaps you could ask me a different question.'

'All right then, exactly how old are you?'

'Ah,' he said, grinning, 'now that really is getting to the nitty gritty.'

He ate another olive, then gave me a look that suggested he was wondering how much to tell me.

'I think we should eat first.'

There was no good in arguing with that. I was desperately hungry, and the smells that were coming from the kitchen were making me feel quite faint with hunger.

While we ate we talked about other things. I told him about the writing course and he said he thought it was an excellent idea; that all artists need some kind of support and constructive criticism and they can't live in a vacuum. We also discussed music and politics and the weather, stealthily avoiding anything too personal or specific.

The food that Will had cooked was one of the most delicious meals I had ever tasted, and yet very simple. It was not gourmet or over-flavoured – it was just good food: baked fillets of salmon with a breadcrumb and garlic crust, creamed potatoes and steamed courgettes in a butter sauce. Everything was cooked to perfection; the fish flaked at the touch of the knife and almost melted in the mouth while the crunchiness of the topping provided a contrast in texture that was utterly sensual. And I had never eaten vegetables with such incredibly intense flavours.

'Where did you learn to cook like this, Will?'

'Cooking is easy,' he said, 'as long as your ingredients are the best quality; all these are locally produced and organic.'

'Isn't that expensive?'

'No – not really. I save on other things anyway – like not having a car.'

'You're very green, aren't you?'

'Not so very long ago, everybody lived like this, and it was normal. There was no such thing as green or organic because everything was green and organic naturally. It was just the way things were, so it didn't have to be defined. I find it amusing, and a little sad, that we now have to label it as a luxury option. But I love good food. I've had a long time to learn, and – it's just one of the things I do.'

'You're full of surprises.'

'Perhaps.'

'Perhaps!' I echoed, mocking him, 'That is the biggest understatement I have ever heard! You're the most surprising person I've ever met!'

'Actually,' he said, 'you're pretty surprising yourself.'

'Me? Why?'

'Turning up in my house like that...'

'Your house...? Oh, yes – well... But I was hoping you were going to explain that to me.' It had never occurred to me that it was just as surprising to him as it was to me.

He laughed, 'don't hold your breath. I have no explanation for that. It's a complete mystery to me. As are many things about my life. I don't have all the answers, Catherine, so don't expect too much.'

'Oh.'

I don't know why I was disappointed. Will was only human – at least, I hoped he was – but there was something about him that was so centred and still that you almost expected him to have the answers to everything.

After an apple pie flavoured with cloves and cinnamon, with a more-ishly short and crumbly pastry and creamy home-made custard, we sat down in the sitting area in the two easy chairs, Will with a glass of claret and me with another tonic water because I was driving. At least tonic water reminded one of gin, even if there wasn't any.

In the corner of the room, I noticed a cherry-red electric guitar, given pride of place and standing as if it was part of the décor. I was not a stranger to the makes of guitars. Jake had been through a few and could go into ecstatic flights of exaltation over a Fender Stratocaster or an acoustic Hagstrom (favoured by Bowie), so I knew a classic when I saw one.

I pointed to it in some excitement.

'Is that...is that *the* Les Paul?'

Will grinned at my excitement. 'Indeed it is.'

'From... I mean, you played that in the Cavern?'

'Yes.'

'In the sixties?'

'Yes.'

'My God, it must be worth something.'

'Probably.'

I leaned back and let out a little laugh. I couldn't help thinking how this would have blown Jake's mind, and I felt just a teeny bit smug. But I didn't want to think about him. More to the point, it was another reminder, and evidence, of Will's strange past. There was no getting away from it. I had to ask some serious questions.

'So – how old are you?' I asked again.

He looked at me for a very long time, and then he said:

'Two hundred and eight years old last March.'

We sat in silence, his words hanging in the air. Outside, I could hear the trees swaying in a sudden gust of wind, and somewhere far away, in another flat, a telephone was ringing, unanswered.

'I see.'

'Do you?'

'No.'

He nodded.

I tried to formulate my next question, but there were so many in my head that what came out was gibberish. He waited for me to say something coherent, calmly sipping his claret and saying nothing. Eventually I managed to formulate some words.

'How... how... I mean, look, if you really are that age – which is pretty far fetched, you have to agree – how do you look... the way you look?'

'How do I look?'

Pretty damned good for two centuries, I thought, but my reply was: 'you look about 35 years old.'

He nodded, staring into the distance as if remembering something.

'The truth is – and I did warn you that I didn't have all the answers – the truth is, I don't know. I don't know why I've lived so long, and I don't know why I haven't aged. It's just what's happened. Somewhere around my mid-thirties I just stopped ageing, and that's all I know.'

'But – don't you have any ideas at all? I mean, have you been to a doctor – or, or – had any sort of research done?'

He shook his head.

'I told you – I have never told anyone else about this before. You are the first person I have ever told – and I don't want anyone else to know.'

'But...'

He leaned forward, suddenly intense. After his calm demeanour, the earnestness of his words took me by surprise.

'Don't you see what would happen? I would never be able to live my life as I have done – with the freedom to be exactly as I choose. If I went to anyone – and it would take some convincing – can you imagine the publicity, even if it was just derisive laughter? I wouldn't mind that so much – but if I was really taken seriously, and it could somehow be scientifically proven – my life would not be my own.'

I thought about it, and I realised he was right. I could even see the tabloid newspaper headlines – whether derisory or sensationalist, it would be the worst thing for Will. He would become a public commodity – and he was a man who liked to stay private. I knew that much of him.

He had leaned back in his chair and spoke in the calm, still voice that I had come to know. 'It took me a while – after our first meeting – to decide whether to trust you or not. And I decided that I would.'

'Thank you.' I was genuinely touched.

Into the silence that followed, rain started to clatter against the window in squalls of gusty wind. I hoped my drive home wasn't going to be too horrible in this weather. But I didn't want to go yet. There were too many things to ask.

'So... I'm the only person you've told... ever?'

'Yes.'

'So – what happens when – I mean, you must have met so many people over the years – don't they, I mean, surely at some point they must begin to think it's a bit strange...'

'I don't allow that to happen. I don't stay around long enough. None of my relationships with anyone has lasted longer than ten years. I have to keep moving on.'

'That must be difficult for you...'

'I don't get close enough for it to be a problem,' he said quickly.

Blimey, I thought, I have met the ultimate commitment-phobe. Thank goodness I hadn't done something silly like fall in love with him or anything like that. Even if I was – just slightly – attracted to him (I had to admit it grudgingly), at least I knew there was no go in that area. I would just make sure that didn't happen.

'Don't you find it very lonely?' I asked.

I could have been mistaken, but for a nano-second I saw something that looked like pain flicker across his face, and then he looked away.

'I like my own company,' he said.

It was the first time I had ever heard Will give anything but a straight answer. The atmosphere became slightly uncomfortable. I decided to change the subject.

'The other thing that is really odd about you,' I said, 'is the way you keep bumping into members of my family. What's all that about?'

He looked back at me, emptied his glass and said with a shrug:

'Search me.'

'You mean – it just happens? You don't even have any say in the matter?'

'No. I just keep moving on, and sooner or later you turn up, no matter where I go. I've come to expect it.'

'But – that's weird.'

'You're telling me.'

'How many of us have you known?'

'Six. Including you.'

'All female?'

'Yes.'

'Going back to...?

His voice was soft as he answered: 'Your great-great-great grandmother.'

I suddenly felt very tired, slightly nauseous and too exhausted to ask any more questions. I had taken in too much – a bit like feeling sick after eating too much chocolate cake. Once again, I had the sense of the world contorting and shifting around me. And this time I hadn't been drinking.

'Are you all right?' he asked, gently.

'Yes... er – no. Yes. Fine. But I think I would like to go home now.'

He glanced at the window. 'The weather's pretty bad...'

'I know. That's why I should go now – before it gets worse.'

'You could stay the night.'

There was a another brief silence. I vaguely wondered why I wasn't saying no.

'I mean – in here. I have an airbed...'

Stupid Catherine. Stupid, stupid, stupid.

'Yes – of course. I mean – no. No, - it's OK. I should go. I've left Charlie on his own. I can't leave him all night.'

'OK.'

I got up to get my jacket, feeling awkward and embarrassed. Then I remembered my manners.

'The washing up – I'll help you.'

'No. It's fine. I don't expect guests to do that. You'd better get going before the roads get flooded.'

We stood at the door of his flat.

'Don't come down. I'll see myself out.'

'OK.'

'Will – thanks for the meal – and everything. I just need to be in the sane world for a while.'

He smiled. 'Is there such a thing?'

'Good point. All the same...'

He nodded. 'I know.'

I turned to go, and then turned back.

'Just one thing. I know nothing about my great-grandmother. Not even her name...'

'Hannah. Hannah Jepson.'

'Hannah. Nice name. Well – I'll see you around, Will. Thanks again.'

'Bye Catherine.'

I sat in the car in the dark, with the rain beating down on the roof and the wind making the car rock slightly.

I wasn't sure I wanted to see him again. It probably wasn't a good idea. The real world was a safer option. Tomorrow I was going to my new class and I'd be meeting new people. Normal people with normal ages and normal lives. People who didn't disturb you and make you feel that you were going mad.

I drove home slowly through the torrential rain, my windscreen wipers beating furiously and adding to my slight feelings of hysteria. Gratefully, I arrived back at Little Dipping and parked the car outside the house, got out of the car as quickly as possible with my jacket over my head and made a run for it.

But when I reached my garden gate I stopped. My hand was on the latch, and immediately such a sense of grief and sorrow and loss came over me that I all but collapsed. I stood, leaning against the wall, drenched in the steady blanket of rain, my hair flat against my face, heaving great sobs. I could see nothing in the dark and the rain, but only the garden gate that was closed to me – closed and locked against me for ever. I was completely alone. There was to be no escape. I could only go back...back to...

And then I heard a dog barking, and somehow, like one slowly coming out of a dream, I looked around me. I saw my car, and for a moment it seemed alien to me, something I had never seen before, but shaking my head it started to make sense and then I realised that it was my dog that was barking. What was his name....? Charlie – of course it was. What was the matter with me? Why was I standing in the rain, crying? What on earth just happened to me?

Chapter 8

Charlie was now barking frantically. I pushed the gate. I almost fell through as it opened easily, and I ran (ridiculously, because I was already as wet as I could be) to the front door and fumbled to find my key.

Charlie head-butted me as I came in, and I sat down on the floor with my back against the closed door, hugging him while he gave me urgent dog licks all over my wet face.

I didn't know what had just happened, but I did know that I was out of breath, emotionally exhausted and that I needed a stiff drink.

I got out of my wet clothes and put a dressing gown on and then poured myself a large gin with very little tonic (I had, after all, had the tonic water earlier). I curled up on the sofa, wishing there was a fire in the grate, but I soon warmed up as I had left the heating on, though it didn't feel quite as cosy.

I wondered if I wasn't very well. I had lost myself out there for a moment, as if I had switched to some other reality, or had some kind of hallucination. Only I knew it wasn't strictly a hallucination because I had not seen anything different, only the gate and the wall and the rain. Yet for a second, my car had seemed like something strange to me.

I pulled my gown around me and invited Charlie up onto my

lap for comfort. I was scared. Perhaps I was losing my marbles, or had a brain tumour or something. All kinds of possibilities, none of them good, entered my head.

But worrying about it wasn't going to get me anywhere. I told myself to pull myself together and get a grip. It was probably Will's fault. Seeing someone like that was bound to make one feel a bit odd. He was spooking me out. So that was another reason for not seeing him.

Feeling a little better, I finished off the gin – which I had drunk incredibly quickly – and decided to go to bed. Tomorrow I would begin afresh. I would start my course, re-start my novel and if I had any more funny turns like that I would go to the doctor and get it sorted.

Feeling marginally back in control I filled a hot water bottle and went to bed.

The evening classes took place at a large secondary school in the centre of Northwick. That oddly familiar smell of polished wood floors and stale school dinners, laced with a hint of adolescent sweat, had me back at my old school for one horrible moment as I entered the doors, and I would almost have turned round and gone home if it wasn't for Maureen. I had to remind myself that I was not going to be standing up in front of a bunch of Year 10 thugs, or do any marking or invigilate a 3 hour exam, and the experience of being within a school building was going to be much improved by the absence of anyone below the age of 18.

As it happened, I noticed that most of my fellow classmates were not much below the age of 55, and, looking around the drab classroom with its ubiquitous maps of the world and posters of French verb tables, and sizing up my fellow students,

I realised that my hopes of meeting writers of similar age and dissimilar sex were going to be severely dashed.

After I had gone through the embarrassing initiation ritual of introducing myself to the class – who had already been together for two classes, enough to make me feel like a complete outsider – we began our first exercise. The tutor, Sue, a tall, willowy lady with long grey hair, was actually a published author which impressed me far more than I felt it should, as I had never heard of her or read any of her books. All the same, I could not help feeling slightly in awe of someone who had actually done it – gone through the process and got someone to publish her books – five of them too.

The exercise involved speed-writing, which I could not get my head round at all. We were supposed to write without stopping for two minutes on something dear to us and just to let the writing flow without thinking about it too much. I chose to write about Charlie, but it was almost impossible for me to write without thinking and planning what I wanted to say, or without making sure that my grammar and syntax were correct.

Sue saw that I was struggling and came over to help.

'You're a grammar teacher, right?' She'd obviously done her homework and looked at my admission form.

'Well – yes. Used to be. Not now.'

'The funny thing is, it's always English teachers who have the most difficulty with this exercise.'

She looked at what I'd written, which, though short, was, I thought, a rather good description of Charlie – his colouring, his wet nose and big 'give me a biscuit now' eyes...

'You know,' she said, 'you write quite well. I can see the dog – but I'm not emotionally engaged. It's very controlled. You need to let go a little, loosen up. That's what this exercise is for. Practise at home – in fact, I'm going to set you this as an extra piece of homework. I think it's exactly what you need, Catherine. Once you stop worrying about the technicalities, your writing will really start to come alive.'

Great. I'd only been in my first class for ten minutes and I'd already got extra homework. I really couldn't see the point of the exercise. I mean, what's the point of writing if you're not going to string a proper sentence together? Still – she was the published writer and I wasn't, so perhaps there was something to it.

In the break we sat round white plastic tables in the canteen and drank disgusting coffee from a machine out of white plastic cups that were too hot to hold. I had hoped to meet up with Maureen during the break, but apparently the evening classes all staggered their breaks so there wasn't too much of a queue for the one coffee machine.

I felt rather alone, as everyone around seemed already to know each other and to have struck up friendships and cliques. Out of fifteen students, there was a whole group of five women who had obviously all joined up together and were laughing raucously at something on the next table. The remaining numbers seemed to be made up of two women much younger than me, and couples in their fifties.

Feeling a little left out, I remembered suddenly the text I had received earlier.

Good luck with your course tonight. Will.

I couldn't help smiling. It was nice of him to remember, and for a moment I did not feel quite so alone.

'May I join you?' said a voice beside me.

I turned to see a white haired man, balding on top with a

craggy, kind face. He was wearing a striped, yellow sweater with a pink shirt collar underneath that clashed disastrously with the sweater. It made me think of something I might have bought for a penny in a sweet shop years ago.

'Of course,' I said.

He introduced himself as Peter Hemming, and we discussed the class, and he told me he was a retired pensions manager who'd never had time to do anything interesting or creative until now, and although he was actually busier now than he'd ever been in his life, had found new energy and enthusiasm for so many things since his retirement that he wished he'd had the time to do them earlier.

'I tell you something else that I've discovered too,' he said, his eyes lit up with enthusiasm, 'last term I did a course here on family history, and it's become a fascinating new hobby, as well as my short-story writing. In fact, I've found that the two things go together. I've found so many people in my family tree that I get lots of ideas for stories.'

'Really?' I said, 'interesting in what way? Murderers? Criminals? Royal Family?'

I had not intended to sound sarcastic, but somehow when I heard the words come out, it sounded so, and I inwardly cringed. Fortunately, he did not seem to notice.

'Oh, no – not at all. In fact, on the face of it, they lead quite ordinary lives. Many of them are agricultural labourers – but there are quite a lot of shoemakers and weavers – but when you see them there on the census, and see where they lived and where they came from, you just start to wonder about what their lives were like, and it only takes a little thing – like a shoemaker married to the daughter of a wealthy merchant, or an illegitimate birth – and you begin to wonder, "what's the story behind that?" and you're hooked! It's like a drug. But I've had plenty of ideas for stories from my family tree.'

'And how do you do it?' I asked politely, realising that I was only humouring him and secretly hoping he wasn't going to suddenly pull out a huge chart of his family tree and start telling me about his ancestors, 'don't you have to travel miles to archives and read dusty old documents?'

'No – no. Well, yes – sometimes. The further back you go, the more you have to use the record offices – that's true. But there's plenty you can do on the internet now. For example, you can see all the census records for every ten years from 1841 to 1911. You just have to put a name and an approximate date into the search engine and away you go. I've done a lot of mine on the internet. I had to get my niece to show me how to use it at first, but it's quite easy once you get the hang of it...'

Something was happening in the pit of my stomach.

'What sort of information does it give you?'

'The census? Oh, lots. Family relationships, ages, occupations – and also where a person was born. You have to be careful though, it's not always accurate, and it can take a while to find someone, especially if the transcriber has made a mistake – it often happens with mis-spelled names and...'

'So – would I be able to find, say, my great-grandmother on the census, if I wanted to?'

'Oh yes – as long as you have a name and have an idea of where she was living. Of course if her name's something like Elizabeth Smith, then it could be difficult, as there would be hundreds...'

At that moment we were called back into the classroom.

'That's very interesting,' I said, feeling slightly weak at the knees, 'I never realised it was so easy.'

Peter was scribbling something on a piece of paper.

'Go to this website,' he said, 'you have to pay a fee, but it's well worth it – and I bet you you'll be hooked by next week!'

He put his folder under his arm and rushed off with the vigour and urgency of a man who had found a new lease of life at a late age and didn't want to waste any of it.

I was left looking at the piece of paper with the website address on it, and a faint buzzing in my ears.

In the car, Maureen could not stop talking.

'Oh, Catherine, I am so glad you suggested doing this – I've so enjoyed myself and I've met some lovely people too. Our tutor is just marvellous and very encouraging. Do you know, she said I had a real, natural eye for details, and – oh, what was it she said? – Oh yes, I already had a good understanding of perspective, which some people find very difficult. She thought if I could just develop my style and become a little bit bolder, I could try selling my work somewhere. Well! I don't know about that, but it was very nice of her to say so, don't you think?'

'Of course. That's wonderful...'

'Oh, and it was so lovely just to spend a whole two hours drawing and painting – I almost felt guilty, but I told myself I wasn't going to. Maureen, I said to myself, it is about time you did something for yourself for a change so you're just going to jolly well enjoy yourself and that's that. Just as you said, and you were quite right. Oh, and there are two ladies there who live quite nearby and they're going to come round for tea and we're going to get together and have little painting parties. I thought maybe we could all go to classes in the same car too.'

'Oh. OK – Yes, that's a good idea.'

'Anyway, thank you so much for arranging this, Catherine, it was such a good idea – but, that's enough about me, I've been wittering on for far too long. Now, tell me all about your class. How did it go dear?'

'Oh – er, very well. It was good. Yes, I – er, I got extra homework.'

'Oh? Did you? Why was that?'

'She said I needed to practise more.'

'Well, I'm sure it'll be for the good. And what were the people like?'

'Oh – nice. I met a very nice man called Peter. He's a family history enthusiast. You'd like him.'

'Oh well – that is nice. At least you had some men in your class – we didn't have any!'

The next day I got out my writing folder and my notes from the class and settled down to try the writing exercises I had been given. I had resolved to do these in the morning and then work on my novel in the afternoon.

When I opened my notebook, a small scrap of paper fell out and fluttered and floated to the floor. It was the website address Peter had given to me. Strangely enough, I had almost forgotten about it, but looking at it again, I felt the same slight queasy excitement in my guts as I had had last night.

It won't harm just having a quick look, I said to myself, and I put my writing aside.

Three hours later I had a small pile of print-outs on my desk and a rather large headache from staring at 19th century handwriting on the computer screen.

And all I had really done was prove that Will was who he said he was. It had taken me a while to work out how to use the site and to find him on each census, but when I realised that his age was probably going to be the same each time, it got easier. There he was on every census: *William Days, 35, lodger, Musician, born in Little Dipping.* There were a few differences on each one, like in 1851 he was described as Actor/Musician, but it basically did not tell me anything I didn't already know, except where he was living each time, which was always in a different place. But he existed. He was real.

I then typed Hannah Jepson into the search engine for the 1901 census, but there were so many Hannah Jepsons – most of them in Lancashire or Yorkshire - of a similar age that it was impossible to tell which was my great-grandmother. I needed more information. Looking at the advice section on the website, I discovered that I could order a birth certificate for my grandmother which would give me some details, and then a marriage certificate for Hannah. But the whole thing was beginning to feel rather complicated and expensive. Besides, I could find out about Hannah any time. It seemed pointless to go to all that trouble for just some minor details, when I knew someone who had actually known her.

Peter had been right. Now I could see her name on the list, I felt tantalising close to her, and I had a real desire to solve the puzzle and pin her down. I suddenly wanted to know more about her, who she was and who her parents were and what they did. I was hooked. Yet, going down the normal routes of ancestry research seemed pointless when all I had to do was pick up the phone.

But I had resolved not to speak to Will. At least, not for a while. Damn the man. It wasn't fair. It wasn't going to do me any good seeing him – it only made me feel weird and I didn't want to have any more episodes like the night before last.

No. Get a grip. I was meant to be writing and it was already lunch time and I hadn't written a single word. I switched off the computer and folded up the papers I had printed and slipped them between two books on my shelf, then I went to warm up a tin of soup.

It took me a while, but I started to get the hang of the speed-writing exercise. Telling myself to forget about grammar and getting it right first time went against a whole lifetime of being a control freak and a complete pedant when it came to the English language. But when I began to let myself go, I found it was strangely enjoyable and exhilarating. At first what came out seemed childish and almost gibberish, but as I wrote, without correcting, without thought, I found myself beginning to get more in touch with the subject matter, and when I read back what I had written about Charlie I realised that instead of a description of a dog, I had written a powerful expression of a relationship with a beloved friend. It looked like a real writer had written it.

After surprising Charlie by waking him from a peaceful slumber to give him a hug and a biscuit, followed by one of his favourite chews, I settled down to try again, while Charlie settled down to dream of another happy wakening.

This time, I tried it on the piece of the novel I was working on. By five o'clock I had finished Chapter 2 and I felt like a bird that had been let out of its cage. At this rate I could write the first draft in a few weeks. Singing the Hallelujah Chorus, I raided the freezer to see what I could treat myself to and nearly made myself sick on double fudge chocolate ice cream.

The next morning promised a beautiful crisp and bright October day with a clear blue sky and air that woke up the lungs and got into your head and made you glad to be alive. Perfect weather for walking.

I put on some wellies, called Charlie, and we set out across the fields, with Charlie racing round in circles in an ecstasy of freedom and energy.

We walked through three fields, along a public footpath that led from Little Dipping to the neighbouring village of Stanton Bridge. The birds were in their full glory of song and even the sheep in the nearby fields seemed happier and less worried than usual, even when Charlie woofed at them from behind a hedge. I was drinking in everything around me, from the birds and wild berries to the gorgeous colour of the autumn trees.

I had intended to turn back after the third field, but ahead I could see that we were very close to Stanton – I could see a few houses on the outskirts of the village. It would only take a few minutes longer to get there and then perhaps we could return via the road and make it a round trip. I would then be ready to start Chapter 3. How good that sounded.

I scrambled Charlie over the stile and followed the track that led down the side of a potato field, towards another gated stile that opened onto a little lane that would presumably lead us to the road.

The lane turned a corner round an old, high wall, and when we came round the bend I stopped, every nerve in my body on edge.

In front of me was a great ruin of a house. It was built of a dark, greyish brick, its turreted walls were three storeys high, and it stood in its own space in what was obviously once its own land but what was now overgrown and surrounded by barbed wire and DANGER, DO NOT ENTER signs posted here and there. I was looking at it from its side aspect, but as I slowly walked along the lane I came round to face the front. A large, crumbling staircase led to a great porticoed entrance. The long narrow windows were boarded up, giving it a soulless look. Some of the wall to the left top corner of the house had fallen down, leaving a dark gap where you could just see torn and faded wallpaper and a blackened empty fireplace. Willow herb, mallow and nettles crowded round its lower walls and in between the steps of the entrance. What had obviously once been a grand approach was now a mud track and at the entrance to the track, high wrought iron gates were now completely brown with rust and tied up with heavy chains and padlocks.

I stood stunned. I would not go any closer. I did not even want to go near its gates. The whole place filled me with a horror that almost made me sick to my stomach.

I don't know how long I stood there but when a tractor lumbered up the lane behind me I came out of my stupor, called Charlie and put him on the lead.

It was then that I realised that I was shaking and was feeling chilly, despite the warmth that I had generated from the walk. I turned and walked away from the house, still aware of its presence behind me, staring at me from behind its boarded windows and it gave me a creepy feeling down my back. I almost wanted to run, as if the house was somehow going to suck me into its festering blackness and trap me for ever.

A cloud had come over the day, though the sky was still as clear and blue as when we had set out.

Stopping at the village post office for a bottle of water, I asked the woman behind the counter about the old ruin.

'Oh, you mean Alderton Hall? It's been like that for ages. The villagers have been campaigning to the council to do something about that eyesore for years. It got bought up by property developers a long time ago, but they never really did anything with it – I think it was going to cost far more than they had realised to get it renovated, so it was just left, abandoned and unsellable. Thankfully, the council have now bought it up and it's going to be demolished and the land cleared for new housing.'

'Do you know who owned it originally?'

'God knows – that would be before I came here. It's been like that for as long as I can remember. Here – don't forget your change...'

I walked home thoughtfully, feeling shaken and worried, but curious.

Three houses now that gave me strange feelings. It was almost getting silly. If anyone had told me that they had odd feelings and semi-blackouts when they looked at certain houses I would have told them it was all in their head and to keep taking the tablets.

But it was me, and I knew that the feelings I had were real – and that somehow they were all tied up with the enigma that was Will.

I had intended to see my doctor if I had another 'turn', but thinking about it now, and imagining the look on my doctor's face if I told her the details, I knew that wasn't the answer. There was something going on that was beyond my – or anyone else's – understanding, and if I didn't get to the bottom of it soon, it could start driving me mad. And there was only one person who might lead me to the answers, even if he didn't know them all himself.

It seemed that all roads led to Will. No matter how much I tried to escape from the absurdity of this situation and lead a normal life, the more I was being turned around and pointed in that direction.

Perhaps, after all, it would be easier to follow the path I was being shown.

'Will – I have another question for you.'

'Go on.'

'What do you know about Alderton Hall?'

He did not answer for so long that I thought the telephone line had been cut.

'Will? Are you still there?'

'Yes. I'm still here. What makes you ask?'

'I went there this morning, and...'

'You went to Alderton Hall? Why? Why did you go there?'

His voice had changed. He did not sound like the calm, still man that I thought I knew. He sounded almost angry, with just a hint of possessiveness, I thought.

'I didn't choose to – I just passed it this morning with Charlie – Why, what's the matter?'

I almost heard him relax, and when he spoke he sounded like himself again.

'Nothing. Nothing at all. It's just an old ruin.'

'Yes – I could see that. But I thought you might know something about it, seeing as...'

'It belonged to the local magistrate and landowner. His son inherited it in 1819. He squandered all his money on drink and gambling and it fell into disrepair. After he...died...his son left it to live elsewhere. That's all there is to know.'

I knew there was something else that he wasn't telling me, and he probably knew that I knew, but I could tell that there was no point in pursuing it, so I decided to change the subject.

'I – er – found you on the census.'

'Which one?'

'All of them.'

'That figures.'

'So, you really are real.'

'I know.'

'I tried to look up Hannah but there were too many...'

'Would you like me to tell you about her?'

'OK.'

Chapter 9 - Hannah's Story

London, 1905

The room was small and stuffy, despite the small window being open as far as it would go, letting in the noise of Woburn Place below: a cacophony of trams, motor cars and horses' hooves combined with the street cries of the woman selling flowers on the corner and a brass band playing in Tavistock Square. It was a clear October day and all these sounds seemed to travel easily through the air to Hannah's desk, where she sat writing, her tongue tip protruding through her mouth, a dog-eared and yellowing copy of John Stuart Mill's *The Subjection of Women* propped up against a pile of papers and text books.

A sudden thunder of footsteps up the bare wooden staircase behind the room announced the arrival of her room-mate Beatrice. She looked at the clock on the mantelpiece and realised that she would never finish the article today. Even the brass band had stopped playing, she realised vaguely.

The door burst open, knocking – as it always did – the sideboard on the adjoining wall with a hollow clash of wood, and Beatrice almost flew into the room, out of breath and with cheeks flushed from coming in out of the cool air and running up two flights of stairs.

'Beatrice – what on earth...? I thought you were out all day...'

'Sorry, Hannah – but I just had to tell you – look!' she brandished the evening newspaper and threw it down in front of Hannah, nearly knocking over the bottle of ink on the desk.

'Look! They've really gone too far now – assaulting policemen of all things – and they're going to prison! Chose to as well!'

'Who's going to prison? What are you talking about, Beatrice?'

'Just look!' repeated Beatrice, her finger pointing to the headline.

Hannah pushed her glasses back up the bridge of her nose with one finger and read: *Suffragettes arrested.* She picked the paper up and started to read the text.

'Oh, the Pankhursts,' she said, as she read, 'they're going to do more damage to the cause with their "deeds not words" than a whole house of back bench Tories could ever do. Look at this – hitting a policeman! They're just going to give us all a bad name.'

'I know – that's what I think too. But, Hannah – do come out for tea. Charles is buying and he's got a friend with him you'll just love. Oh, do come!'

'But, Beatrice, you know I've got a lecture at 5 and I really wanted to get this piece finished...'

'Oh, really, Hannah, can't you just miss one lecture? Charles does it all the time – you don't always have to prove something just because you're female. And you can finish that later – the cause can wait for one little article. Oh, please come – they're both waiting for us downstairs and I promised I'd persuade you!'

'Really, Beatrice, you mustn't go round making promises like that – but...' she sighed and took her glasses off to wipe her tired eyes,' I suppose I could do with a break. And I have to say I am rather thirsty and a cream cake wouldn't be out of the question if Charles is buying.'

'Hoorah! Then we shall be four for tea and you will wear your best hat!' she cried, picking up Hannah's straw hat with its single feather.

Hannah laughed.

'Best hat indeed! It's just about my *only* hat!' and pulling an overcoat over her shoulders and quickly glancing at herself in the mirror, she followed Beatrice out of the door and they ran, giggling, down the stairs.

Beatrice's brother, Charles, was waiting for them on the street, still wearing the dark suit and cap that was the uniform of the brass band. Beside him in similar dress was a man about ten years older than Hannah with a thick, dark moustache and the most amazingly intense blue eyes that she had ever seen. Both men raised their caps as the two young women appeared, rather breathlessly, onto the pavement.

'Good afternoon, Miss Jepson,' said Charles, raising his hat again nervously, 'er - allow me to introduce my friend and musical colleague Mr William Days.'

'How do you do, Mr Days,' said Hannah, grinning a little at Charles' awkwardness. He had had a slight crush on Hannah for some time, but she had rejected all of this advances. She had no intentions of ending up married and losing any hope of the independence she fought for.

'Charles, dear!' said Beatrice, taking him by the arm, 'such formality! We are all to be on first name terms now – and if anyone calls me Miss Pearson I won't speak to them. Come on,

Hannah, do take William's arm – you have been introduced – oh how silly it all is.'

William offered his arm to Hannah and she took his elbow and followed Beatrice and Charles.

'I do hope you are not offended by my friend's forwardness, Mr Days – William,' said Hannah to her walking partner, 'she has no respect for the niceties of society.'

'Not at all,' he replied, 'indeed, I find it quite refreshing.' He looked back and up at the building they had just left. 'You have rooms here?'

'Yes – if you can call a cupboard a room. Beatrice and I rent them for a cost that feels more like we should be living in Buckingham Palace – but it does for now. So you play in the band with Charles? What else do you do?'

'I am a musician all the time,' he said with a grin, 'I work in the theatre in the evening – at the Vaudeville on the Strand.'

'Oh, good for you!' she said, 'I do think that it seems to be the most difficult thing to do the thing you would most want to do in this life – whether you're a man or a woman.'

He turned to her and fixed her with his intense eyes as they turned into Euston Road.

'And you? What is it that Miss Hannah Jepson would most like to do?'

'Oh, I would write – all the time – oh, and do a little drawing as well. But write things I want to write, like a novel. But time just seems to be taken up and I can't see that I could ever be able to earn a living from it.'

'Do you write now?'

'Yes – but I'm afraid it's only the occasional article for the NUWSS magazine, and I illustrate some of the pamphlets and posters too. Voluntary of course – but the rest of my time is taken up by some part-time teaching and a part-time course at the University College. I'm afraid I don't have wealthy parents, so when I return home to Manchester I will have to earn my own living – which I am quite determined to do – or get married, which I am not. Are you a supporter of the cause, Mr Days?'

He nodded.

'From what I know of your sex, I see no reason why women should not have the vote or work in whatever field suits their nature – whether that may be managing an organisation or managing a home. Most women I have ever known have an intelligence far beyond even their own awareness, but I am afraid that society appears to be rather blind to the capabilities of women. What a waste to put women such as yourself on a pedestal and expect them to do nothing, while the women of the labouring classes work themselves to death raising large families and working in factories for half the pay of their husbands and sons.'

Hannah stopped in the middle of Euston Road and turned to him.

'Well said, sir! And I rather think you have helped me enormously by providing me with an ending to the article I have been working on all morning. Would you be kind enough to allow me to use your words?'

'Of course.'

They had reached the tea room and inside Beatrice tugged at Hannah's sleeve and whispered in her ear:

'What do you think of our William? Is he not dashing?'

'Very. And intelligent too. A rare combination.'

'And he obviously has taken to you Hannah. I've never heard him talk for so long upon anything. He's usually so quiet and shy. You must have touched on something close to his heart.'

Heavy, black clouds loomed above Hyde Park, and fitful gusts of wind tugged at hats and skirts and caused the black white and gold banner that Hannah was helping to carry lurch this way and that. Hannah's boots and lower skirts were already caked with mud from earlier rainfall, but it looked as though there was more bad weather to come.

Despite this, Hannah's heart felt full to bursting with pride as she looked around her. There were crowds of women all around her – probably thousands – filling the park with their banners and marching colours, colours all chosen to represent their own group or society. The NUWSS colours were red, white and green, but Hannah had chosen to wear the colours to represent writers, and was proudly wearing a white blouse, black skirt and overcoat and a black hat with long golden feathers. The mixed colours all around stood out against the muddy park and the grey day and a group of fascinated bystanders was growing rapidly, keeping the police force busy in maintaining order.

As the clouds burst and torrential rain descended onto the crowds of women and onlookers, the march set off, undaunted by the weather, amongst cries of 'Votes for Women!' and 'Liberty!' and a band of musicians started a stirring marching song. Hannah, flushed and smiling, felt every nerve tingle and an incredible sensation of chills down her spine as she began to march; a sense of belonging, and a feeling of being involved in a noble cause, with all the anger, pride and determination that had brought this group of nearly three thousand women here on this wet February day in 1907 to march for their rights.

Beside her suddenly appeared Beatrice, who had been running to catch up with her and was holding on to her hat with one hand and an umbrella with the other.

'Oh, I thought I'd never find you,' she gasped, 'Hannah –

there are thousands! This is going to be one in the eye for the new PM, surely!'

'Let's hope so, Beatrice. But could you hold that umbrella so it's not in danger of knocking my eye out?' She had to shout to make herself heard above the noise and rain.

'Sorry – but it's so difficult to control with this rain and wind. Oh, what a foul day! But what a glorious one too – what a turn-out! Oh, I just saw Charles and William, that's why I was late. They both said good luck and sent their best wishes. And Charles was worried about us catching pneumonia.'

Hannah laughed, but it was too difficult to talk any more. The effort of shouting above the din, coupled with the extra effort of keeping her banner straight and her hat on were too much to carry on a conversation, and even now she was feeling the extra heaviness of mud on her skirts, hampering her movements and making walking difficult. She had noticed at least two women had turned up in trousers, and she wondered why it was thought of as so outrageous. It seemed to her, especially right now, that trousers would be so much more practical and comfortable; perhaps not always, but certainly on days like today.

As the march turned out of Hyde Park and into Park Lane, Hannah's thoughts turned to William and the friendship that had developed between them since they had met just fourteen months ago.

He was one of those people who just seemed to turn up in one's life now and then. Sometimes he would be there with Charles – at a party or a dinner – and sometimes he would just turn up, bringing her cakes or a roast chicken, and on a couple of occasions a bottle of claret. He seemed to have a knack of knowing the best bakers and butchers, and whenever they were out, he always seemed to know the best places to eat.

Beatrice was quite convinced that William had fallen in love with Hannah, which meant of course a rivalry between himself and Charles, which Beatrice (whose romantic imagination surpassed even her ability to talk easily to anyone and everyone) had built up into a tortured dilemma, believing William to be torn between his love for Hannah and his honour towards Charles, yet on the brink of proposing at any minute.

Hannah was not convinced. It was certainly obvious that William thought very highly of her – even admired her to a certain extent – but could he really be in love with her? There were times, she had to admit, that she caught him looking at her with a far away look in his eyes and once or twice he had responded to something she had said with a funny kind of sad smile, as if it was the tone of her voice that had affected him rather than the words she had used. But apart from these things he had said nothing to her that suggested a romantic attachment.

'But he does visit you regularly, doesn't he?' Beatrice had asked recently when they were discussing the matter.

'Regularly, perhaps, but not frequently. He seems to be perfectly happy to be able to live without my presence for weeks at a time. No, Beatrice I believe he is interested in me so far as my work and my personality are concerned, but I do not believe it goes any deeper than that.'

Disappointed, Beatrice sipped her tea in silence for a moment or two, and then turned to Hannah with fresh hope in her eyes.

'But you? How do you feel about him? Don't you feel happy when he's with you? You have to admit he is very handsome. And don't you miss him when he is not here?'

Hannah thought for a while to honestly explore her feelings.

'No – if I am honest, Beatrice, I don't miss him. But I do like his company, and he has been a great help with the articles I've been writing, and he is so insistent that I must write and not sacrifice my writing for anything. No – he is a very dear friend, but he is not and never will be a lover. And besides, you know full well that I am determined never to marry, so the whole conversation is academic anyway.'

Hannah thought she had never been so wet in all of her life, but by the time they reached Trafalgar Square and were turning into the Strand, it hardly seemed to matter. She could not get any wetter anyway. The march was an obvious success and the atmosphere was thrilling. Even the few onlookers who jeered, grimaced or even spat at them, had not taken away any of Hannah's feelings of elation that she was taking part in something so exciting, and there did seem to be at least some people in the crowds who supported the cause and even started to march with them.

As they approached the Corinthian columned doorway of Exeter Hall, Beatrice poked her in the ribs and started waving and pointing, making Hannah duck to avoid being blinded by her umbrella. When it was safe to do so, she looked up and saw William in the crowd with Charles and several other members of their band, all dressed in their uniforms and carrying their instruments. As the march approached, they struck up a fanfare of welcome, and in that moment Hannah could almost have fallen in love with William; it was the most welcoming sight she had ever seen.

'I don't know what to do,' said Hannah, gloomily sipping coffee, 'I really want to stay in London. I've made so many friends here, but I can't afford to keep up the rooms unless

I work full time, and if I work as a teacher here, I will never write anything! So I suppose I *have* to go home and help my parents and continue with The Cause there – but either way, it's a compromise. What do you think I should do William?'

William looked straight at her across the table. They were sitting in the Euston Road tea room for the last time as Hannah's course was finished and she had to decide whether to stay and build a life in London or return to Manchester and assist her mother and father in getting their own works published.

It was April; over a year since the march that had become known as the 'mud march' and felt to be successful enough to set the ball rolling for many more demonstrations. But Hannah felt frustrated and impatient, and above all she was tired and run-down. Despite being almost constantly in the news – mainly because of the activities of the Pankhursts – The Cause did not seem to have progressed any further, and now Asquith had become Prime Minister, a man known to be against votes for women, victory seemed to be further away than it was a year ago. Added to that, unspeakable things were happening to those suffragettes that had been sent to prison, and although Hannah did not agree with their tactics, she could not condone their brutal treatment, which reduced them to common criminals.

William still had not answered her question and she stared out of the mullioned windows onto the busy street where the cherry blossoms outside of Euston Station were in bloom and brightened up what was otherwise a cold and colourless day.

'Perhaps the change would do me good,' she said, almost to herself, and sighed, turning back to William.

'Last year everything seemed so easy – I felt as though my

life had meaning and purpose, but everything feels different now, so difficult to decide what to do next. Oh dear, what on earth is the matter with me?'

'Nothing,' said William, pouring more coffee into her cup, 'you're just at the end of one phase and the next one hasn't started. It will do. You just need a little patience.'

'You're always so wise, William. What would I do without you? But – what should I do while I'm being patient? That's the question.'

'In my opinion – which is yours to do what you like with – you should do whatever comes easiest in times like this.'

She pondered this.

'I think it would probably be the easiest thing to go home right now – though it's not...'

Hannah had been vaguely aware as she was speaking that the bell above the door of the tea shop had tinkled as someone entered, but she had taken no notice of the newcomer until he approached their table and interrupted her.

'Well, bless me, if it isn't William Days as I live and breathe! My God, you don't look a day older than when I last saw you at the Garrick in '99. How the devil are you, old chap?'

William was standing and a man in his thirties dressed in a tweed motoring jacket and cap, and sporting a reddish blonde moustache, was pumping his hand up and down as if he was trying to strike oil.

'Reid! What a pleasure!' William returned, and immediately introduced Hannah to the man, who he told her was Michael Reid, an old friend of his in the days of the Garrick Theatre's opening, when Reid had been a theatrical journalist working for one of the evening papers.

The man whisked off his cap and turned to Hannah, and she

was instantly struck with the kindness of his face. His green eyes were immediately friendly as he smiled and produced a set of laughter lines along with a mischievous twinkle.

'Miss Jepson,' he said, giving her hand a firm shake, 'I am absolutely delighted. Delighted.' He looked strangely at her for a moment and seemed to have forgotten that he was still holding her hand.

'Forgive me,' he said, still holding on to her hand, 'but have we met before? Your name rings a bell. Hannah Jepson... I know I've seen that name recently... it was in the paper – why yes! Wasn't it you who wrote that brilliant article about the Waste of Womanhood in *The Times* not so long ago?'

Hannah blushed.

'I have to admit that it was, Mr Reid – and how kind of you to remember it.'

By this time he had let go of Hannah's hand and William had drawn up a chair so he could sit down.

'Oh, not at all. It was an inspired piece of writing. Now then – this is an amazing piece of good luck – oh, thank you Daysy old boy,' (this to William who had bought him a coffee), 'oh, I'd better order a cake or two – that was what I came in for after all. Cakes all round, I think.'

While he spoke to the waitress, Hannah mouthed 'Daisy?' to William, who just grinned and shook his head.

'Now, as I was saying,' continued Michael, 'this is an amazing bit of luck bumping into you like this. You see, I'm the editor of a little magazine that reviews events of all kinds – plays and music hall, that kind of thing. But I've been wanting to start a section on political events and I need a team of writers to go to demonstrations and things of that nature to report on what's happening. I'm particularly keen to employ a woman to get a female viewpoint – especially with a view to the Votes question. Now, the pay isn't much, I'll be honest with you, and you can spit in my eye and tell me it's beneath you if you like, but after seeing your work, the offer's on the table, if you want it.'

Hannah caught William's eye, and he raised his eyebrows with a quirky grin.

She turned back to Michael, her eyes wide. She could not quite believe what he had just said.

'I... do you mean... I would be a journalist?'

'Well, yes, that's what you'd call it I suppose.'

'And – how much time would this take up?'

'Oh, it won't be full time by any means, hard work with deadlines and everything, but you would still be able to work on other things, write for other papers and whatever else you need to do. What do you think?'

She looked at William again.

'It seems that new phase might be closer than we thought,' he said.

Working for Michael Reid was like entering a maelstrom. She had never known anyone so energetic, so spontaneous and so able to make friends with anyone he came into contact with, and she had never worked so hard in her life. She had also never been happier.

Within a few days she found herself reporting on demonstrations at the House of Commons, interviewing suffragettes who had been force fed in prison and even attending a court appearance by Bernard Shaw in a row over censorship. The days went by in a constant flurry of activity and every night she fell, exhausted but happy, into her bed.

But the best moments of all were when she saw her new boss, which she did frequently at work and at social events. When she walked into a room where Michael was, she instantly felt alive. He had a genuine interest in people, which drew them to him naturally, and a spontaneity which constantly kept you on your toes and which Hannah found exhilarating.

Never more so than when he looked up at her one day when she was describing an idea for an article on Mary Wollstonecraft, and asked her to marry him.

Chapter 10

I scraped the last remnants of froth from the bottom of the soup-bowl sized cup and put the spoon in my mouth, savouring the last little taste of chocolately sweetness on my tongue.

'That,' I said, 'was the best cappuccino I have ever had.'

'And,' I continued, wiping my mouth with a paper napkin, hoping I had not left a moustache, 'I can't believe that my great-grandmother was a writer.'

We were sitting in a small café-restaurant in Clayford and Will had been telling me about the life of Hannah Jepson.

'Yes,' he said, smiling, 'and a very talented one too. You have something to live up to there, Catherine Burns.'

'I think it's wonderful. I mean, you wonder, don't you, where it comes from – the desire to do something – or a talent, or whatever, but it always puzzled me that no-one else in my family seemed to write at all. Well – actually, my brother John does, but that's advertising copy and not the same thing at all, though he'd hate me for saying so. But, there she is; obviously the genes do make their way though, and you know what?'

He looked lazily at me across the table, leaning back in his chair, one foot on his knee. He raised a questioning eyebrow.

'It makes me feel validated as a writer. I mean, all this time

I've been wondering whether I've got it in me or whether I'm just kidding myself, but knowing that one of my direct ancestors was actually a writer, well I just feel that, oh, I don't know, like I've been handed some kind of baton and I have to run like hell with it.'

'Good,' said Will, leaning forward to pour himself more tea. 'More coffee?'

'Better not. That was my second and I'll be bouncing off the walls soon. But Will, there's so much more I want to know about Hannah. Did she ever write a novel, and if so, was it published? And what happened about my great grandfather? Didn't she marry twice? Grandmother Elizabeth said she had a stepfather, so, what happened...?'

'It might be better if she told you the rest herself.'

I stared at him.

'What do you mean?'

Will put his hand inside his jacket and pulled out a very scruffy looking envelope which he put down in front of me.

I looked down to read, in a firm but feminine hand, the name 'Mr William Days' followed by a London address. I picked it up. It was postmarked Manchester, September 1916 and had a stamp bearing the head of George V.

I looked up at Will.

'She wrote to me when she returned to Manchester as a widow with a two-year old daughter – your grandmother,' he explained. 'Go on, read it.'

'Oh my God,' I whispered, gently removing the neatly folded pages within and opening them out.

While Will quietly watched me as he sipped his tea, I read the words written ninety years ago by my great-grandmother.

Ardwick, Manchester

2nd September 1916

Dear William

I can only hope that this reaches you at the last address I have for you, and that it gets sent to you, wherever you are. The war has driven us all apart, and I hope that you are safe, whatever you are doing.

It seems a very long time since we last met, and I feel great sadness that the first time that I should contact you in all this time is with tragic news. Forgive me for the omission; the last few years have brought little time for letter writing.

Knowing your previous friendship with Michael, I thought that it was only right for me to inform you of his death on the battlefields of the Somme on 1st July of this year.

As you will see from the postmark, I have finally returned to Manchester with little Lizzie to stay with my parents until I can decide what I should do next. I have closed up the apartment in Bloomsbury and I do not think I shall return. I want to keep the memories fresh.

It seems almost selfish to mourn so much the loss of one, when so many of our young men will never return from France. I heard with sadness the loss of Charles at Gallipoli, and I know that you will miss his friendship deeply. Beatrice was inconsolable, but continues to work as a clerk at the War Office, refusing to be broken.

But I cannot help thinking how wonderful a father Michael would have been and to think of all the coming years that we could have had together. We had so little time together as man and wife. You will remember how determined I was to remain a single woman, and Michael – persistent as ever! – had to propose three times before I gave in. You always said that I would lose nothing by marrying a man like Michael, and you were right, as you so often are. How silly that it had to take the threat of war to bring me to my senses.

Can it really be nearly four years ago since I last sat down to write to you, thanking you for your very delicious wedding present, and my regrets that a sudden illness had prevented you from attending? How much everything has changed since then.

I wish, William, that you could see my daughter, Lizzie. She is so like Michael in looks, with her green eyes and light colouring, but her temperament is more like mine – quiet and sensible (!!) I do not know how I would cope with the months and years that are to come without her with me, and my mother and father completely dote on her, so she is going to grow up very spoiled if I am not careful!

I know that you would advise me to continue writing, but my career in the last few years has been so tied up with Michael that it seems too painful to continue as I was. I told you once that I would like to write a novel, and perhaps that will be my next step, though heaven knows I need an income, and father's new book does not bring in enough to keep us all in bread and comfort. For the moment, though, I may take on some war work, and I am investigating the possibilities. Perhaps the one good thing that will come out of this war is the recognition for the work women have done – who knows?

Perhaps, if you receive this letter, you would be kind enough to write to me and let me know that you are safe and well.

Yours fondly

Hannah Reid

I slowly folded the letter up again and passed it back to Will.

'Did you write to her?' I asked.

'Of course.'

'What did you say?'

'That I was well and safe. That I was sorry to hear the news about Michael and that I hoped she would continue to work at the one thing she loved. That he would have wanted her to.'

As usual, when I was with Will, so many questions crowded my brain that I found it difficult to decide which to ask first. While I hesitated, Will paid the bill and we stepped out into a cold, grey day. It was not the kind of weather to suggest going for a walk and we dithered on the pavement while I arranged my scarf.

'What now?' I asked.

He stood with his hands in the pockets of his black leather jacket and looked up at the sky where dark clouds threatened rain. He looked back at me.

'Can you give me a lift?'

'Sure. Where to? Home?'

'Brighton.'

I looked at him, wondering whether he would ever cease to surprise me.

'What?'

'Well – home first. I need to pick up my guitar and some gear. Or I could get the train. If you're busy.'

'You're going to Brighton?'

'Yes – I'm playing at a gig there tonight.'

'Tonight? What time?' I asked, mentally working out travel times.

'Late. I don't think I'm on until 10. If you give me a lift I'll get you in for free. And I'll pay for petrol.'

'But...'

Once again, I was finding it difficult to form a sentence. Will seemed to have this effect on me. He answered my unasked question.

'We can drop by your place and pick up some overnight stuff. That's if you want to come. But, if you don't want to, you can just give me a lift home. It's no problem.'

'No... I... But there's Charlie...'

He nodded.

'Never mind. It was just a thought.'

'No – wait.'

I dug my mobile phone out of my bag and hit Maureen's number in the memory list.

'Hi Maureen, it's Catherine. Listen, I know it's terribly short notice, but something's come up and I'm going to be out all night. If I come over later with Charlie, do you think you could look after him – just for tonight...?'

An hour and a half later we were on the A44 and I was thinking how exciting life was when you weren't tied to a job or a restricted routine, and you could be leading a steady day-to-day existence one moment and in the next be heading off to Brighton on a whim to go to a rock festival. This was the way life should be, I thought, full of surprises and different experiences. Besides, given the choice of rock concert in Brighton or an evening at home watching repeats of American sitcoms, it was a bit of a no-brainer. And I was still a rock chick. Just.

Soon my thoughts turned back to Hannah and the letter I had read nearly two hours ago.

'There's something I want to ask you, Will.'

'There usually is.'

I couldn't help laughing.

'Ain't that the truth?' Well – as usual, there are several, but I'm just curious about this.'

'Well?'

'What did you do during that war? How did you avoid enlisting?'

He said nothing while I negotiated the Wolvercote roundabout and headed onto the A40.

'I didn't.'

'Oh.' I accelerated, changing gears until I was settled in fifth. 'So – you fought in the war? I didn't know.'

He stared out of the window.

'You couldn't look 35 and walk around as a civilian without questions being asked. At first I just carried on working in the theatres – there was a lot of work for musicians. You have to understand that any official paperwork has always been difficult for me, and I had seen the results of too many wars to feel the enthusiasm of most of the young men who rushed off to enlist in 1914, and I couldn't run the risk of someone questioning my details.

'Not that it was safe in London. The Strand Theatre where I worked was almost hit by a bomb in 1915. But by 1916 it started to become too difficult to do nothing. The numbers of casualties were so great that there was a shortage of men on the killing fields and the government made enlistment compulsory in order to make up the numbers. So I had to choose between conscientious objection and enlistment. And I wasn't a conscientious objector.'

'So...'

'I lied. I had to. Date of birth, my age, my family. Nothing was said, and I was sent off to France.'

I said nothing for several minutes. Then he said:

'I was 111 years old. I had seen enough of life to know there is nothing glorious about war, but nothing could prepare anyone for that experience. I watched hundreds of young men dying – some of them as young as 15, covered in blood and mud, crying for their mothers – and I kept thinking, *it should be me, I've lived long enough, they haven't….* The fact that I managed to get out of that show alive convinced me that there is no justice in life. And, it also confirmed for me something that I had always thought.'

I turned to look at him. His face was pale, staring out of the window, and I knew he was not seeing the Oxfordshire countryside, but the barren war-ravaged fields of France.

'What?' I asked, quietly.

'Sounds strange, coming from me – but it reminded me that life is short, and you don't know what will happen in your life, so you had better get on and do whatever it is you want to do, no matter what. What you do with your life is so much more important than money or status, or even just being comfortable and secure.'

His words hit me in the gut, and before I knew it my eyes had misted up and I had to blink a few times in order to see where I was going.

Those who were supposedly close to me, my ex-boyfriend, even my parents, had judged me on taking the risk of losing money and security in order to do what I wanted to do. And I knew that inside I had been beating myself up about it; telling myself I was a fool. But here was Will, validating me in his passionate belief that life was not here to be wasted in settling for comfort, a boring job just because it has a good pension, so you can sit and do nothing for the last 20 or 30 years of your life. Suddenly I saw how incredibly illogical it all was, to settle for security, to be 'sensible', to work at something you hate because it paid well…for what? So you can gather possessions about you, to holiday in St Tropez, to have a big car? It was all so meaningless, and ultimately, joyless.

My inner doubts had been holding me back. Perhaps that was the reason for my difficulty in writing. I had been brought up to believe in job loyalty and getting a good pension; no wonder I had allowed those beliefs to undermine my creativity. Well, my parents had chosen to give up a musical career for a safe life, I was damned if I was going to do the same.

'Thanks Will,' I said, 'I needed that.'

'I know,' he said.

We drove on for several miles and it wasn't until we had joined the M25 that I felt able to start up the conversation again.

'So did Hannah write her novel?'

'I think she did, but I don't think it was ever published. If it was, I never knew and it would be long out of print by now. It wouldn't have been easy for her. Her father became very ill and she had to care for him as well as bring up Lizzie. After the war servants were difficult to find and she and her mother had very little money to pay for them anyway.'

'But she could vote at last.'

'Yes. There was that.' He smiled. 'I know very little after that, except what I heard from Lizzie many years later. I think she continued to write for local Manchester papers but with her second marriage and more children, and then the Depression, it must have been a struggle.'

The traffic on the M25 was sluggish and I had the opportunity to look at Will as he talked about her.

'You were fond of her, weren't you?'

He cocked his head to one side and ruffled his hair, looking out onto the flat Middlesex countryside.

'She reminded me of someone.'

'Who?'

'Her grandmother.' He continued to stare out of the window.

'Ah. A future instalment. Or rather, a past one, ha ha.'

'Yes.'

He turned to me, his head still on one side.

'You look a bit like her too. You have the same jaw line, the same colouring.'

'Really?'

We said very little for the rest of the journey, and I thought for a long time about Hannah who was a writer, who was a suffragist, who Will was fond of, and who looked a bit like me.

The concert was held at a small rock and blues venue near the sea front. The show was a one day festival of artists from all over the country, and had been going since six. We got there at eight.

Will had done some phoning from the car and got me a ticket and a room for the night in a small hotel in Hove, his own hotel being fully booked.

After checking in at the hotel and driving back to the venue, I went with Will backstage to pick up the ticket that had been left for him at the stage door. As we stood outside in the dark, arranging how we were going to meet afterwards, someone appeared from the stage door and lit up a cigarette. The lighter flared to show a haggard looking, gaunt face with thick, black spiky hair.

'Hey, Will,' he said, with the cigarette in his mouth, 'all right?'

'Hi Ronnie – catch you later.'

We walked towards the entrance of the theatre.

'Do... do you... do you know who that is...?' I whispered incredulously.

'Er – yeah.'

'That... that's Ronnie Wood. I mean, for real – right in front of me.'

Will then did something that I'd only ever seen done on comedy shows. He put his finger under my chin and closed my mouth. My teeth snapped together and I blinked several times.

'Yes,' he said, 'but that is not a cool look for you.'

'Right. OK. But – don't tell me the rest of them are here... The Stones?' I lowered my whisper to more hallowed tones.

'No. Ronnie's promoting his solo album. They don't do gigs like this.'

'And – you're on first name terms!'

'It's no big deal. You'd better go in. I'll see you later.'

The auditorium was packed, and I wondered how Will had managed to get me in. There was a folk band playing when I went in, doing covers of fifties stuff. They were pretty good, as were all the other bands, including the band that Will was playing guitar with, who played great blues and jazz. It was turning out to be a day of surprises, because Will had not told me that he would be playing solo as well, and when he came on alone my heart started thudding with excitement.

I knew, as soon as he started playing, that he had an amazing talent. He played two songs he had written himself and I recognised the roots of folk that came through in the first song, hitting on the blues and touching the rock ballad. Only I knew how many years of experience had produced such excellence, and as he got into the number the audience became so quiet

I could have shut my eyes and felt like I was the only person there. He had a voice that made me think of Bruce Springsteen, and the song appeared to be about the passing of time and the passing of old friends. No surprise there then.

The second song was a little more upbeat and had the audience moving and swaying. I heard the Beatles, but I also heard the distant echo of music hall. At the end the audience cheered and applauded and stamped their feet, and Will said a modest thank you, and was gone. He was followed by another folk band, and then Ronnie Wood, who, of course, brought the house down.

I met Will at the stage door, and after locking his guitar safely in the car, we bought a bottle of wine from the bar and took a walk along the promenade. After the stuffy atmosphere of the theatre it was refreshing to feel the sea breeze and hear the roar of the breakers on shingle, but after a while I was shivering with cold and Will lent me his leather jacket.

A couple caught up with us and recognised Will, insisting on shaking his hand.

'Amazing, mate. Really amazing.'

Will smiled and said thanks, and they disappeared into the night.

'They really liked you – the whole audience,' I said, feeling for the first time since I had met him, slightly shy and in awe. 'So did I – I was really impressed.'

'Thanks.'

'I'm amazed you're not famous by now.'

I felt him turn to me.

'You know why.'

It was true. I did. It didn't take much to work out why he had avoided the recording contracts that must have been offered him. The possibility of becoming a success could throw him into the celebrity lifestyle that would be impossible for him. His face, a public commodity in the world of fame, would be remembered by past friends and colleagues, and future generations would notice the lack of ageing. Sooner or later, questions would be asked – about his background, his family, his early life. His life would become about avoiding the truth, and his fame would become about his looks rather than his music. It would kill him.

We sat on a bench, passing the bottle back and forth like a couple of old tramps and Will leaned back and shut his eyes for a moment, winding down from the high of performing.

I looked at his face, vulnerable in its sleep-like pose, and I thought of all I had learned from him today and all I had seen, and I felt a rush of admiration mixed with sympathy. And something else, which I hurriedly denied and pushed away.

I looked out to sea, focusing on the light of a distant ship, but the smell of Will's leather jacket remained, disturbing me.

'We'd better go,' I said, getting up and handing him the bottle, 'you finish this – I've got to drive you to your hotel, and me to mine.'

Chapter 11

I arrived home the next day feeling as though I had had a week's holiday. Despite all the driving, I felt relaxed and refreshed, and when I picked Charlie up he greeted me as if I had been away for a month, licking my face furiously and then running round Maureen's living room like an athlete taking a victory run.

I had picked up some flowers on the way back to thank Maureen.

'Oh, it was no trouble at all, dear. He was as good as gold. He pined a little at first, but he was quite happy once he realised I had the dog biscuits!'

'I'm so pleased,' I said, fondling Charlie's ears as he lay panting at my feet, 'I would hate to think of him worrying and thinking I was never coming back – you never know with rescue dogs, do you?'

'No – he was quite happy. And it's nice to see you looking so happy yourself, Catherine. Have you had a nice time?'

To my horror, I found that I was blushing, though I couldn't think why.

'Oh, yes... it was just a friend who was playing at a concert in Brighton and needed a lift down. It was a good evening, and we had a good drive back; even the M25 was clear.'

It had been a pleasant drive. Being a Sunday and having no time pressures, we had driven home in a leisurely way, stopping for coffee and muffins and to read the Sunday papers. We had chatted easily, and I told Will about my teaching career, and about Jake and how and why I'd decided to move from London. He told me bits about his own career, how he always managed to keep a hold on the music business, playing in bands, filling in, sometimes playing solo – but never allowing himself to become so involved that he would become too well known.

It was relaxed, like two normal people finding out about each other. We did not mention Hannah or any other of my ancestors. For once, being with Will did not fill me with a sense of surrealism and apprehension, but was – well, it was easy.

'Well,' said Maureen, 'if you ever want me to look after Charlie again, I'd be quite happy to. You know – if you're staying overnight somewhere...'

I could have sworn she had winked, and I wondered whether she thought I'd made the whole Brighton thing up because I was too embarrassed to say that I was sleeping with someone and I blushed again, which was really annoying because she would obviously think she had hit the nail on the head.

That afternoon I did some Google research and found that my great grandfather Corporal Michael Reid had been among the over nineteen thousand British men who died on that first day of the Battle of the Somme. The details of the conditions, the mud, the trenches and the continual bombardment, and the lack of adequate communication resulting in bungled orders, sending thousands of men to their deaths for the sake of a few miles of territory made me feel sick and grief-stricken. I remembered the history lessons I'd had at school, but I cannot remember having such strength of feeling before. But then it had not been personal. Now I knew that a member of my own family, who by first hand account was a lovely, open-minded, talented and friendly human being, had died horrifically in the mud and slaughter of Picardy. He was not just a name on a family tree, or a statistic of war, but a man of flesh and blood, and he had loved my great grandmother. I didn't even berate myself when I shed a few tears for him.

Feeling chilled, I made myself a cup of coffee, then had a look at the 1901 census. This time, with the right details to hand, I found Hannah straight away, aged 16 and living in Manchester with her parents, Henry and Anne Jepson. Henry's occupation was described as Teacher and Writer, but no occupation was given for Anne. Hannah had one older sister living there called Elizabeth.

On the 1891 census, I found that Hannah had at least six older brothers and sisters and that they were living at this time in Anston in Yorkshire where Hannah had been born.

I could have tried to find out more about Hannah's parents, but it was getting late and there was a film I wanted to watch and a meal to be cooked first. I had done no writing for two days, but tomorrow being Monday I felt I could start afresh and really get a move on with my new found sense of drive. No doubt I would find out about Anne and Henry all in due course, and it was something to look forward to. Perhaps I would wait for Will to tell me anyway – it was far more interesting that way.

It was two weeks before I heard from Will again.

In that time I had written the whole of Chapter Two and

I had been to two more writing classes. Sue said that my speedwriting exercise was an excellent improvement, but she was less enthusiastic when she read the two chapters I had taken to show her.

'It's a good effort for a first attempt at a novel,' she said, 'but the writing's a little thin. You need a few more descriptive passages so the reader can feel themselves in the classroom. We're doing some work on that next week, which will really help. But I would suggest you start out with some short stories before embarking on a complete novel.'

I decided that I did not like the words 'effort' and 'attempt'. They made me feel like a rank amateur. Which I had to admit that I was. Then the horrible thought I had next was, 'How on earth can I expect to write a bestselling novel and run a country house as a rank amateur?' Then I remembered that I had used exactly the same words myself when I had been a teacher and I thought what a terrible teacher I must have been. Bad teacher, amateur writer. It all felt a little sad and hopeless. And I did not want to write short stories. They just didn't interest me. My doubts started to creep back; I felt that I had bitten off more than I could chew and again I began to feel a rising sense of panic.

But I thought about what Will had said in the car, and I thought about Hannah and her determination to be independent, and how difficult it was, but how she would not have been stopped by two words like 'effort' and 'attempt'. I decided I would take inspiration from her and keep on fighting. I would develop my writing and carry on regardless.

Peter asked me if I had taken his advice about family history, and I told him I had found out lots about my great grandmother (more than he could possibly realise) and he said 'I told you

you'd be hooked.'

After the third class, I came out of the room chatting to Peter about other sources that he used in finding his family tree, and Maureen and her two friends, Betty and Janet, were waiting for me at the main entrance. I introduced them to Peter who told them all how adult education had changed his life as we walked towards Betty's Peugeot 207. I stood and waited while these four people in their sixties talked about the importance of having a hobby during one's retirement, and I yawned, not with boredom or tiredness, but with fear.

I liked these people, but despite my recent new-found confidence, I could not help the internal dialogue inside my head: *It's all right for you; you probably have great pensions and have paid off your mortgages. I don't write as a hobby, it's my life – my chosen career, and I don't even know if it will bring me an income. I no longer pay into a pension and I'm paying a mortgage I can't really afford. You are all normal, and I am completely out of my mind.* But then I remembered Will's words, and I tried to tell myself I was really OK.

In the car the three women discussed Peter and what a nice man he was, and how right he was about having a hobby and making sure you kept active and interested in things.

In my head I was screaming, *I want to be active and interested in things now, not just when I'm 60! I don't want to have a hobby, I want to have a life. Is it too much to ask? Is this really totally unrealistic?*

I suddenly wanted to talk to Will. I knew that when I was with Will I felt calm and sane. Funny that, given how insane his own life was.

I decided I would ring him tomorrow. We seemed to be good enough friends for me to do that without it looking like I had any kind of agenda. I would invite him over for dinner. I had never cooked him a proper meal and I could do my favourite recipe, the spicy lemon chicken that could never fail, and he can tell me all about my next ancestor whose name was Anne.

I suddenly realised that I was being spoken to.

'Catherine – oh, she's miles away,' said Maureen, grinning knowingly, 'somewhere nice, I think, judging by the smile on her face.'

'Ah,' said Janet, 'no doubt there's a young man involved...'

'Er – no... sorry,' I mumbled, 'I was just thinking about my novel and the class tonight...'

'Of course you were,' said Janet, looking at the others in a way which meant she didn't believe me for one moment. They were all being very nice, really – but I couldn't wait to get out of the car.

Luckily, Maureen and I were the first to be dropped off, and after we'd waved goodbye, Maureen said, 'I hope you don't mind a bit of teasing, dear. They don't mean anything by it – women are terrible in a group aren't they? But don't take any notice of us – we're just glad to see you looking so happy, that's all.'

I mumbled something and fled into the house.

I did not phone Will the next day because I received a letter from him. It was written on blue notepaper in a steady, slow hand.

Dear Catherine

I'm going to be away for a few weeks, in Scotland. I have a couple of gigs there and I thought I'd stay up there for a while to have a break.

I know you will be expecting me to tell you more about your family. I will do in time, but I hope you will understand that digging up these memories is sometimes difficult for me. I have in the past tried to forget certain things, but have not been able to. For some reason, I have felt compelled to tell you everything, but this gets more difficult the further back in time I go. I need to take some time out for a while.

In the meantime, you could perhaps look up Hannah's parents on the internet. Their names were Anne Corbett and Henry Jepson. They lived in Yorkshire and Manchester, but before her marriage Anne lived for several years in London with an uncle.

Thanks for the trip to Brighton. It was a good couple of days.

Best wishes

Will

I read the letter over and over again while I drank my morning coffee. I searched for something that wasn't there. The letter was friendly in tone, but felt as cold as the November frost that was currently whitening my garden.

What did I expect? I asked myself but seemed unable to reply. I knew I felt let down. And somehow left out. I also knew I felt angry – but I could not say why. It was a reasonable letter. Friendly, polite and god-damned reasonable.

I got up and kicked the fridge door, putting a dent in it and making Charlie leap up in surprise and stare anxiously at me with his large, dark eyes.

'Sorry, Charlie,' I said, crouching down to rub his ears. Then I put my head on his warm neck and said into his fur, 'men are the pits.'

I realised that my eyes were wet, and I stood up briskly.

'This won't do. This is definitely not the thing. How very ridiculous. Charlie, my boy, you have a very silly owner indeed.'

Charlie wagged his tail enthusiastically.

'No need to agree. But – you're right. Time to end all nonsense. We're going for a walk.'

Charlie pricked up his ears and wagged his tail even more.

'And then we are coming home and we're going to get on with the business of making me a writer. And everyone else can all go to Hell!'

Charlie danced and barked with excitement.

When we returned, the letter was where I had left it on the kitchen table, sitting amongst several unopened bills. I carefully folded it up without reading it and stuffed it back into its envelope. I then took it upstairs and slipped it between some books in my study where I could not see it.

I sat in front of my computer and opened up my novel. I did not want to look for Anne and Henry. I did not want to do anything connected with Will. It was time to move forwards, not backwards.

In bold letters, I typed the words, CHAPTER 3.

For the next few days I barely left the house except to walk Charlie. I wrote like I was possessed. I introduced new characters who had unique backgrounds and personalities, I wrote descriptions from memory of the school, people's homes and environments, and one day my main character started to take over and have her own ideas and started doing things that didn't seem to have come from my imagination but from hers, and I knew I had created someone real and human. It was very exciting. Instead of my writing sessions being a struggle and a chore, I began to enjoy them, even more so when I let go of control and allowed my pen to write what it wanted to.

CHAPTER 11

I had taken to writing in longhand, with a biro, sitting at the kitchen table looking out onto the garden. It was warmer in there, but also I liked the organic feel of pen on paper as opposed to the clinical coldness of the keyboard.

In three days I had a third chapter and was beginning to feel like a real writer. I had almost been successful in pushing Will and my family to the back of my mind but he would keep popping into my head. Then I would go and make a coffee, or pour a glass of wine, depending on the time of day, and carry on writing or put the television on very loudly to drown away my thoughts.

On Sunday I was running out of food so I got into my car to go to the supermarket at Clayford. As I sat in the driver's seat I remembered it was three weeks ago today that Will and I had driven back from Brighton on that sunny, relaxed day.

I looked at the empty seat beside me.

The car felt cold. I turned on the ignition and turned up the heating dial.

It was as I turned out of the bottom of Mill Lane and onto the main road that I noticed something for the first time. Turning left into the road took me to Clayford, and the right turn led towards the hamlet of Stanton Bridge and the ruin of Alderton Hall. Across the road was a small lane leading off the main road, and as I turned I noticed for the first time that the name of the little road was Corbett Lane. The name Corbett sang in my head. Surely that was the maiden name of Hannah's mother?

I crunched my gears as I gathered speed along the Clayford road and felt my skin tingling all over. I felt for a moment that I couldn't breathe.

My head swam and I had to concentrate very hard on the road in front of me.

'It's a coincidence, of course,' I said to myself out loud, 'the name's common enough.'

And yet something about that name, and it appearing like that in front of me, here at Little Dipping, filled me with a sense of dread. I didn't know why. But I did begin to think about Will's connection with Anne Corbett and the fact that he had been born in Little Dipping. Could there be a connection, or was it just a coincidence that was messing with my head? But if there was a connection, why hadn't he told me?

I wandered round Tescos in a daze, picking up packets to read the ingredients and seeing nothing. I managed to fill my trolley with all the essentials: bread, coffee and wine, as well as a few vegetables and fruit, and by the time I had left the check-out I had made up my mind.

I would have to give in and do what Will had suggested. I would look up Anne on the internet and see if there was any connection with the village. Otherwise, it was going to stick in my mind and possibly drive me crazy, if I wasn't already.

After unpacking the food, I poured myself a large glass of Merlot and settled down in front of the computer to start my investigation. I felt quite excited, and I remembered what Peter had said about the anticipation of finding something new about your ancestors: who they were and what they did and where they came from. I felt a bit like a detective investigating a crime, only it wasn't murder I was looking for. At least I hoped not.

I had already seen Anne's details on the 1891 census, but now I looked more carefully at the details of her place of birth. I had been so interested in Hannah before that I hadn't really taken much notice, and had been expecting to get all the information from Will anyway.

As I looked at the column headed Place of Birth and checked it against Anne's details, a chill ran down my scalp and down the back of my spine. I took a large sip of wine.

The name of the place where Anne was born was given as Aldercote, Gloucestershire.

I quickly went through the remaining censuses. I found out that she'd had about twelve children (which had me reaching for the wine glass) and Hannah had been her last child when she was 48, that she must have been married some time between 1851 and 1861, and that before she was married she had lived in St James Place in London with her uncle, Captain James Corbett and his wife, Agatha.

'Sounds a bit posh,' I thought.

The last census was 1841 where I tracked her down at Aldercote. This census had less information than the others, but as the thick, black handwriting appeared on the screen and I scrolled down to find Anne's name, my hands went numb and I felt the blood drain from my face. For there, as her place of residence on the left side of the page were the words, Alderton Hall.

Chapter 12

Of course, I should have known. It all made sense. If Will had known six generations of my ancestors then it was going to be quite likely that he met them where he once lived. It had just never occurred to me.

But why did the very name of Alderton Hall fill me with such dread?

I had almost forgotten the day that Charlie and I had come across the old ruin, until now. And I remembered now how cagey Will had been when I mentioned it. What was that all about?

As usual, all roads seemed to lead to Will, but he was in Scotland and had said he didn't want to talk about anything at the moment. What was all *that* about?

The details on the census gave nothing away. There did not seem to be another inhabitant who could be a parent of Anne; just a housekeeper and various servants, even though Anne was no more than seven years old.

I tried Googling Alderton Hall, but found nothing except one line in a website entitled 'Great Houses of the Cotswolds', saying, 'eighteenth century building, now in ruins, once belonging to the Corbett family.'

So tell me something I don't know.

So presumably, the owner that Will had told me had drunk and gambled away the family fortune, was one of my own ancestors. Great.

I looked at the almost empty glass on my desk and wondered whether I had inherited the Corbett degenerate gene. But I didn't suppose that doing the Lottery once a week could be classed as hard gambling.

My head was spinning. I didn't know what to do next. I knew Peter had mentioned some other ways of getting ancestral information, but I couldn't now remember what he'd told me. I suppose I hadn't really been listening, smugly thinking I had my own source of information far beyond anything the internet could give me.

I had to speak to Will.

Presumably he had his mobile phone with him.

He answered almost immediately.

'Catherine?'

I clocked that I was on his phone memory list.

'Hi. How's Scotland?'

'Cold. How are you?'

'Confused. Why didn't you tell me Anne came from Alderton Hall?'

'Ah... I wondered when you'd find that out.'

'Why didn't you tell me?'

There was a pause.

'I don't know. I thought it might be more fun for you to find out on your own.'

'But...'

'Why, what's the matter?'

Of course, I hadn't told him how I felt about the place.

'Will, when I saw Alderton Hall, that day I told you about when I was walking Charlie, I got a sense of terrible... oh I know this sounds stupid, but I hate the place – it made me feel – I don't know – trapped or something. It scared me.'

'Really?' he said, so quietly that I could hardly hear him.

'Yes – it really does sound silly now, saying it out loud, but it gave me the creeps.'

'I suppose ruinous buildings can do that...'

'No, it was more than that, I'm sure. So finding out that my ancestors actually owned it is a bit of a shock.'

'Yes... I suppose it would be.'

'Will, I need to know. I need to know about Anne – and all the rest. I know you didn't want to talk about it right now, but it's doing my head in.'

'Right. OK. But – not on the phone. Not right now. I'm on stage in a few minutes.'

'Oh.'

'Listen, I'll have to think about this, and I'll call you back. It's all a bit difficult right now.'

'Well, OK. But, Will...'

'Yes?'

'You will phone soon won't you? I want to know – it just seems important to me that I know, that's all.'

'I'll do my best.'

I put the phone down. He obviously wasn't going to make any promises. He was, in fact, avoiding making any kind of commitment. I'd had enough telephone conversations with men in the past to know that.

But, infuriatingly, I knew the sooner he told me everything and just got out of my life, the better. Will and his darned 200 years of bumping into my family was driving me potty. If only he would just get it over with and then go and leave me in peace.

I tried not to listen for the phone to ring on Monday, I really did. I spent all morning pretending to write Chapter 4 and writing barely two paragraphs. I made too many cups of coffee and consequently felt hyperactive and jumpy by lunch time.

In the afternoon I gave up trying to write and occupied myself by scrubbing the kitchen and the bathroom until the tiles and units gleamed and dazzled my eyes, but the phone remained stubbornly silent, despite my glaring at it from time to time.

Exhausted by my efforts, I tried reading, but that was no good. I could not concentrate and had to keep going back over the same page until I threw the book down in a rage.

'This is ridiculous,' I said to myself, 'I'm behaving like a love-sick seventeen year old, and all because I want to know more about my ancestors.'

Perhaps Peter was right about family history being like a drug. Perhaps in my case it was even worse: I was getting so much information it was like taking an overdose, and then I was more and more desperate for the next fix.

I looked nervously at the computer. If I was so desperate, I supposed I could find out about other ways of researching. But somehow, it wasn't how I wanted to find out. I knew that any answers it gave me would only open up more questions, questions that could only be answered by one person. It would be just a way of making me more crazy.

No, the best thing to do was to just drink more wine and immerse myself in mind-numbing television. So that's what I did.

That was the night I started to have the dreams.

The dream started out pleasantly enough, as most nightmares do. I was in a house, and I was walking through the rooms, which were many and full of beautiful furniture; button-back chairs with gorgeous floral fabric, bureaus and desks with elegant carved legs. There was music playing somewhere, and I was trying to make my way to the room where the music was playing. But the music seemed to be getting further away, and the rooms got darker. When I tried to look at the furniture, it turned out not to be beautiful, but to be broken with the fabric torn and rotten. In one room, a baby's cot was rocking in a corner, and when I looked inside I found a doll with staring eyes and a hole in its wax head, its hair half pulled out. I walked through a door into a passageway and then I knew that at the end of the passageway was something terrible and frightening that would harm me. I turned to go back but the door was no longer there. The only way out of the corridor was through the door at the end.

That was when I woke up sweating with the duvet over my head.

'You all right, dear?' asked Maureen when we met to go to our next class on Wednesday evening, 'you look a bit peaky.'

'I'm fine,' I said, 'just haven't been sleeping too well.'

'Ah... well...' she said, her eyes widening with unspoken connotations.

I decided to ignore any knowing glances or veiled suggestions that Maureen and her friends might make. It was clear that any protestations on my part would just feed the fuel of speculation about my love life. How could I possibly explain what was really going on?

As it turned out, the focus was off me that night.

'So, Maureen', said Janet, sitting with Betty in the back of Maureen's Toyota, 'when is Peter coming over to sit for you? And is it going to be head and shoulders, or full frontal?'

She and Betty collapsed against each other in a heap of wheezy giggles.

My god, I thought it was the young who were supposed to be sex-obsessed, I thought to myself. And then I saw Maureen's reddened neck and a little bit of a dither as she navigated the parked cars along the narrow streets of the school, and I realised there was actually some truth in what they were saying. Well, not literally perhaps – I hoped, putting the image of a full frontal of Peter firmly out of my head.

'We've just been for coffee together, that's all,' she said, 'and we're going to go to the theatre one night. We're just friends, so you girls can just calm down.'

But I could see from the secret little smile on her face that there was more to it than that.

I felt a pang of jealousy.

The whole world seemed to be having a normal life, except me.

The class that evening was quite enjoyable. We did a writing game that was similar to the game of Consequences, where we had to write a short introduction to a story, describe two characters, some dialogue and then an ending, but pass the paper round in between each step. It was an exercise in writing structure, but the results were hilarious, and I came away from the class feeling euphoric and relaxed after the hilarious laughter that had dominated the evening. It helped enormously with my mood, and when I got home I felt less fraught about the unanswered questions and the silent telephone.

But that night I had the dream again, and I awoke at four in the morning in a cold sweat, and then could not get back to sleep. I started worrying about my life and the way it was going; my rapidly dwindling bank account, the potential need to get a job within a few months, and the fact that the only social life I had was a group of sex-crazed sixty-year-olds and a 200-year-old man who only seemed concerned to put as much distance between himself and me as he could.

At nine o'clock I eventually gave up on trying to catch any sleep and dragged myself to the kettle to make coffee and put some food in Charlie's bowl.

At nine thirty I was still in my dressing gown and finishing off the remains of a bowl of crunchy nut cereal when the doorbell rang. Thinking it was the postman with a parcel or something, I opened the door.

He was leaning against the door frame in a familiar black leather jacket.

Instinctively, my hand flew to my head and attempted to smooth the inevitable haystack arrangement I knew to be there.

'Will.'

Charlie flew out and leapt up at him, whimpering with delight, his tail a blur.

He looked down to pet Charlie, but I knew he had already clocked the dressing gown and the 'bedroom' hair.

'Good morning.'

'But.... You're in Scotland.'

He gave me a sideways look.

'Then you must be hallucinating.'

Actually, it wouldn't have surprised me if I was, but I resisted the urge to pinch myself. Not even in my wildest hallucinations would I have allowed this scene to take place whilst wearing my dressing gown.

'I...er...got up late,' I said, pathetically.

'Evidently. Am I interrupting something?'

I would have given anything at that moment to have been able to say, 'Yes, as a matter of fact, you are. Perhaps you could call me another time.' But knowing Will as I did, God only knew when I'd hear from him again. So I sacrificed the potentially delicious moment of revenge.

'No, you're not. Not today, anyway.'

'OK.'

His breath was coming out in steam, and I wasn't dressed for the outside world.

'You'd better come in.'

He came in.

'Put the kettle on while I go and get dressed,' I said, and fled upstairs.

I nearly fell over in my attempt to dress too quickly, but managed to find a clean salmon pink jumper that enhanced my skin tone. I put a hairbrush through my hair, cleaned my teeth and applied the slightest touch of lip gloss. I couldn't do much about the sleep-deprived eyes, but what did it matter? This wasn't exactly a seduction scene.

When I got downstairs, Will was sitting in the chair by the empty fireplace with a cup of coffee by his side.

'I made you one,' he said, nodding to the table by the sofa, 'you looked like you might need it.'

Thanks.

'Thanks,' I said.

I sat down on the sofa and picked up my coffee. It was exactly as I like it; strong and milky, without sugar, in my favourite, paw-print mug.

'You were going to ring me,' I said, hoping I didn't sound too much like a jilted lover.

'Yes,' he said, looking at me over his coffee mug, 'but I'm here instead.'

There was no arguing with that.

'Why aren't you in Scotland?'

'It was too cold.'

I sipped my coffee and waited. Will was being at his most infuriatingly evasive best, but I wasn't going to go chasing. I did have some dignity. Not a lot, after the dressing gown episode, I had to admit, but some.

'I thought we could go for a walk,' he said eventually.

'Walk?' I repeated, while Charlie looked up at us hopefully. I looked out of the window where a low November fog was obscuring everything beyond the houses opposite. Will followed my gaze.

'This will clear by ten,' he said, 'these light fogs are common here, but the sun's behind it and it will clear within the hour.'

Something about the way he spoke reminded me that he had been born and bred here when it was nothing more than a small farming community – people who knew the countryside and were familiar with the idiosyncrasies of local weather patterns.

I melted, just a little.

'All right,' I said, 'where do you want to go? Not to Alderton Hall – I don't want to go there.'

'Nor do I,' he replied, 'I wasn't thinking of that. I thought we might go into Clayford first, have a coffee and then walk along the canal.'

'Why Clayford?'

'I want to show you something. I'll buy you lunch as well, if you like.'

It seemed like a fair deal.

In Clayford High Street, Will told me to turn into the car park of the Fox and Goose pub.

The Fox and Goose was one of those large eighteenth century pubs that had once been a coaching inn. It had a narrow, arched drive down one side where the coaches used to enter and was now the entrance to the pub car park.

We sat in the car, behind the beer garden, where empty wooden chairs were tipped up for the winter against round wooden tables, and a children's play area with swings and a slide lay dormant and frosted.

'This is where I first met Anne Corbett,' he said.

'What,' I quickly rejoined, 'in a pub car park?'

He grinned. I liked it when he found me amusing. Not everyone did.

'It's not much to look at now,' he said, 'but then it was the main coaching stop for the stage to London. It was a busy, exciting place, full of noise and bustle. The railways came soon after and the coaching business faded away. Most of these old inns have never been the same since. They lost their character. It was a time when many things were changing.'

I looked at his pensive face and contemplated the mind-boggling amount of change he must have witnessed in his lifetime. It was almost inconceivable.

'Shall we have coffee here?' I asked, 'I'm getting cold.'

'Yes, OK,' he said, 'but I draw the line at coming here for lunch. I have a much better place in mind.'

'On that subject I will trust you completely,' I said.

We left a very indignant Charlie in the car and entered the pub through the back entrance.

I could see what he meant about the loss of character. The pub was part of a chain, decorated in what was supposed to be a 'traditional' style, with dark red patterned carpets, lots of alcoves at different levels and red-shaded wall lamps to give it a 'cosy' atmosphere. Slot machines and juke boxes flashed away in corners, and bartenders and barmaids – who looked barely old enough to visit a pub themselves – wore smart white blouses and shirts with black trousers or skirts. It was pleasant enough, but it had no soul, no individual touch. It was run smoothly to a model, without heart.

The laminated menus on each table looked like they belonged in a fast food restaurant.

'I see what you mean about the food,' I said, glancing at the menu, 'and I don't suppose the rest of it is anything like what you remember?'

He laughed, almost choked on his coffee.

'Unrecognisable. It's like something that's been anaesthetised. It was full of life once: the warmth of log fires, smoke, noise, smells of roasting meat and sawdust, the shouts of the innkeeper and the laughter of drunkards. Now, it's – well, to quote a favourite musician of mine, 'comfortably numb'.'

'Ah, there's nothing like Pink Floyd for a musical quote when you need one.'

He smiled.

'That's pretty true.'

'So...' I started, cautiously, 'you met Anne here.'

'Mmm. Not in here exactly. She was with her governess, who wouldn't have allowed her to step foot inside an inn for one moment. Though I have every reason to believe Anne would not have hesitated to make a bold entrance and order a pint of ale had she been alone.'

'Really?' I said, fascinated, 'she was a bit of a wild child, then?'

'Wild she certainly was. And she was barely seventeen when I first saw her, so in many ways a child, and in many ways, not. But she was certainly what you'd nowadays call 'feisty'.'

'She sounds fun.'

He hesitated.

'That's one way of putting it.'

Chapter 13 - Anne's Story

'I really do not understand why we could not have travelled to London by railway,' said Anne, sulkily pulling her shawl a little tighter round her shoulders, 'this carriage is cold and these seats are hard. The whole journey will be quite unbearable.'

'Oh, do be quiet, Anne,' said the woman with her, who was about fifteen years her senior. Her face was thin and pinched looking, and she looked around her nervously as if expecting calamity at every second. 'I have explained to you that I will not travel in a tin box on a steel track that travels at break-neck speeds; it cannot be healthy for anyone. If one must travel, it should be at a civilized pace; I do not hold for rushing around the countryside like a lunatic.'

Anne turned her face to the window and mouthed to herself a mocking repetition of her governess's words: 'I do not hold...' and mimicking with some exaggeration the expression on her face.

It wasn't fair. But then, nothing in her life had ever been fair. If her uncle wasn't so weak and didn't listen so much to Sarah – who after all was only a mere servant – she, Anne, would be able to order her to do whatever she wished. Instead, Sarah behaved as if she were in charge. It was not right at all.

Everyone travelled by railway now. You only had to look at the amount of people that were here today – the inn's yard was empty and no-one else seemed to be boarding their coach, either outside on the cheap seats on the top, or inside.

Rubbing at the murky window, she found she was mistaken. More cases were being loaded onto the back of the carriage. They were to have a travelling companion, it seemed. Perhaps that might make the journey more interesting.

The carriage door opened and Anne turned to see who was going to enter. The open door let in more cold air, for although it was early spring, the air was still cold and that morning there had been a frost on the ground.

A man in a morning coat and top hat climbed up into the carriage, tipping his hat to both women and issuing a polite, 'Good morning' before sitting opposite them. Anne was pleased to see that, although old – in his thirties at least – he was nevertheless rather handsome, with short, dark brown sideburns and a small moustache. His eyes seemed to linger on Anne for a moment as he sat down. She was glad she was wearing her new wide brimmed bonnet, and that she had written to her uncle previously to insist on some new travelling clothes before the journey.

No other inside passengers being due, the coach set off, bumpily and noisily echoing through the arched passageway of the Fox and Goose Coaching Inn and onto the cobbled main street of Clayford. Anne sighed and gripped the straps at the side of the carriage. It must be so much smoother in a railway carriage, she thought.

Next to her, Sarah had opened a book to read, one of those silly romances that governesses read, she supposed. The man had opened out a newspaper and commenced to read it.

Anne sighed again. It was going to be an interminable journey.

Her eyes strayed over the back pages of the newspaper that were in front of her. Advertisements for liver pills, hair oils and ladies' dancing schools covered the page, but she noticed a different advertisement which was written with larger, bolder type and had a picture of a huge glass palace, like a giant greenhouse. 'The Great Exhibition!' shouted the advertisement, 'Created by Prince Albert and housed at Hyde Park in the grand and spectacular Crystal Palace built by Joseph Caxton. From the great Steam Hammer to the most delicate Wedgwood pottery, the best of British and International technology will be on show for the general public. Grand Opening by Her Majesty Queen Victoria on May 1st!'

Anne leaned forward.

'Excuse me, sir.'

Sarah's head shot up and she glared at Anne in horror.

'Anne!' she whispered loudly.

Anne ignored her, and repeated more loudly above the noise of the carriage wheels and horses' hooves.

'Excuse me, sir!'

The man lowered his paper and looked at her with a steady gaze. She was glad to see that he did not seem at all shocked that she should be addressing him.

'Tell me, sir, are you travelling all the way to London?'

'Yes,' he said, 'I am. But I will be changing at Oxford to take the train.'

'Oh, that is unfortunate for us, for we will be on this coach for the full journey.' She gave a meaningful look to Sarah. 'And when you are in London, will you be visiting the Great Exhibition?'

'Anne!' repeated Sarah, and then turned apologetically to the stranger. 'Please forgive my ward, sir, for her impertinence.' Then she turned back to Anne to begin admonishing her.

The man tipped his hat and said, 'Please, it is of no matter. The young lady has asked an interesting and apposite question, for I am indeed planning to go to the Exhibition, and will in fact be in employment there.'

Anne turned to Sarah with a look of triumph.

'But,' he continued, 'I should introduce myself if we are to engage in conversation. My name is Mr Days. Might I be forward enough to enquire as to your own identity? Your face seems familiar...'

Anne was about to answer, but Sarah interrupted her.

'Pardon me, sir, but you should understand that I am under strict instructions that my young companion should speak to no strangers on our journey...'

'Oh, Sarah,' cut in Anne, 'I am not going to sit here for three hours all the way to Oxford in total silence. Forgive me, sir, but my governess will insist on following instructions to the most ridiculous extremes...'

'Anne, you are the most impudent child. Don't think that your uncle will not hear about your rudeness...'

'Oh, Sarah, I don't care...'

'Well, I think that a girl of your age should care and should be made to care.' She turned back to Mr Days. 'You can see my problem, Mr Days. But, if we are to enter into such intercourse, might I ask you your profession?'

Anne looked out of the window at the fields passing by, rolling her eyes in embarrassment.

Mr Days smiled gently and looked straight at Sarah.

'I am an actor and a musician.'

Anne grinned. Sarah looked as though she was going to faint.

'Oh, but...' she began, but had nothing else to say. She fumbled in her purse for a handkerchief and held it to her nose.

Anne stared at her new friend with pure delight.

'But how exciting!' she said, ignoring the stifled exclamations coming from behind the silk handkerchief, 'allow me to introduce myself. My name is Anne Corbett, and this is my governess, Sarah.'

Sarah shook her head, her eyes closed.

Mr Days looked at Anne, and she thought his skin seemed a little paler.

'Corbett?' he said, 'not the Corbetts of Stanton Bridge? Your father...'

'...was Andrew Corbett, yes, of Alderton Hall. It is... was my home. My father is dead sir.' She made this last statement without emotion, but as a matter of fact.

He continued to stare at her in a curious way, looking extremely discomforted.

'I am sorry...' he began in a gruff voice.

'Please do not be, sir. My father was a drunkard and a gambler. He died from a fall from his horse coming home late across the fields in a drunken stupor. Nobody mourned his death. He loved no-one, and no-one loved him.'

Days gave a single nod of understanding.

'And your mother...'

'My mother is dead too, sir.' This time Anne's voice was softer.

'Yes,' said Mr Days, his voice equally as soft, 'I know. I once knew her.'

Anne's eyes widened.

'You knew my mother? But then, sir, you have the better of

me, for I never knew her. I am sorry to say that I was the cause of her death, for she died in childbed at my birth.'

'Yes,' said Mr Days, and turned away to look out of the window.

'You see, Sarah?' said Anne, 'Mr Days knew my mother and is therefore perfectly respectable and not a stranger at all.'

Sarah only sniffed, and buried her nose in her book.

Anne turned back to Mr Days.

'I am delighted to make your acquaintance, Mr Days. I know very few people who knew my mother. Tell me, was she as beautiful as they say?'

'Yes,' he said, with a slight smile, 'beautiful and accomplished.'

'Oh, I am glad to hear you say so.'

They travelled in silence for several miles.

'May I ask what takes you to London?' asked Mr Days eventually.

'I am going to live with my uncle, Captain James Corbett, in St James Square, and learn how to be a lady and find a husband.' She laughed, and leaned towards him. 'But I will let you into a secret, Mr Days, I have no wish to find a husband and I plan to live a full life and break many hearts. Why should I not, if my uncle is kind enough to allow me to live under his roof and let me eat his food. After all, he has allowed me to linger all this time at Alderton Hall without caring anything about me or my older brother until we were of an age that was more interesting to him, for he has no interest in children, and merely paid for the staff to look after our welfare. My brother John now has a commission in the army, and I think it is quite reasonable therefore that I should take advantage of my uncle's hospitality now and for many years to come, do you not think so?'

Mr Days' eyebrows lifted in some surprise at the young lady's statement of intent, but he smiled slowly and bowed his head slightly in acknowledgement, if not in collaboration.

'Well,' said Anne, leaning back, 'that is what I intend. I have lived for seventeen years in complete boredom, and I intend to live the next seventeen at least in some excitement. Oh, but, you must have lived a very exciting life, Mr Days, in your line of work. Tell me what the life of an actor is like? Is it as scandalous and exciting as they say?'

They were interrupted by a series of tuts from Sarah, which were ignored.

'It can be,' he replied, 'for some. But most of the time it is very hard work. I do not wish to disappoint you, Miss Corbett, but we provincial actors spend most of our time travelling, rehearsing and painting scenery – oh, and performing as well. The life leaves very little time for anything else.'

'Oh,' said Anne, feeling a little disappointed, 'well, do tell me about your employment at the Great Exhibition. I am fully intending to have my uncle take me. I believe it is going to be the grandest exhibition ever.'

'I believe it will, Miss Corbett, and I have the honour of playing at some of the concerts that will be held in the central transept.'

'Oh, I do hope that we shall see you there.'

They continued in polite conversation all the way to Oxford, and Mr Days told Anne about life in the theatre; he explained that many provincial theatres were really just converted barns, but there were also many purpose-built theatres in the larger towns which were warmer and pleasanter to work in. He described the long walks between towns and shocked her with the amount he spent on cobblers' bills each year, because only the famous actors, or women who were with child travelled between theatres by coach as most of them could not afford to. He also explained that the popularity of the railways had caused a decline in audiences in the smaller theatres because they all now wanted to travel to the more comfortable theatres in the bigger towns, so he did not think the travelling theatre circuits would still be in existence in five years' time. This was why he had looked for other work as a musician – which was what he wanted to do most of all – and luckily knew someone who was able to get him employment at the Crystal Palace.

Anne tried to ask him about her mother but on that subject he was not as forthcoming. All he said was, 'I did not know her that well,' and stared out of the window.

At Oxford Mr Days left them at the railway station and told Anne that he hoped he would have the pleasure of meeting her again at the Crystal Palace. The coach then called at an inn for a change of horses and to enable the passengers to eat luncheon. Sarah was very quiet and would hardly even look at Anne, so the ensuing journey to London was a long and uninteresting one, and Anne slept for most of it.

Living at Uncle James's large house in St James was very different to living at Alderton Hall. Anne had to get used to a more strict regime, with set times for breakfast, lunch and dinner, and rules for dressing differently for each part of the day. Without parental guidance she had been able to do very much as she had pleased at the Hall, running rings around the servants, getting up late and annoying her older brother who had avoided her as much as possible. Sometimes she came to dinner in the same muddy dress that she had walked the fields in.

At Captain James's house she was to be tamed and turned into a presentable young lady who would be able to play the piano and sing at parties. This meant having to practise daily with tutors for hours, being measured for dresses and accepting invitations for balls and other social gatherings.

The last of these arrangements she did not mind at all, but she found daily practice to be tedious in the extreme and she missed the freedom she had had at Alderton Hall, which surprised her, as she had not expected to miss anything about the Hall at all. She was constantly now being chastised for rudeness to her tutors, and two piano teachers had walked out within a month of her being there, much to the dismay of her Aunt Adele, who lost no time in telling her that theirs was a respectable house and she would not countenance the wild behaviour that Anne had obviously inherited from her father. Anne was mortified by this remark, and secretly thought that she would try to be nicer, but did not want to admit this to her aunt, so she became merely sulkily compliant.

However, whenever they had visitors, her behaviour was exemplary; she smiled, she blushed, she spoke only when spoken to and she played pretty little pieces on the piano. The friends of Captain Corbett were captivated by his young niece, and Aunt Adele bowed her acknowledgement to their praises. Only in private did she mutter that the girl was a 'little madam' and deserved taking down a peg or two.

On 16th May her uncle and aunt took her to the Great Exhibition at Hyde Park.

She had never seen anything so large and glorious as that great glass house. It seemed to stretch as far as the eye could see. Great fountains around the park threw water high into the sky and statues of enormous and strange animals could be seen as they approached. She was shocked by the crowds of people of all classes who were making their way to the entrance.

Sarah had come with them on the trip and she was alarmed at the type of people who jostled past them.

'Anne, keep hold of your purse and take my arm. Goodness knows who might be....Oh really!' she exclaimed, as a young man with a peaked cap ran past almost knocking her over and causing her bonnet to shift over one eye.

Anne stifled a giggle.

'Do try and enjoy yourself, Sarah. Look at all the people and the grandeur of this place! Does it not make you feel quite dizzy?'

'No, it makes me feel quite queasy. But I suppose if you learn something from it, it will be worth the money, so do please remember that this is an educational excursion and not an opportunity for enjoyment or making goggle eyes at young men.'

'Why on earth learning should have to be so devoid of enjoyment, I do not know,' said Anne, gasping as they entered and saw more fountains and statues within the palace, as well as some huge elm trees actually growing underneath the roof. 'You see? Is that not something to marvel at and enjoy? Oh, look up there! There are galleries – oh, there's so much to see, isn't it magnificent? Such colours – oh the fountain! Look at those statues!'

They wandered through the exhibition, gazing in awe at the colours and richness of the fabrics in the Indian and African courts, being astounded by scientific inventions and enlightened by agricultural and factory machinery. It was almost too much to take in and after two hours they flopped into chairs in the refreshment rooms for tea.

'Can we not go to the concert at four, uncle?' asked Anne, as soon as their tea arrived, 'I do believe they have a fine group of musicians playing Schubert, and as you know I have great difficulties with that composer. It would be very helpful, I think to listen to professional musicians...'

'Captain Corbett is far too busy to linger here much longer, Anne....' began Sarah.

'Oh, I don't know,' said the Captain, who was enjoying himself immensely (several young ladies had smiled at him in his military uniform and he did like to be seen to be patronising such events), 'I think if Anne wants to improve herself by listening to music, we should only encourage her.'

They wandered back through rooms full of machinery, fabrics and pottery from all over the world. It was difficult to walk quickly, partly because of the amount of people, and partly because there was always something interesting to look at.

By the time they reached the central transept they could hear music already playing Schubert's Trout Quintet.

'Look, Sarah!' said Anne, 'it's our friend Mr Days playing the piano! Doesn't he look grand?'

'Hmmm,' was all Sarah replied, but Captain Corbett turned to Anne.

'Do you mean to tell me you know this fellow?' he said, 'he plays very well.'

'Yes, uncle, we met him on the coach on the journey to London and he was a friend of my mother's. He is perfectly respectable and a very pleasant travelling companion.'

'Is that so? Then perhaps you might introduce us...'

Sarah cleared her throat.

'I must inform you, sir, that our travelling companion,

though indeed he gave the demeanour of a gentleman, introduced himself as being of the...' she cleared her throat again, '..of the *theatrical* profession.' The word 'theatrical' was spoken in a whisper, as if the word itself might carry a dread disease when spoken aloud.

Captain James Corbett threw back his head and laughed. Several people turned towards their party and 'shushed', while Adele nudged him in the ribs.

'Ah yes... pardon me. A theatrical eh? In that case, Anne, I insist that you introduce us. I think it might be rather jolly to invite such a fellow to a few of our little soirees, do you not think, Adele?'

'If you say so, James,' said Adele in a voice that was not at all sure.

Anne was aware of an attempt by Sarah to pull herself up to her tallest and look indignantly shocked, but Anne thought that she merely looked slightly ridiculous and pretended to ignore her. At the same time, her respect for her uncle had increased a thousand fold.

So William Days became a regular visitor at Number 11 St. James Square, and sometimes gave piano recitals at the parties that Adele gave, and which had become very popular within their little wing of society.

He also, once the Captain and his wife had decided that he was a man who was to be trusted, became Anne's new piano teacher and under his tutelage her playing slowly began to improve.

One hot summer's afternoon Anne was struggling with a very complicated piece of Bach, while William sat patiently by, issuing gentle guidance and making her go over bars that she found particularly difficult by adjusting her fingering. A shaft of sunlight from the long French windows fell across the sheet music, and Anne frowned and squinted as she concentrated on the notes. The more she tried to get the notes right, the more she got them wrong.

Finally, she slammed the lid of the keyboard down and crossed her arms.

'I do not feel in the mood for playing the piano today.'

William looked at the piano lid for a moment, and then stood up and went to the window. A long, orderly garden stretched away from the windows, joining the sides and backs of other gardens. The effect was that of a large square of trees and greenery surrounded by the backs of the elegant houses of the area. Close to the house a gardener was dead-heading roses.

'Unfortunately,' he said eventually, 'the purpose of my being here is to teach you to play the piano. If I do not fulfil my task, I am being paid for doing nothing, which...'

'Oh, don't be so stuffy,' said Anne, 'uncle can afford it. Anyway, I refuse to play another note today, so there. What will you do about it?'

William eyed her thoughtfully. Sometimes she reminded him so much of her mother he did not know how to respond.

'Nothing,' he replied, you are apparently in a stubborn mood today. There is nothing I can do about that.'

'I suppose my mother was able to play the piano perfectly.'

Memories came back to him; the sound of Mozart floating through an open window, across a gravelled drive; a falter, an exclamation of frustration and then the continuation, potent in its expression.

'Not perfectly, but very well,' he said.

Anne got up and walked down the side of the long room,

fingering books on the shelves as she passed.

'You must have been very young when you knew her, Mr Days.'

William's eyes slid away from her.

It was not the first time someone had commented on his age. People who had known him ten or fifteen years ago met him with looks of puzzlement. 'Willie,' they would say, 'have you found the secret of eternal youth? You have not changed a bit...'

He knew he looked and felt no different than he had done nearly twenty years ago, yet he had just this year passed his fiftieth birthday. His peers complained of stiffness, grey hair, wrinkles and gout, but none of these things had come to him.

'Perhaps I am older than I look,' he said, moving out of the sunlight and into shadow, 'but I do not believe it is normal for people to discuss each other's age in polite society, Miss Corbett. Perhaps we could discuss how we are to fill the rest of this hour, or would you like me to inform your uncle that you no longer require my services?'

'Oh, no! Please do not do that!' Anne said with feeling, 'couldn't we just talk for a while? Tell me more about the theatre.'

'I would have thought you would be tired of that subject by now.'

'Oh, no. Not at all. Please tell me what the women are like.'

'Miss Corbett, I hardly think...'

'Oh, I just cannot bear the life I am expected to lead!' she burst out, holding her head between her hands, 'I thought that being here would be so much better than at Alderton Hall, and of course it is, but I was able to do as I pleased there even if I was nearly driven mad with boredom. Now I am almost driven mad with all the rules and ways I am expected to behave. I wish

I had been born a man, I truly do. Men have so much more opportunity and freedom...'

'It is not always so...'

'Oh, don't try to tell me it's not that easy. All men should know what it is to be a woman!'

An awkward silence followed.

'I take it,' said William, softly, 'that your plan is not working as you would have liked?'

'Plan? What plan?'

'I seem to remember that you were going to live very happily upon your uncle's generosity and break numerous hearts whilst doing so. Was that not what you told me?'

'Oh, curse you, Mr Days, for having an excellent memory. Yes, I did say that and... well it has not... I have not begun the plan properly yet. Perhaps we should continue with the piano lesson.'

'As you wish.'

She sat on the piano stool but did not raise the lid.

'You know, what I would really like is to be an actress on the stage.'

'Your uncle would not...'

'I know perfectly well that my uncle would not allow it! I do realise that despite his interest in people like yourself and his natural ability to socialise with all classes, he would not tolerate... After all, does he not treat you more like a servant than an equal?'

William inclined his head slightly.

'That is how the world works, Miss Corbett.'

'Well I wish it did not! Why should a person – man or woman – not do as they wish? Why, if I ran away from home and joined the theatre, and do not think it is not something that

I have contemplated, I would be ruined in society! People with whom I now exchange polite and dainty words with, who bow graciously over my hand, who clap prettily when I play the piano, those same people who actually go to the theatre themselves, would turn their heads away and pretend not to know me on the street! Such hypocrites people are! I would be treated as no more than a common prostitute...!'

'Miss Corbett...'

'Well, do you think it is fair? Do you?

William looked at her levelly.

'No. I do not think it is fair.'

'There!'

She sat silently on the stool. Her eyes were moist and she seemed to quiver with an eternal rage that William knew he had only just seen the surface of, like the tip of an iceberg.

But he had no words of comfort to give to her. She had spoken the truth. The rules of the class she had been born into were strict and harsh for the female sex if they had intelligence and an independent spirit. Yet he could not advise the course of action she had suggested. He had lived long enough to see many actresses end their lives alone and destitute, once their looks were gone, unless they had achieved some degree of fame. And, it may be the one career for women that offered autonomy and freedom, but most actresses he knew had been born into it and grew up with the necessities of hard work and rough living. The few women who came from middle class backgrounds rarely survived.

He drew up another stool and sat facing her drooping head.

'Listen to me, Anne.'

She raised her head at his use of her Christian name.

'I know you have had to grow up without the guidance of a

mother, or, indeed a decent father.'

She nodded.

'Well, I did know your mother... a little. And I suppose I knew her well enough to know that she would have taken pride in you.'

'Oh,' said Anne, her hands flying to her face, 'do you really think so?'

'Yes, I do. I know so. She would have loved your intelligence, your wit, your determination to be nobody else but who you are. But I think that she would have given you some advice as well. Would you like me to tell you what I think that might have been?'

'Oh, please do.'

'I think she would have told you to be very cautious about throwing what you have away. It is very easy to look over at another world and think it better, but that other world can look very different from the inside, when you find there is no way back.'

William stopped speaking. He rose and went to the window. Outside, the gardener had started to trim the hedge that surrounded the garden. He remembered a garden long ago, where his own dreams had been destroyed.

'I'm sorry,' he said, turning back to her, 'you are young, and you can only see that the things you want are blocked by seemingly idiotic conventions and rules. I may be a man, but I am not a stranger to such feelings. But all I can say is that you must take what you have and make the best that you can with it. Do not run from it, but do not give in to it either. You are strong and clever, and sooner or later you will find a way to make it work for you.'

'I don't know how I can do that.'

'I know. But, trust me, Anne. Have patience and listen to what your heart tells you. No-one can take that away.'

She looked down at her hands. She seemed saddened by his words, as if they were not what she had wanted to hear, but at the same time she appeared calmer than she had been five minutes ago.

She began to speak but in the same moment the clock on the mantelpiece chimed the hour, signalling the end of the lesson.

William picked up his hat and his case.

'Keep practising those bars of the Bach, Miss Corbett, and I look forward to seeing some improvement next week.'

He bowed politely, put his hat on his head and left the room.

Chapter 14

'So,' I said, 'you became a kind of mentor as well as a tutor.'

We were walking along the bank of the canal, Charlie racing up and down the towpath, glad to be free of the restraints of the car. The fog, as Will had predicted, had cleared, leaving a clear blue sky and a residue of rime on the leaves that we kicked as we walked. Crisp in the cold air, they cracked loudly beneath our feet.

'I suppose so,' said Will, 'but I was mainly her piano tutor. That was what I had been employed to do.'

I looked at him in his jeans and leather jacket, a dark red scarf tied beneath his chin, and tried to imagine him as a Victorian, with a top hat and frock coat. I had to squint a bit to get the picture and the image I got made me smile.

He caught my look and turned to me.

'What?'

'Nothing. I was just picturing you as a Dickensian character.'

'Ah,' he said with a grin, 'dear Charles.'

I stopped walking.

'Now you're having me on, aren't you? Are you going to tell me now that you knew Charles Dickens?'

'Passionately fond of the theatre, was Boz. It's not surprising that our paths should cross.'

'Really? You're not just teasing me?'

He smiled broadly.

'Well, maybe just a little. But I did meet him once.'

'Oh, my God! What was he like?'

'Genial, enthusiastic – with the energy of a young dog.'

We both looked at Charlie, who had caught the scent of something – probably a fox – and was quickly following it, his nose down, tail up, running from one spot to another.

'Of course, that was when he was still quite young himself. I would have liked to have known him better,' said Will.

I was quiet for a while. Knowing I was only two handshakes away from one of my favourite writers – even if he had been dead for about 140 years – was pretty awe-inspiring.

But that was a conversation for another time – if there was to be another time.

'So, what about Anne? Did she stay at her uncle's house, and did she break any hearts?'

'She stayed. Whether hearts were broken or not is a matter best known to the owner of the relevant hearts, but she certainly had many offers of marriage.'

'Which, obviously, she turned down?'

'Yes. Which caused many heated arguments with her aunt and uncle.'

'Could they not have forced her to marry?'

He smiled warmly.

'The idea of forcing Anne to do anything she did not want to is an amusing one. Besides, perhaps you've read too many historical novels – or even too much Dickens – but it didn't happen that often. I'm not denying that forced marriages did happen, but most of us Victorians were not quite as horrid to women as you like to think. And, even if Captain Corbett had threatened her with homelessness, it would have been no real threat to Anne. She would merely have taken herself off to join a theatre company. I do believe she would almost have welcomed it.'

'But, they did try to get her to marry against her will?'

'Oh, yes. It's true that money was often the main reason for marriage in the higher classes, and feelings were often dismissed as of secondary importance to a good marriage. Women who knew their own minds were usually thought of as 'difficult' in society. And Anne certain knew her own mind.'

'But, she did marry.'

'Eventually.'

'How did that happen?'

'I can only tell you from what I heard years later. The thing is, Catherine, my body's refusal to grow old was just beginning to be a bit of an embarrassment to me, and I was finding it increasingly necessary to break contact with people after a certain period in order to avoid comment. I had to move on after a few years and find new work. With Anne's knowledge of my connection with her mother, it was obvious that she would notice my lack of ageing quite soon. We parted company in 1856, by which time she no longer needed a tutor anyway.

'But the way I found out about Anne was through the most extraordinary coincidence – and quite worthy of a Dickensian plot.

'Some time before I met Anne, I had known a young man who did some work as a playwright. He was a friend of one of the members of the theatre company I was with and had written several plays and sketches for our repertoire. His name was Jepson, Henry Jepson; a quiet, shy fellow, but quite a philosopher. I liked him very much, and we had been drinking partners on many occasions. He had many ideas about reform and was a follower of John Stuart Mill. When the circuit theatres began to break up he found some employment up in Yorkshire and that was the last I saw of him for years.

'Then, two years after I had left the Captain's employ, I was in Leeds for the opening of the new Town Hall there. They had put on a big music festival in which I was taking part, and I spent several days in the city and one night took myself to the Theatre Royal to see a Shakespeare production – I think it was *Macbeth,* but I could be wrong.

'Anyway, I was just coming out of the auditorium after the final curtain, when I saw Henry coming towards me...'

'Willie? Willie Days? What a pleasurable surprise!' said Henry, 'my word, sir, you have not changed a bit...'

'Henry!' exclaimed William, noticing wisps of grey hair around the man's temples, 'this is a surprise! How goes it with you? Are you still writing?'

The two men shook hands.

'Now and then, when I get a commission, but it's a difficult business, you know that, Willie. I earn a living as a teacher of English in the grammar school here, which takes up much of my time. What about you, Willie, are you still in the theatre? Things have changed so...'

'Yes, when I can,' replied William, 'but I find as much employment as I can as a musician. I am in fact here for the festival.'

'Oh, but of course. The city has been festooned with bunting for days in honour of the Queen's visit. There has been a lot of excitement about it.'

They came out into the cool night air.

'Where are you staying, Willie? I hope you have good rooms here.'

'They are sufficient.'

'Well, I would press you to visit, but unfortunately, well, fortunately for me as it happens, I am bound for London on the morrow.'

'London? What takes you there?'

Henry looked bashful, but his eyes twinkled with mirth.

'A young lady. I am to be married, Willie; to the most beautiful and intelligent woman you have ever met.'

'And the name of this lucky creature?'

'Anne. Anne Corbett...'

'Anne Corbett?' Will stopped and faced Henry, and they stood staring at each other under the light of a gas lamp.

'Surely you do not mean the niece of Captain Corbett of St. James Square, the daughter of the late Andrew Corbett of Alderton Hall?'

'Why, the very same! Do not tell me that you know the girl?'

'Why, yes, indeed I do. I was her piano tutor in London for five years.'

'But what a wonderful and extraordinary coincidence! I am sure she will be delighted that I have met you!'

'And I am delighted that she has met you, Henry. The last time I saw her she was about to turn down the third offer for her hand in marriage. She was quite determined not to marry. However, I could not have wished a better match for her, my friend.'

Henry laughed warmly as William shook his hand again.

'I must admit, I hesitated at first. After all, I am a socialist, and she is from – well, she is from the family she is from. It seemed the strangest of matches, yet I could not get her out of my mind, and eventually I had to propose. I was in fact deeply surprised when she accepted me – and even more surprised when her uncle consented to our union, given my station and so forth. Fortunately for me, he has a liking for those of our profession, Willie, and I rather have a suspicion too that he had begun to despair of Anne ever accepting anyone.'

'Yes,' said William, 'I remember him well, and I think they had hoped that she would marry earlier. But my warmest congratulations to you both. I know you will have great happiness.'

'Thank you, Willie; but, do you know – the most extraordinary thing! I have only this moment remembered. You see, I once asked Anne why she had chosen me over all her other suitors – after all, the teaching profession provides only a modest income and the income I receive from writing is very small indeed. I happen to know that many of her previous offers had been from men of some considerable means. So I asked her, why me? Why not a man with a fortune to keep you in fine gowns and bonnets and grand houses for the rest of your life? And do you know what she said?'

A smile was playing around the corners of William's mouth. 'Tell me.'

'She said, "Some years ago I had a very wise, and indeed handsome..." (but she only said that to tease, you know, Willie) "...piano tutor, who once advised me that I should follow my heart. And so, that is why I am marrying you, dear Henry, because I have followed my heart." Now then Willie, my boy, that would not happen to have been yourself would it? It certainly sounds just the sort of thing you might say.'

William's smile had been steadily growing as Henry made

this little speech.

'I am bound to say that I believe I did say something of the sort. It seems that Miss Corbett was perhaps a better student of philosophy than she was of the piano.'

Henry laughed again.

'That she still is, Willie, and in fact she has expressed a passionate desire to assist me in writing my pamphlets and books. And so she shall!'

'I wish you the very best, my friend. I am overjoyed, truly.'

The two men shook hands once more and soon parted company, each going on his way, happy for his own different reasons.

'That is an amazing coincidence,' I said, calling Charlie as we turned round to return to the car, 'fancy you having known Henry all along, and then meeting him like that. You wouldn't believe it if you read it in a book.'

'I know. But my life seems to be full of such coincidental meetings, such as the fact of my meeting every one of your direct female ancestors for six generations. How does one explain that?'

He was asking me?

'Christ, Will, I don't know. It's almost as if – oh, crumbs – as if it's all meant to be, somehow – but I don't... I've never believed in that kind of thing, you know – fate or destiny. But it makes you think. Hell, do you think in thirty years' time you're going to meet my daughter? That means I'd better get a move on...'

Will did not reply, and we walked on in silence. I felt I had said something that he wasn't comfortable with, and I felt suddenly awkward.

'So, what happened? Did they live happily ever after? Did you ever see them again?'

'Anne and Henry? No, I never saw them again.'

He did not speak for a few moments, then he said,

'I think, from what I heard later, they were happy enough. They had ten surviving children, of whom Hannah was the last. But I think it was a struggle for them financially. Some of Henry's books were published, but sales were minimal. Anne, I think, wrote a lot of the stuff, but of course, her name was never given as co-author. Women authors were not good publicity. It must have been galling for her, to say the least.'

'Her and Mary Anne Evans too,' I said, 'but I suppose she must have been kept very busy with all those children.'

'Yes.'

Again, he was quiet for a while.

'I need a beer,' he said, eventually.

We were almost back at the car now, and we rounded Charlie up and headed off for a little pub Will knew of, which he described as friendly and unpretentious.

He was dead right. Unlike the Fox and Goose, which had lost all sense of history in its quest to be 'historical', this was a small, privately run pub with original oak beams, wooden settles and a flag stone floor. In one corner there was a very welcoming inglenook with a crackling fire, and we took our real ales over and sat next to it, while Charlie curled up under the small table.

'This is more like it,' I said.

'The food's good too,' said Will.

We ordered a couple of hotpots and settled down to stare at the fire. I felt a warm glow on my cheeks after all the cold air, and sitting by the fire after all that walking made me feel relaxed and cosy.

I looked at Will.

His head was resting back on the stone wall behind us, and he was staring into the fire, a red glow dancing over his fine cheekbones. He looked far away, lost in his own thoughts.

'Are you OK?' I asked.

He turned his head slowly to look at me.

'It's funny,' he said in a low voice, 'people would pay thousands to find the secret of eternal youth, but if they really thought it through, they'd realise it would be more like a curse.'

This was a new Will. A Will in a dark mood. I didn't say anything, so he continued.

'Have you ever said goodbye to someone knowing you'll never see them again, but not being able to tell them?'

'No,' I said, 'I don't think so.'

'Can you imagine what it's like knowing that everyone you meet, every friend you make, you will only be able to know for a short time, and then years later to hear that they have died of old age, while you are still young and healthy?'

'I'm sorry, Will,' I said, 'it must be...' I was going to say 'difficult', but it seemed too much of an understatement.

'This is why I wrote to you from Scotland. I didn't want to bring back all these memories. It was the worse time, that time when I was just beginning to realise what was happening to me... or rather, not happening. I realised I could never see previous friends or acquaintances again. I could have got in touch with Henry and Anne – I liked them very much – but I knew I could not continue our friendship and watch them grow old, while I...'

He downed his beer.

'Would you like another one?' I asked.

'Yes.'

I got another beer from the bar and put it down in front of him.

'Thanks. I'm sorry to be so... but I told you it was difficult for me.'

'But you came back anyway, and told me all the same.'

'Yes. Don't ask me why. I feel compelled to...' he looked at me, '...confide in you.' He looked away again.

'I feel honoured. Seriously.'

At that point our hotpots arrived, sizzling in deep earthenware bowls and drizzled with melted cheese accompanied by chunks of wholemeal bread and pats of butter.

'Oh, boy. I'm ravenous,' I said. For a while we didn't speak except to say how good the food was and to thank the waitress when she came to check everything was OK.

After soaking up the last remnants of the stew with the last piece of bread and butter, I sat back with a contented sigh. The waitress cleared our plates and Will got us two more beers.

'Do you mind if I ask you a difficult question?' I asked after he'd sat down, 'you don't have to answer if you don't want to. I'm just curious.'

'There's a surprise,' he said, 'go on, what is it?'

'What about women? I mean, what about girlfriends... what – I mean, you must have had some relationships, surely?'

He sighed and leaned his head back again.

'Sure. Girlfriends, lovers, whores... I am a man, after all.'

'But, were any of them...?'

'Serious? No – I don't allow that to happen.'

There was something very final about the way he said it.

'Right. Sure. Of course.'

I followed a grain of wood in the edge of the table with my

fingernail.

'It makes sense,' I said, taking a swig of beer.

'What if they already knew?' I asked, staring up at the ceiling.

He turned to me slowly.

'No,' he said, softly, 'especially not. How would you like to see the person you love grow old and die and then have to go on living for ever without them? And it wouldn't be fair on her either.'

'No,' I said, 'of course not.'

We both stared at the fire.

'Just one more to go, then,' I said.

'Yes. One more. And the most difficult.'

'You're not going to disappear again, are you?'

He turned to look sideways at me.

'Is it really that important to you?'

I stared into my half pint glass.

'Actually, yes. I don't know why – I've never been particularly interested in my ancestors before, but somehow, since you've started telling me all this, I have felt that I need to know, that something that's puzzling me will somehow be answered.'

'What is it that's puzzling you?'

'Oh, only everything. Like, why I hate Alderton Hall so much.'

A frowned passed across his face.

'I did tell you that I don't necessarily have all the answers...'

'Oh, I know that. But... I think I need to know the final instalment – or rather, the first instalment, I suppose. You know, my writing teacher told me the other day that I should always follow my instincts when I'm writing, and just lately I've begun to think that that applies to everything else in life; and I do have a strong instinct about this. It's important that I know the full story – and I don't know why. It just is. Will you trust me on this, Will?'

He nodded.

'Yes, I will – I do trust you. Anyway, I suppose I started it, so I have to finish. It was my own instinct to tell you after you. But it doesn't make it any easier.'

'Well,' I said, staring rather bleakly into the fire, 'at least it will soon be over.'

We finished our beers in silence.

Chapter 15

I knew Will would need some time before he came to me again, so with a determination not to pressurise him, I distracted myself with other things.

There was the book to get on with of course, and I spent most of my mornings working on Chapters three and four, trying to use all the techniques and advice I had been given by Sue. I also bought myself some books on writing, and sat down to read for an hour each day. Having found at least three writers in my ancestral tree I was now determined to follow the path that I now knew to be in my genes and turn myself into a professional writer, worthy of my own bloodline.

The more I worked on my writing the more excited about it I became, and this excitement fuelled my motivation and kept me going. My confidence was growing little by little and I knew that every day that I wrote, I was developing my skills.

The other distraction was the approach of Christmas. It was now late November and in Clayford all the shop windows were full of Christmas trees and fairy lights, and by four o'clock every day the town's Christmas lights brightened up the darkening streets, arching from building to building with colourful stars, bells and ribbons.

It was time to start thinking about Christmas shopping.

CHAPTER 15

The big question was, should I buy a present for Will? And if I did what on earth do you buy for the discerning double centenarian? Would he be embarrassed? Or would it be more embarrassing if he had bought me a present and I hadn't bought him one?

I didn't worry about it for too long. It was early days yet, and maybe by Christmas I'd know what to do. Perhaps it would be irrelevant by then. He might be out of my life.

There was another thing that was on my mind too.

The dream was becoming more and more frequent. It was waking me up at three or four in the morning at least twice a week with a sense of foreboding that kept me awake until about seven thirty. I would eventually fall into a deep slumber, only to be woken half an hour later, groggy and grumpy, by Charlie, desperate to be let out for his early morning pee. On those days it was much more difficult to get going and my progress would be slow.

While I got on with writing, did bits of Christmas shopping here and there, or sat in the evening with Charlie in front of the fire, I was aware of something constantly in the back of my mind; a feeling that something was incomplete and needed to be sorted. It was like a background hum, or like the interference on a TV transmission, niggling and irritating, and despite the progress in my writing, it left me feeling in a permanent state of dis-ease, irritable and short-tempered, and it grew daily in direct proportion to the growing frequency of the dream.

I knew that I needed to speak to Will, and to hear the last story. But I had promised myself not to contact him, so every day I tried to keep myself busy, but each day it got more difficult.

One morning after a particularly bad night, feeling very restless and unable to settle to anything, I decided to pop across to Maureen's and see if she'd like coffee. I hadn't seen her for some time, except on our way to class and back, and I felt a little guilty that maybe I'd been neglecting her.

When the door opened my jaw must have dropped a couple of inches, for there on the threshold instead of Maureen was Peter, and he was looking very smart.

I had, in a vague disinterested way, noticed that his dress sense had been improving over the last few weeks, and the colours he wore clashed less and suited him more. Today he was wearing a deep red shirt under a charcoal grey jumper with a dark grey tweed jacket. His hair was neat and he looked almost dashing.

'Good heavens!' I said before I could stop myself.

'Hello Catherine! Do come in. The other half is just finishing off her 'toilette' upstairs and promises me she won't be long.'

The other half? Blimey, she didn't waste time, did she?

As I entered the kitchen Maureen came down stairs dressed in a cashmere top, wool skirt and boots.

'Who's that, darling? Oh – Catherine, dear, it's you! How lovely! Do sit down for a bit, though you've come at a bad time, as we're just about to go out. Peter's taking me into Clayford to do some Christmas shopping and a slap-up lunch. Isn't he a dear?'

I was still sitting with my mouth open, but managed to pull myself together to say,

'Yes, how lovely.'

Peter took a tweed cap that was hanging on a hook by the door and winked at me.

'Well, the old dear is going to go and get the car out of the garage...'

'Oh, you are a tease, Peter, you know I didn't say 'old' dear –

isn't he naughty?' she said, turning to me.

Her face was flushed and she looked the picture of health, like one of those women in an advert who has taken lots of vitamins.

I smiled a response and as Peter went out of the door, Maureen sat on the edge of the chair next to me.

'I'm so glad you introduced me to Peter, Catherine. Really, my dear, since you've arrived so much has happened – I have a new lease of life and it's all down to you!'

'So, when did you and Peter...'

'Oh, well, I'm sure you think it's all rather sudden, but you know at my age you can't afford to wait around for too long. We've been seeing each other nearly every day now for about two weeks. I'm surprised you haven't noticed. I'm sorry, I've been such a bad neighbour, but...' she tapped my knee knowingly, '...*you* know how it is.'

'Er...'

'And how are things with your young man, dear?'

'My young......?'

'Now don't try and tell me there's nothing going on there! I've seen him with you – I actually saw you both in Clayford the other day, but I didn't interrupt you – you seemed so wrapped up in each other.'

'Oh, but he's not...... Really?'

'Yes – and a very handsome young man too, if you don't mind my saying so. I would hold on to that one if I were you.'

A car horn pipped a couple of times outside.

'Ah, my carriage awaits! We'd better go – he's already told me off once for taking ages to get ready. It's lovely to see you, Catherine. Perhaps we could all go out one evening – at Christmas perhaps, and make up a foursome? Cheerio, dear.

Have a lovely day! Don't do anything I wouldn't do... ha ha!'

She kissed me on the cheek and I waved them both away, still feeling slightly dazed.

I wandered back into the house and shut the door behind me, Charlie snuffling my ankles to see where I'd been. I stood leaning on the door for a few moments.

So, Maureen had a boyfriend.

He was probably fairly normal too, with few hang-ups and the usual kind of age.

I supposed I'd have to have coffee on my own, then. I walked into the kitchen and put the kettle on.

I was really glad for her.

I filled the cafetiere, got my paw-print mug out of the cupboard and a pint of milk out of the fridge.

She thought Will was my boyfriend.

I sat down at the table.

There was no way that was ever going to happen.

I sipped my coffee and imagined the evening out she had suggested, the foursome. The one that I knew could never be.

I wondered why there were tears on my face.

It seemed I had been here before. Every time I resolved not to call Will, I ended up calling him.

I tried all kinds of tactics to avoid it first. I rang two friends in London to see if they wanted to come up and visit. When I had left London I had given open invitations to all of my friends and there had been many promises of weekend visits, but nothing yet had come of it and I wondered whether they needed a little encouragement.

I had two long conversations with my old friends Angela and Kirsten who were full of London gossip and told me all the finer details of who was sleeping with who. Apparently, Jake had a new girlfriend who, according to Kirsten, was blonde and gormless and followed Jake around and hung on his every word. Kirsten reckoned that Jake would soon tire of such devotion and said she wouldn't be at all surprised if he turned up on my doorstep one day. I told her that, to the contrary, Jake was perfectly comfortable with sycophantic devotion and that if he ever came looking for it from me I would send him packing. In fact, I thought it sounded like he'd found the perfect match. Kirsten sounded slightly disappointed by this reaction, as if she had hoped me to be prostrate with grief.

Before she could ask me if I had someone new, I asked if she wanted to come over before Christmas.

'Oh, I'd love to – it would be a scream to get together – but I don't think I can fit it in, Cath. There's so much happening here – I'm booked up every weekend for weeks. Maybe in the New Year some time?'

It had been the same with Angela. They were both full of parties and boyfriends and were far too busy to spend two days of peace and quiet in the country.

Neither of them had asked how my book was getting on.

I wondered whether I'd actually ever had any real friends – of my own age, that is. Had I really been that shallow myself, and had I changed so much since I moved from London?

Finally, to put myself out of my misery, I bit the bullet and phoned Will.

I was relieved when his voice sounded warm and friendly, as if he was pleased to hear from me.

'Hello, Catherine.'

'Hello, Will. I just wondered how you are. I hope you don't mind me ringing...'

I cringed at myself. I sounded like I was about seventeen.

'Of course I don't mind. I'm glad you have actually.'

'Oh...?'

'Yes – I've meant to ring you several times and then chickened out. So you've kind of forced my hand.'

'Sorry – I don't want you to think I'm pushing you into...'

'No – and I don't. I'm a complete coward, that's all. I've lived all these years and I still find it difficult to talk about... certain things. Remember, you're the only person I've spoken to about this.'

'I know. I've often wondered why.'

'Because you somehow make it easy. Or, easier, anyway.'

'That's nice, I'm glad.'

'So when shall I come over?'

Tomorrow. This evening. Now.

'Er...'

'Shall I come now?'

Was he telepathic or something?

'If that's all right with you?'

'Of course.'

'OK.'

'Catherine...'

'Yes?'

'Do stop apologising for yourself. You're all right, you know.'

'OK.'

I thought he looked paler than when I last saw him, more drawn; not as relaxed as the Will I had met nearly three months ago.

He came in and gave Charlie a stroke and a pat, but he didn't take off his jacket.

'Coffee?' I said, 'or do you want some lunch?'

'No. I want to show you something first. Leave Charlie here and come with me.'

I got a jacket and scarf from the kitchen and we left the house and headed towards the church. We said nothing to each other but he stopped at one point and waited for me while I pulled my scarf around my neck. The temperature had dropped since this morning and I was wishing I had put on a hat.

We passed the manor house with its giant blue spruce and lichen-covered walls, and entered the churchyard.

Will led me to the old part of the yard, down the side of the church where stone headstones crumbled under the ancient yew tree. He stopped by two small stones, the inscriptions long since faded, and stood looking down at them.

'My parents,' he said.

I said nothing. All I could think of was that Will had taken me to meet his parents and I wondered whether it had any significance.

He pointed to two even smaller stones, sunk well into the earth.

'My younger brothers,' he said, 'John and Robert. They died young.'

I felt a little sick.

'Did you have any other brothers or sisters, Will?' I asked.

'No,' he replied, 'my mother was never very well after Bobby died, and she died when I was about sixteen.'

'I'm sorry,' I said.

He smiled sadly. 'It's a long time ago. And in those days it was a common enough occurrence. Death was always a large part of life.'

'That doesn't necessarily make it any easier, does it?'

He shook his head.

Suddenly he took my hand. It was so unexpected I gasped.

'I have something else to show you.'

He pulled me away and closer to the church. I had a sense of foreboding so strong that my head began to pound. I found myself pulling back, resisting.

He stopped and looked back at me. His own face was pale and his skin seemed tight around the eyes.

'What is it?' I said.

He turned and pointed to a large and ornate headstone, its inscription written in a flowery script. It stood alone in the shadow of the church tower, half covered in moss and ivy at the back, though the front had been kept clear, leaving only tendrils of ivy curling round its front.

'Please,' he said, giving my hand a little pull, 'come and meet your ancestor.'

Hesitantly, I allowed him to pull me closer, though the pounding in my head was worsening and I felt as though I couldn't breathe.

We drew close and stood in front of the stone.

'This,' he said, his voice thick and low, 'is Grace.'

Grace. The word was like an echo. Where had I heard that name before?'

I read the inscription:

Sacred to the memory of
Grace Corbett
Wife of Sir Andrew Corbett
Of Alderton Hall
Beloved daughter of
Jonathan Bailey

CHAPTER 15

Departed this life 3rd August 1834
Aged 27

The headstone seemed to sway in front of me and I felt my head would burst. I could not breathe. The ground lurched...

'Catherine? Are you all right?'

I felt his hand tightening and I gulped the cold air.

'I need to sit down.'

I felt his arm around me and I leaned against him as he led me to the bench that was in front of the churchyard wall.

'Take some deep breaths,' he said, rubbing my hands with his. I was shivering violently and could not stop. I tried to breathe.

'You're freezing,' he said, 'when you feel able to stand up we'll go home and I'll get a fire going. Have you eaten?'

'Not since...' I remembered I'd got up late and hadn't had breakfast, '...no, I haven't.'

'No wonder...' he fished around in his pockets, 'here – eat this. The sugar will help.'

It was a toffee, still in its wrapper, but slightly sticky on the outside, as if it had been in his pocket a long time. I suddenly wanted to cry. Perhaps I was pre-menstrual or something.

'Oh, Will...'

'Come on, take it. I'm getting cold too, and you need to get home.'

I chewed the toffee, feeling a little like a child. The rush of sugar seemed to go to my head and I felt a little better.

I stood up slowly and managed not to fall over. Will took my hand and we walked home like an old couple out for an afternoon stroll. As we walked I tried to work out in my head what had just happened. I have never been prone to fainting fits and there were plenty of times in my life that I had gone without breakfast or sleep and remained standing until lunchtime. Nor was I normally the type to be stricken with awe by an ancestor's grave. It just wasn't my style, and I was pretty annoyed with myself.

'I'm sorry,' I said as we entered the house, 'I feel really stupid. I feel OK now – I don't know what happened. It was as if – like a reality shift or something. It sounds so silly, but – honestly, I don't usually do that kind of thing.'

'Sit down, will you, and stop being sorry. I'll make some coffee and something to eat and then I'll light a fire. It's freezing in here.'

'I know – I keep the central heating down because it's so expensive. Oh my God, that sounds so pathetic...'

To my great embarrassment and disbelief, tears ran down my face. I tried to wipe them away before he could see, but it was too late.

He sat down next to me on the sofa and gave me one of his candid looks.

'Catherine Burns,' he said, 'what's the matter? Is all this troubling you? Is there something on your mind? Was today a bad day for me to come?'

'No,' I said, finding a tissue in my pocket and blowing my nose, 'it's not your fault. I just – I haven't been sleeping too well. I have bad dreams, and I'm worried about money and whether I'm a good enough writer, and then Christmas is coming and all my friends are too busy to see me...'

He leaned forward suddenly and his mouth was on mine.

It was a brief, sweet kiss with a promise of passion behind it that left me speechless and dazed.

'Sorry,' he said, avoiding further eye contact, 'but you worry so much and I wanted you to stop.'

I reached out my hand to turn his face to me, but he caught it, turned it over to kiss my palm and then laid it back on my lap.

'No,' he said, 'my mistake. I crossed a line and I'm sorry. I can't do this, Catherine. You know I can't. I like you too much.'

Words stuck in my throat.

'I'm going to make coffee and whatever you've got in your fridge, and we'll just forget that I did that. After we've had lunch I'll tell you what happened with Grace, and then I'm going to go.'

He got up and went into the kitchen, leaving me curled up and confused on the sofa. Charlie joined me and rested his head on my lap while I fondled his ears.

When Will came back into the room, he had distanced himself as only a man can. He had made a pot of coffee and some cheese and pickle sandwiches, and while I nibbled the edge of one he built a fire and got it going. He did not make eye contact, and he did not speak. His movements were brisk and efficient. Despite the warmth from the fire, I felt chilled. My headache had returned.

He sat down on the armchair and ate a sandwich. I poured us both some coffee.

The silence between us was like a yawning chasm, creating an unbreachable barrier. I managed to make my way through one quarter of a sandwich washed down with coffee, but my appetite had gone and the rest remained on the plate.

Eventually, I said, 'You'd better tell me, then.'

Will put down his mug, stood up and went to the window. He stared out of it for a moment or two, his hand on the window frame, as if he was expecting to see someone there, and then he leaned his forehead against the cold glass. I saw him shut his eyes.

'Yes,' he said, 'I'll tell you about Grace.'

Chapter 16 - Grace's Story

It was the summer of 1822 when Will and his father pulled in at the manor house to receive the morning's post from Squire Bailey's household. The chestnut tree on the village green, where Will had once collected conkers as a child, was in full leaf. It was a warm, bright day and the scent of honeysuckle that climbed over the stone walls at the entrance to the house wafted across the morning air.

As the pony and trap came to a stop at the door of the half-timbered building, the sound of piano music could be heard through an open window.

Will had heard the occasional sound of a piano at the manor house, but he had never heard anything like this before. It had a kind of joy; a sense of running and jumping and teasing, as if the person who had composed it was playing a game with the listener.

A servant came out to hand the mail to John Days. The music faltered, a girl's voice uttered a curse, and then began again. Will smiled.

John Days issued a command to the pony and the trap began to move away.

The music halted abruptly.

In the next moment, a girl of about fifteen came running

out carrying a letter. Her light brown hair was in ringlets and uncovered, and she wore a light dress clipped in at the waist and laced high on the neck. Her cheeks had a flush of heat in them.

'Oh, Mr Days, please stop!'

Will's father reigned in the pony.

'Miss Bailey?'

'I nearly forgot. I have a letter here to go at once. I was so late for my piano lesson I forgot to leave it for you. It's very urgent. It is for my cousin – his poor friend Mr Shelley, the poet, has died tragically in Italy and I had to write my condolences immediately. Good morning, Will.'

She smiled up at him, shading her eyes against the sun with her hand.

Will touched his cap.

'Miss Bailey.'

John Days dismounted in order to put the letter in the bag behind him.

Will coughed.

'Excuse me, Miss Bailey, but was it you I heard playing on the piano just now?'

Will saw his father frown out of the corner of his eye, but ignored it. The music seemed more important right now than etiquette, or indeed his own shyness.

'Oh, did you hear it? I was playing that piece while my tutor was out of the room. It's by a composer he does not like,' she said in a low, conspiratorial voice, 'no-one seems to play him very much these days, but I just adore his music. Mozart is his name. I am sure one day he will be popular again. Isn't there something just deliciously wicked about it?'

Will grinned again.

'It's the most wonderful thing I ever heard.'

'Why, William Days, you have a musical ear and a voice! All these years and I never heard you speak before!'

Will looked down, suddenly shy. He was six years her senior, but in class she was his superior.

Mr Days was ready at his seat again and touched his cap.

'Good day to you, Miss.'

'Goodbye, Mr Days. William.'

Will turned as they rode away from the house and watched Miss Bailey waving after them, her hand still shielding her eyes.

It was the first time he had ever noticed that Grace Bailey had threads of pure gold in her hair, and a dimple in her chin when she smiled.

Without any siblings, Will was the only help for his father's courier business. Since his mother's death they had a single servant to cook, clean and carry out other household tasks, but Mr Days could only afford to pay Mrs Gibbs for four days a week, so Will had persuaded her to give him a few lessons in cooking a roast or a game pie.

'It's not the sort of thing a young man of your age should be doing, Master William,' she would grumble, 'now why don't you find some nice young girl you can marry and do all this. A kitchen is no place for a man, except for eating in.'

Will said nothing, and would sit and watch her while she plucked, gutted and prepared a chicken for roasting. He watched as she mixed flour and water for pastry and rolled it out to just the right thickness and then used it to cover a pot of rabbit stew, deftly trimming the edges and glazing it with a little milk.

At weekends, Will used his growing knowledge to experiment

and cook food for himself and his father, occasionally with disastrous results, but more often ending with clean plates. John Days, a taciturn man, who spoke only when necessary and with a soft voice, would look up and nod approvingly and then fall asleep in front of the fire in the front room, a tankard of ale by his side.

Every morning Will got up and went out into the small yard at the side of their small house in Mill Lane, and feed and water the pony where he lived in a single stable. He would then harness him to the trap and after breakfast father and son set off on their rounds to gather the day's mail at the village post office and several of the grander houses, and take it to the large office at Clayford. Sometimes they would have to go further afield to take something urgent or fragile.

Since that day at the end of July when young Grace Bailey had come running out into the sunshine with her ringlets bouncing, Will had looked for her at every visit to the manor house. Every Sunday morning in church he would sit looking at her back in her place in the family pew, with her best poke bonnet and lace collar and remember the way she squinted up at him with the sun in her eyes.

Sometimes, after his work with his father was ended for the day, he would take a few minutes to visit his mother's grave, and as he walked past the gates of the manor house, he would strain his ears to hear the piano music again. Occasionally he would be rewarded, and he would linger at the gate, listening to the sounds that had such power to make you feel happy or sad, inspired or fearful. The idea that just these notes, put together in different ways had the power to bring such a variety of feeling was wondrous to him, and he longed to hear more, or even – though it seemed out of his reach – to be able to produce such sounds himself. But he was only the courier's son. He had no piano and music was for the entertainment of the upper classes who had time on their hands for such frivolity.

For two years he continued in this way, listening for the music, searching for Miss Bailey, his heart skipping a beat if she should chance to pass him on her pony or in her father's carriage. But if she ever turned towards him, he could not look at her as he had done so boldly that day. He would look down at the ground and take off his cap as she passed by, muttering only a polite response to her greeting.

As Grace grew older, Will saw her out on her own more frequently, riding her pony through the village or sometimes galloping through the pasture fields at the back of his father's cottage.

It was on a Sunday, an hour after church that he stood one morning leaning against the stone wall that divided the yard from the fields, watching her gallop a distance away, her hair falling out behind her. She looked like a free spirit snatching a few moments of freedom from the governesses, tutors and social duties that ruled her life. It always made Will smile to watch her. Like the music she played, watching her invoked a variety of feelings in him which were at once delightful and disturbing.

The day was fitful. The sun came in and out of scurrying clouds, while a fretful, restless wind blew the branches of the elm trees that lined the brook running along the side of the field.

It was a small branch, breaking in a sudden gust of wind, that fell on her and knocked her sideways. The animal stopped and reared, and Will watched, horrified, as she was thrown from the pony while it shied and reared.

Will turned, wildly.

His father was seated on a stool, repairing a wheel on the trap.

'Father! Go fetch Dr. Thomas! It's Miss Bailey – she has fallen from her horse.'

John Days got up and without a word opened up the stable door and mounted the pony. Before he was out of the yard, Will had jumped over the wall and was running across the fields.

She was lying very still, one arm awkwardly beneath her, her riding hat skewed over her face so he could not tell if she was alive.

He kneeled, almost fell, beside her.

'Miss Bailey! Speak! Can you hear me?'

A low groan issued from underneath the hat. He removed it gently. Her face was cut and bruised, and blood was already staining the grass by her head.

'Miss Bailey, you've had a fall. Tell me, are you hurt?'

'My arm,' she cried, her voice weak, 'my arm...'

Will looked to where her left arm was caught at a dangerous-looking angle and trapped beneath her.

He looked back at her face, where pain was beginning to crease her brow and draw back her mouth. The blood was forming a pool.

'The doctor is coming, Miss Bailey. He won't be long. My father has gone to get him. Can you move at all?'

Tears were streaming from her eyes, but she managed to look at him.

'Mr William? Is that you? My horse...'

'Your pony is safe, Miss, and grazing quite happily. Can I do anything for you?'

'Can you... can you wipe my face, Will? I think it's bleeding and it tickles so... Oh, my arm...!'

Will had no handkerchief on him, so he pulled the sleeve of his shirt down and softly wiped the trickle of blood that ran from her cut mouth. He looked at the more serious wound.

'Wait here,' he said, and ripping off a piece from the bottom of his shirt, he ran quickly to the brook.

He returned with the damp fabric and attempted to staunch the bleeding from the side of her head.

'I would lift you,' he said, 'but I am afraid I would hurt you more. Can you wait until the doctor gets here?'

She nodded, and then opened her eyes briefly.

'Will,' she whispered, through gasps of pain, 'stay with me, won't you? Don't leave me.'

Then she shut her eyes.

They carried her, unconscious, back to the manor house, and Will retreated to the back door, waiting for the doctor to come down. The servants were too busy to notice him, either running to prepare poultices or whispering together about what had happened.

The doctor was a long time in attendance upon Miss Bailey, but at last Will heard his step on the staircase and he ran through the hall to meet him as he stepped out into the front drive.

'Dr. Thomas.'

'Ah, Will. There you are. What a business, eh?'

'How is she? Is she...? Will she...?'

'She'll recover. She had a nasty blow to the head, and it's a jolly good thing you were there, young man. If you had not have come when you did, she could have bled to death in a very short time. You did well, Will.'

'Thank God. And her arm...?'

'Not broken, thankfully – just badly sprained. With rest it will be completely recovered.'

Will went home, relieved, but every morning for the next few days he enquired from the downstairs maid how Miss Bailey was, and was pleased to hear that her recovery was going well.

On the fourth day after the event, Will and his father received a visit from Squire Bailey himself.

He came through into their living room, lowering his head to enter because he was a tall, if stout, man. Father and son rose to receive him.

'This is an honour, sir,' said John Days, 'can I get Will to bring you something – a tankard of ale, perhaps?'

'No, no, John. It is young Will I have come here to see, as well as yourself. And the honour is all mine. Let me shake you both by the hand – my wife and I are indebted to you, much indebted. If it had not been for your quick actions, well...'

'I am only glad I happened to see her fall, sir,' said Will, 'it was my father who got the doctor so quickly – I merely...'

'You saved her life, Will. I will never forget it. And nor will my daughter. In fact, I am ashamed to say that it was at her bidding that I am here today – otherwise I would have forgotten to thank you amidst all the to-do. She asked me to bring you something as a token of all our thanks...'

He called outside for his coachman, who appeared with a crate. John Days' eyes widened as he saw its contents.

'The very best claret from my cellars,' said the squire, 'John, Will, it is a small gesture...'

'Why, I do not know what to say, sir.'

'Say nothing, John. We wish you joy of the wine, that is all. As for you, young Will, if there is anything at all we can do for you, you only have to name it.'

Squire Bailey was on his way out of the door.

'Actually, sir, there is something.'

Bailey turned, and Will's father looked at him askance.

'Well?'

'I would very much like to learn to play the piano, if that is at all possible, sir.'

The two older men looked at Will as if he had grown another head.

'Will...!' said his father in a concerned whisper.

'Learn to play the...! Well, bless my soul – of all the...' exclaimed the squire. Then he laughed. 'I suppose it could be arranged – Grace's tutor is unemployed at present. If that is what you really want?'

'Yes, sir, it is,' said Will.

So for one hour every other day, Will was allowed to be taught by Grace's tutor while Grace was still indisposed. And when she was finally able to resume her own studies, they practised together. Because Grace was well in advance of Will in her piano, she would sometimes teach him herself, while the old tutor took the opportunity to nod off in the corner of the room.

Will began to live for his hour with Miss Bailey. He woke up every morning of his piano days with the joy of knowing he would see her that day. And perhaps she would lean over him to correct his fingers or to turn the page and he would feel the warmth from her skin and perhaps her hair would brush his face momentarily.

'Will! You are not concentrating!' she would cry as he hit a wrong note. Then she would look at him with softened eyes and say, 'but all the same, Will, you do learn quickly.'

After several weeks of this, Will began to feel that it was not enough. If only he could see her alone, to touch her face or stroke her hair. Then he would truly be in heaven.

One day they were playing a simple duet together that Grace had taught him, and as they came to the end they laughed together, then both looked over at the tutor to make sure he had not woken.

Will looked back at her and spoke softly.

'Miss Bailey... I...'

What is it, Will?'

'I would very much like to see you alone.'

She looked down, but he could see that she was smiling, and a blush was spreading on her cheeks.

'Mr. Days. It is not possible.'

'It must be. I have to see you alone.'

'But, Will...'

'Every evening I go to visit my mother's grave at eight o'clock, after supper. Will you meet me there?'

'But, if someone should see us...'

'There is a stile into the field. If we take a walk, no-one will see us then.'

'You are very bold, Will.'

'You have made me so.'

The piano tutor suddenly coughed in his sleep and woke up. Grace stood up.

'No, Mr Days. You will have to practise that piece again. From the beginning...'

Just before eight o'clock, Grace made an excuse to her mother and her three younger sisters that she needed some fresh air and would go for a short walk alone.

Her mother, watchful ever since her riding accident, looked up.

'Grace, are you feeling quite well? You do not have a headache?'

'I am perfectly well, mama, the air is just a little stuffy and I would like to take a little walk, that is all.'

'Would you like Isobel to go with you?'

'No, mama, please do not fuss. I am quite happy on my own and I will only be gone for a few minutes.'

'Very well, dear...'

Grace slipped out into the twilight, hoping that her father or any servants had not seen her go.

By the yew tree, Will was waiting. She felt a stab of excitement in her guts and her heart seemed to be beating inside her head. She had always thought him handsome, ever since she had first set eyes on him as a young girl, but since he had miraculously appeared by her side that day when she fell from her horse, her feelings had become stronger and it seemed there was an unspoken bond between them that felt unbreakable.

'Grace,' he said simply, as she appeared at his side. Then he fell silent. He looked shy and awkward, unsure of what to say or do.

'I can only be gone a few minutes, Will, or else mama will send the servants out to look for me. She has been very protective since the accident.'

Will said nothing, but took her arm and led her silently to the stile and helped her over.

They walked a short distance, keeping close to the hedge, and then Will stopped and turned to her. He did not speak at first, but stood looking at her, while she looked up at him as the sky grew darker and his face faded into shadow.

'I had so many things to say,' he said at last, 'but now I can remember nothing, except that I must be with you. I...'

'Shh,' she said, putting two fingers against his lips, 'don't say anything, Will. It is the same for me. I long to see you – but anything beyond this is impossible.'

He took her hand away from his mouth and kissed her palm.

'All things are possible,' he whispered.

'In another world, perhaps. Not in mine, my sweet, not in mine...'

But he had taken her in his arms before she could say any more and was kissing her on her mouth so sweetly and yet so urgently passionate, that she thought she would faint from the strong sensations racing through her body.

At last he pulled away, and she leaned against him, trying to get her breath back along with her sense of reason.

'I must go home,' she said.

'When can I see you again?'

'The day after tomorrow, when you come for your piano lesson.'

'No. When will I see you alone, like this?'

She had meant to say that it was not possible; that tonight was the only time they would ever be alone; that their paths led in different directions, but when she looked up at him to speak, all she could think was that she wanted him to kiss her again like he just had, and soon.

'Tomorrow,' she said, 'the same time.'

Grace told her mother that she found her twilight walk refreshing and that it helped her to sleep. She said she would like to go out at the same time most evenings.

'If it makes you feel better, my love. Though I thought you looked a little flushed when you came back last night.'

'The air was cool, and I had been walking quickly,' was Grace's quick reply.

She and Will met after that almost every evening and walked and talked and kissed; and in the day they exchanged glances while they played piano under the rheumy eyes of the piano tutor.

It was several months after this that the Bailey household began to receive calls from a landowner in the neighbouring hamlet.

Grace was at an age when her parents were looking for a suitable marriage for her, and Sir Andrew Corbett of Alderton Hall seemed a likely suitor. He was rich, had a large house and grounds and came from a family who had created wealth through industry. Sir Andrew's grandfather had owned an iron foundry in Derbyshire which had allowed his children and grandchildren independence. Sir Andrew's father had bought Alderton Hall with inheritance money and then sold his share of the business to his brothers so that he could live as he wished. Andrew was his only son, who had lived without any need for work all his life. He was not unhandsome, and had obviously taken a strong liking to the oldest daughter.

Will was growing frustrated by the brevity of his meetings with Grace. He began to feel that if he could not see her all of every possible day, his life had no meaning.

'Marry me, Grace,' he said one evening after a tender embrace.

She pulled away.

'Will, you know I cannot. Please do not ask me.'

'I love you.'

'I know. But I cannot marry you. My father would never allow it.'

'Your father likes me.'

'Oh, Will!' she said, 'of course he likes you! You saved my life. And who could not like you anyway? But marriage is a different thing entirely. He cannot marry me to... to someone without...'

'...money and status. Of course I know that. I am not stupid, Grace. But... if you... if we went away together, were married in secret, with a licence - there'd be no need to call the banns – perhaps they would come to...'

'Oh, but you are being stupid! My father would disown me and we would be penniless. Besides I would have to be 21 before we could marry without consent. It is out of the question...'

'I would wait for you.'

'This is nonsense, Will. Have I not always said to you we can never go further than we have done?'

They were silent for a few moments.

'I must go home now. I do not think we should meet again like this for a while. Goodbye Will – I will see you on the morrow, at the piano.'

She was cool towards him after that, and despite his attempts at every lesson, she avoided making eye contact.

He knew it was hopeless; that marriage between them was out of bounds. He had spoken in desperation because he wanted her to know how much he felt for her. It was all he had, but she had not understood.

It was two weeks later that she one day said to him after

practice:

'Mr Days, would you care to take a turn in the garden with me? I have something I wish to discuss with you.'

His hopes rose. Perhaps she had relented. Perhaps she would renew their meetings.

He followed her into the walled garden and under the blossom of a peach tree she turned to him without looking at his face.

'I have some news for you, Will. You must be pleased for me. I am betrothed to be married!'

She was looking at him with a smile on her face, her cheeks flushed. Will felt as though he had been punched in his stomach. He thought his heart had stopped beating, yet he remained standing. He stared at her, dully wondering if he had heard her right.

'I am to be married in July, Will. But I won't be moving far away, only to Stanton, to Alderton Hall. I will still see you now and then in church. Sir Andrew Corbett has asked for my hand in marriage and I have accepted and my father has consented. Is it not exciting, Will?'

She looked up at him and he tried to look into her eyes, but she faltered, and looked away. She continued to smile though, and playfully punched him on the arm.

'Do say you're pleased for me, Will.'

They were like two friends who had never shared any intimacy.

'You never loved me, then,' was all he could say, his voice coming out choked and hoarse.

'Oh, Will, do not speak of love. Or, if you really love me, be pleased for me. Let us be friends and be happy....'

'Friends! How can you...'

'Please, Will, someone will hear. Yes, Will, please...' she looked him in the eyes for the first time, '...it is the only way. Don't you see? It could never go on. Of course I was bound to marry some time. It has just come sooner than I thought. I do want us to be friends, Will, and not quarrel. Please.'

She touched his arm and he felt his anger melting. Of course she was right. This day had always been bound to happen. Yet he could not speak.

'Will, you will always be very dear to me and close to my heart. I would like to know that you will always be here at Little Dipping in case – well, in case I ever need a friend...'

Of course, it was the only way that it was ever going to be. How could he expect anything else? The choice was his: to remain her friend or to say goodbye for ever.

'...promise me Will.'

'I promise,' he said, and then he turned and blindly walked away without looking back.

Chapter 17

'She married Andrew Corbett in the summer of 1828.'

Will swallowed, still staring out of the window.

'If only I had known, if only her parents had known what kind of a man Sir Andrew really was. If I had taken the trouble to find out, to make enquiries, perhaps I could have saved her life for the second time.'

I frowned.

'What do you mean, Will?' Didn't she die in childbirth? How could you have prevented...?'

'Yes,' he said. His skin was almost white as he turned to look at me. 'Yes, she did die in childbirth, but I believe it was only because her body was weak from... from the way he treated her...'

'You mean, he beat her?'

'That... and worse...'

'But how do you know?'

He came back into the room and sat in front of the fire, warming his hands and staring at the flames.

'After a while, I decided she had no need for me. I saw her occasionally riding in her fine carriage and that was all I ever saw of her, except at church, when she came in on the arm of her husband, all smiles. She never looked at me. I thought she was happy and had forgotten me. I had nothing to offer her any more. When my father died, I left the village. It was only years later when I returned that I heard the news of her death and then the rumours of his violent temper and cruelty.'

He stopped and stared at the fire.

'In nearly two hundred years I have not forgiven myself for allowing her to marry him. I was weak. I should have... done something.'

I had been curled up on the sofa, my head against its arm. Now I sat up.

'There was nothing you could have done, Will. Not then, not in that society.'

He did not reply.

'Is there anything else you have to tell me?' I said.

'No. That's all I have to tell you.'

He stood up and retrieved his jacket and scarf from the arm of the chair. My heart sank.

'That is all there is. And now I must go.'

'But...' I stood up too, still feeling light headed, '...but, there's so much more I want to know...'

He shook his head.

'There is nothing I can tell you. I have told you all I know about your predecessors, and I have nothing left to say.'

His face was a blank, and he would not meet my eyes. I stood in front of him, desperately trying to think of something to say, to ask, that would make everything clear, or keep him in the house for a little longer. Nothing came.

'Will I see you again?'

'No.'

He looked at me, and seemed to regret this abrupt reply. He sighed and took my right hand, squeezing my fingers in his large, strong hands.

'I did think,' he said, 'that we could be friends. I thought that after all this, after I had told you my story, that we could carry on in a similar way – seeing each other now and then. Having someone – having a friend who knew my background would be great. But, here we are at the end of the story I had to tell you, and I know that friendship with you is impossible.'

'Why?' I asked weakly, already knowing the answer.

'You know why, Grace. For all the reasons we've talked about...'

I looked up at him.

'You called me Grace...'

'Did I? I'm sorry...'

I suddenly remembered why the name Grace had sounded vaguely familiar.

'You called me Grace once before. When we met and you had fallen off your bike, you looked up and said, "Grace".'

'I did? Yes... I remember. You were standing in front of the manor house and for a moment I thought...'

'Will – are you telling me that I look like Grace? Is that why...?'

He dropped my hand.

'There is a strong resemblance.'

'Oh,' I said, 'I see. I understand. Well, I suppose that's it then. If there's nothing more, you'd better go.'

'Catherine...'

'It's OK. It's been nice knowing you. Really – it has. Thanks for everything, Will. I hope everything works out for you.'

His eyes were sad as he leaned forward to kiss my cheek.

And then he was gone.

Charlie stood beside me, staring at the closed door.

'He's gone, Charlie boy,' I said, 'that's it.'

Charlie looked up at me with his large brown eyes. His tail slowly drooped towards the floor, and then he sighed, flopping to the ground, his nose pointing to where Will had just disappeared.

There was a hammer pounding in my ears. I cleared away the coffee cups and the plate of unwanted sandwiches, putting the cups in the sink and wrapping the sandwiches in cling film in case I needed them later. I put the kettle on and poured myself a hot water bottle. Then I went to the drinks cupboard and poured a large whisky. Calling Charlie, I climbed the stairs, took a couple of headache pills with water from the bathroom, and then I got into my bed, fully clothed, and pulled the duvet over my head.

I stayed there for three days. I did not sleep much, but when I did the dream came back to me, worse than before. Now, the music had gone completely, and all around me I could only see rotten wood, peeling wallpaper and ornaments that crumbled to dust if I touched them. The dark corridor came earlier each time I dreamed, and the room that terrified me was closer, its door slightly open and there was nowhere else for me to go but towards the flickering candlelight that lay behind it...

I would wake up with a start, for a moment thankful to be awake and in the next moment wishing I was not. I had no energy to do anything, and poor Charlie had to be content with the occasional race around the garden for exercise as I did not want to leave the house. I knew I was allowing myself to sink into a spiral of depression, but there seemed to be nothing I could do about it. I tried to eat a little, but Will's stale sandwiches were tasteless and dry, and the only other food in the house were a few tins of tomato soup.

My head seemed to be going round in circles. I had thought that somehow, when Will had told me the final instalment, I would understand something, that there would be some sense of clarity. But all I knew was that the only reason Will had ever liked me – the only reason he had kissed me – was because I reminded him of Grace. All along I had thought that there was something special about me, that he really cared for me. But, no – all I was to him was the painful reminder of a past memory.

What had the past few months been about? Why did I ever leave London and buy this god-damned house? Why had I left my friends and thrown myself into a solitary life where I knew no-one of my own age? Wouldn't I really be better off back in my own job and back with Jake? But he'd moved on now...

I sat up in bed and wiped away the tears. I told myself to pull myself together. I'd allowed myself to wallow in this state for too long. If things weren't going well, then it was time to make a change. If buying this house had been a mistake, then I must remedy it. I could change things. I could move on and put the house and the village and Will all behind me and forget it ever happened.

All I needed to was to move house – to the kind of place I should have bought in the first place. A nice, modern flat in the outskirts of a town - not Clayford – somewhere nowhere near here – nearer London perhaps...

I had got out of bed and into the other room to look for estate agents on the internet when the doorbell went. Charlie woofed and flew down the stairs. I followed slowly, wrapping myself in my dressing gown and hoping I didn't look as bad as I felt I did.

I opened the door a crack. There was Maureen.

I suddenly remembered what day it was. Wednesday – the day of our class. I had completely forgotten.

'Hello, love – are you ready?'

I opened the door a little more.

'Maureen – I...'

She saw my face.

'Oh, Catherine, dear – are you all right? You look awful.'

I let her come in.

'I'm so sorry, Maureen. I should have let you know – I'm not feeling too well, so I don't think I should come tonight.'

'Of course not, dear. Not if you're unwell. I'll let Sue know – what is it, 'flu or something?'

'No – I don't know...'

'You don't look like you have a temperature...'

'No – I'm feeling a little better.'

'Sit down, I'll make you a cup of tea.'

'Oh, no – it's all right, you need to get to class. Isn't Peter waiting?'

She opened the front door and I heard her telling Peter, who was waiting in the car, that I wasn't well and she'd just be ten minutes.

'There now. I've got plenty of time anyway. I'll just put the kettle on and you can tell me what's happened. You're not actually physically ill, I can see that.'

There was no point arguing.

When she brought me my tea she sat on the edge of the armchair.

'There's nothing much to tell you, really. I'm just being really pathetic.'

'Is it your young man?'

'My...? Oh, well – yes, I suppose so. I won't be seeing him again anyway.'

'Oh no! That's too bad. What on earth has happened?'

'It's nothing really. Seems he only liked me because I reminded him of someone else. Someone he knew a long time ago.'

Maureen's eyes narrowed.

'I find that difficult to believe.'

'Well, it's true. He was very much in love with her, and I'm the spitting image. But I'm not her, so there wasn't much point. In any case, it wasn't going anywhere. He wasn't interested in getting involved. It's all rather complicated, but it's really pretty hopeless. Anyway, don't worry about me, I'm feeling a lot better now and I'm going to get up and pull myself together and...'

'What a lot of nonsense.'

'Pardon?'

'I said, Catherine, that it's all nonsense.'

'Well...'

'Now, just you listen to me for a moment. I may seem old and out of touch to you, but I do know something about men. Good heavens, I lived with one for forty years and he wasn't exactly my first, and not my last either. Not only that, but I've seen my own girls fall in love and make mistakes, and I've seen their boyfriends, and I could always tell whether it was going to work or not – and I've never been wrong. If there's one thing I do know is when something is genuine. And – I may have only seen you together once, my dear, but if that man doesn't have genuine feelings for you and you alone then my name isn't Maureen Spenser.'

'But...'

'There are no "buts", Catherine, when it comes to love. It's either there or it isn't and that's all there is to it. And as for you looking like someone else, I've never heard anything so ridiculous. Men are full of nonsense. They'll say anything to give them an excuse to run away from their feelings. Believe me, I know all about it. That man loves you, he just doesn't want to admit it.'

'But he didn't...'

'Call me an old fashioned romantic, but I sometimes think men *are* attracted to someone because they remind them of a previous love, but I think that sometimes, if not most of the time, it's because the first person reminds them of the person they've yet to meet. I know it sounds like something out of a slushy film or novel, but it makes sense to me. You mark my words, this young lady he knew before – well, why couldn't she just be a forerunner, like a kind of practice run for the real thing?'

She leaned forward and gave me a warm smile.

'A kind of Catherine Burns pre-model.'

Something clicked in my head. My skin was prickling all over and I felt cold and slightly nauseous.

'Oh, my God...' I said, half to myself.

'That's right. It's you, my dear. You're the real thing. Now, promise me you won't just let him get away. Promise me you'll go after that man of yours and make sure he doesn't get away this time.'

'OK. I promise.'

'Good girl. Now, there's Peter tooting on the horn. Such impatience! I'd better go. You look after yourself, now.'

In a daze I went upstairs and got dressed.

Memories came back to me of the day I had first arrived at Little Dipping: the manor house with its old wooden front gates and the stone wall covered with honeysuckle and bramble, the cottage and its mesmeric effect on me, and finally, the terrifying, gloomy edifice of Alderton Hall.

Maureen's words had cleared something in my head, and the more I thought about it, the more it seemed to be right. It was time for me to tell Will something.

I turned off the computer with its screen full of estate agent listings, put on a jacket and told Charlie to stay and look after the house. I picked up my car keys and left the house to get into my cold and dark little car that had been abandoned for days on the road.

'Please start,' I whispered. It coughed and wheezed, the engine cold and lazy, but then suddenly roared into life.

Shivering, I headed towards Clayford.

I had rung Will's doorbell twice, but the intercom remained silent. I tried his mobile phone but it was switched off and there was nothing I could think of to say in a voicemail message that would make any sense. I stood in the cold doorway, pulling my jacket around me tighter and wishing I had put on a scarf. I wondered how long I would have to wait. Perhaps he was out at a gig – but if someone would just let me into the building, I could at least hang out in the corridor in moderate warmth.

After twenty minutes a young man with his arm around a girl the same age – her skirt merely a strap around her hips – appeared out of the darkness and he got out a key and began to let himself in.

'Excuse me,' I said, 'but do you know Will Days in Flat number 16? He's not in, but I'm a friend of his, and I wouldn't mind waiting if...'

'Oh, what – you mean the musician guy? Third floor?'

'Yes, that's right.'

'Nah – you'll be waiting a long time then. He left this morning.'

'Left?'

'Yeah – packed up all his gear in a van this morning.'

'This morning?'

'Yeah. You his girlfriend or summit? Looks like he's done a runner...'

The young girl giggled and they disappeared into the hall, closing the door behind them.

'Thanks,' I said to the closed door.

I drove home. There was nothing I could do. I tried his mobile again but either it was switched off or he was not receiving my calls. It was no point trying again, it just would look too pathetic.

I had to face it. I had lost my chance. I might as well carry on with my plan and move to somewhere that had no memories of any kind.

The gate was shut when I arrived home and the now familiar light headedness and nausea came over me in waves. There was no light in the street, and no light came from the house. All was silent and still, and the cold seeped into my skin and crept around my bones like icy fingers.

I had lost all sense of time or identity. I only knew that if I could not get to the house I may as well die here in the cold, but I knew the gate was locked before I touched it. The house was empty; weeds grew between the paving stones, no fire was in the grate and no light at the window.

I fell to the ground, knowing that my last chance had gone. I had lost the only thing that could ever bring me the happiness and peace that had now gone for ever.

I closed my eyes.

'Catherine?'

I opened my eyes.

Miraculously, the gate was opening.

The familiar voice belonged to a familiar figure, who now crouched down beside me.

'Catherine – what are you doing out here?'

Dazed, my mind struggled to comprehend the reality of the moment, so I barely recognised my own name.

I looked at his shadowy face in the darkness.

'I came to see you, but you were gone.'

He peered at me and I could feel his puzzlement.

'You're not making any sense. Here, let me help you.'

He took my arm and we struggled to a standing position. I could hear a dog barking somewhere. It seemed to be coming from the house. Slowly, my mind retrieved the facts. It was my dog. What was his name?

'Charlie...' I said.

'Catherine – I don't think you are quite yourself. Can you find your keys? Let's get indoors – it's freezing out here.'

'My keys? Oh, yes, of course.'

I looked into the bag I had with me and found a set of house keys.

Will gently took them out of my hand.

'Come on, let's get you home. I knew I shouldn't have left you – not the way you were, so pale and strange-looking.'

'Home,' I repeated, looking at the cottage in front of me,

'yes... home.'

He opened the door and let Charlie out, who greeted us both madly with equal affection.

I felt a wave of warmth as I entered my house with Will.

The first thing he did was to make me sit down and then he poured me a large whisky and handed it to me, saying, 'drink this. Now.'

I obeyed, and the strong liquid burned my mouth and warmed my insides as it slid down my throat. I coughed a little.

'Take another sip,' he said, like a doctor issuing medicine to his patient.

I did so, and the warm, heady aroma this time seemed to clear my mind, filtering through my sinuses and into my brain, returning me to my senses and to reality.

Will stood in front of me, a look of deep concern on his face.

'Will,' I said, 'what the hell are you doing here?'

He smiled with a look of relief.

'Well, you sound a little more like yourself.'

He sat on the arm of the sofa.

'What happened? What were you doing out in the street?'

I tried to remember. This time the thoughts and the memories were clear.

'It's not the first time it's happened,' I admitted, 'I come back to find the gate locked – only, of course it isn't really. I think... I think I'm beginning to understand. I think I can explain... or try to. That's why I went to see you. I wanted to tell you.'

'You went to see me? At Clayford? I left this morning.'

'Yes, I know. I found that out. But – what are you doing here?'

He stood up and went to the fireplace and started arranging

kindling and logs.

'I came back because... because I wasn't strictly honest with you. I thought I had told you everything I needed to tell you. But there is something else. Something I didn't want you to know.'

He lit a match and soon the fire was burning, and I felt the warm glow on my goose-pimpled skin. Will remained kneeling by the fire.

'I was going to disappear. I'd put all my stuff in storage, and I thought I'd just take off, with just some gear in a back-pack and see where my bicycle took me for a while. But as I was cycling along I realised that nothing felt right. Something was incomplete. And for the first time in my life I realised that I had no purpose.

'I've always known – despite the amount of time I've been walking round on this earth – I've always known where I was going next. There's always been a plan for the next episode of my life. I've always known what I want to do, from learning to play the piano, to which town to head for next, to what job I was going to take on. There has always been something to move towards, whether it's a goal or an opportunity that has arrived out of nowhere.

'But this afternoon it hit me that I had nowhere to go and nothing to aim for. It all seemed completely pointless.

'And I realised that there was this one last thing that needed to be said, and unless I came back and completed the story in its entirety, I would not be able to plan ahead. I need to complete the past first.

'So I turned my bike around and I came back here. You weren't in so I sat on your doorstep and waited until you turned up and... and kind of collapsed outside the gate.'

I looked into my whisky. He had returned to tell me something that was all. Not for any other reason.

'There's something I want to tell you too,' I said.

'I think,' he said, 'that you should wait and hear what I have to say. It might change everything.'

'All right,' I said, 'pour yourself a drink and make yourself comfortable. Then you can begin.'

Chapter 18 - Will's Story

My father died in the winter of '29. I carried on with the business for a while but my heart was not in it. I needed a change. I needed to get away from the memories.

I had seen advertisements in the paper about auditions for the circuit theatre that travelled the area then. I had always been fascinated by the stage ever since my parents had taken me to see a pantomime at the little theatre at Clayford – I don't mean The Royal, that wasn't built then – this was a small building next to the Fox and Goose and little more than a fitted-up barn.

When I heard that Grace had given birth to a son, I decided that she had no need for me to stay around. As I said, she had not communicated with me or even looked at me since our last meeting. I decided to take my chances and audition for the theatre. I took the pony, paid up the rent and locked up the house for safety until new tenants should arrive.

The auditions were held at the Fox and Goose, in a back room. I don't know whether I was that good an actor, but the manager was very impressed by the fact that I had a pony and could play the piano.

'Why, my dear fellow,' he said – his name was Marsh...

Montague Marsh, that was it... 'my dear fellow, audiences will flock, flock I say, to see a live animal on the stage! Has he been on the stage before?'

'Er... no,' I said.

'Well, this will be a new venture for him – give him a new lease of life. Once you've been on the stage, sir, whether you be man, beast, woman or child, you are never the same again! Never! Now, then, you say you play the piano?'

'A little, yes, sir.'

'SHARP!'

I was a little alarmed at this response, but it turned out he was calling to a man named Sharp, who was sitting in a corner of the room practising on a fiddle.

The man got up and walked over to us.

'Sharp! – Ah, there you are. Can you play the piano, Sharp?'

'Er – no, sir.'

'Then it's time you learned. And in return for his services of tuition, you shall teach our newest recruit the fiddle, and so the Marsh Theatre Company will have an orchestra! Pidgin! You can put that into the next allotment of posters – a new orchestra! And a pony! Now, to find a play with a pony...'

So that was my introduction to the theatre and my new career as an actor/musician.

I could not believe that I had ever worked hard before. The theatre company kept me busy from early in the morning until late at night. It was hard, tough, exhausting work. If I wasn't learning a new instrument, I was painting scenery, or walking to the next town, or learning lines or promoting the next new production. Then there were the performances – rabble-like audiences who shouted, jeered or laughed at every possible moment, filling the auditorium with the smells of the farmyard and orange peel. There was no time to think of the past or mourn my losses. I did not forget Grace – I could not. She was with me every time I laid my hands on a keyboard; every time I played a lover's scene, and every night when I shut my eyes. But the sheer intensity of the work numbed the pain of loss, and I grew to love the theatre, its larger than life characters and the women who had never known the restrictions of normal society. I loved the fact that I was learning all the time; I was playing the piano every night – for a living – and learning the violin. Sharp and I experimented: Irish jigs and ballads, folk songs, classical. We tried everything, and in our thirst for music we began to learn new instruments and widen our repertoire.

It was one of the best times of my life. I was involved with something I could believe in and every day was full.

Then, in 1833, the great tragic actor, Edmund Kean, died on stage at Covent Garden, and Montague Marsh, who had seen him once at Drury Lane, declared a week of mourning and closed the theatre for two days.

I decided to visit Little Dipping and lay flowers on my parents' graves, and see if there was any news from Alderton Hall. I felt a little guilty that I had been away for so long, and I wanted to make sure that Grace was all right.

When I came back into the village, it was as if I had never been away. The past five years melted away and it was as if I had only left with that pony and the audition advertisement the day before. There was the church, the old manor house with all its memories of my first meetings with Grace, and Mill Lane with our old cottage, now re-inhabited. Nothing appeared to have changed when I first set my eyes on it all.

I was about to enter the churchyard when I saw one of the

manor house gardeners approaching me from the house. I knew him quite well. He had been a gardener for the Baileys for many years and we had often passed the time of day when my father and I had come to the house with deliveries.

'Why, if it isn't young Mr William! Very pleased to see you again, Will. Thought you'd gone for good, we had. 'Twas a bad business with your old man passing away so sudden – he was a quiet man, your father, but much loved I can tell you that – and then you disappeared so sudden too, we all wondered where you'd gone. You're looking in fine health, Will, you do indeed.'

'Thank you, Sam. And how is your good wife, and the master and mistress?'

'The wife is the same as ever, Will. But Master Bailey is not too good as it happens. He hasn't been the same since... But, of course, you won't have heard the bad news?'

He looked at me with a curious sideways glance, and a chill came over me. With a growing sense of dread, I told him I had heard nothing as I had been so very busy I'd had no time to read many papers.

He shook his head solemnly and looked at the ground.

'Oh, it was a bad business, Mr Will, a very bad business. Not that these things don't happen, because they do, and only God hi'self knows why, and I suppose He has a plan, but the master was taken so bad with the news he wouldn't leave the house for days, and even now...'

I grabbed his arm.

'Sam – what is it that has happened? Is it Mrs Bailey?'

'No, Will, she's well enough – though of course she was grief-stricken at the time. No, Will, it was the young lady. The Miss Bailey that was – or I should say Lady Alderton. Why, she's dead, sir.'

The sun seemed to go out in that moment. I stared at the man and my face and limbs felt numb. My mouth was suddenly dry. Time stood still.

I don't know how long I stood staring at him, my hand still gripping his arm, but after a while he said,

'Mr. William, sir, are you all right?'

I dropped his arm. The world seemed to be reeling. I leaned against the church wall.

'What happened, Sam?'

'She died in child-bed, Will, after a long and difficult labour.'

'And the child?'

'Oh, the child survived. A strong'un that one – three years old now, but mightily strong-willed from what I've heard. A little girl called Anne. Looks like her mother too.'

My head was in my hands.

'I'm that sorry to break the news to you, Will. I knows you and Miss Bailey were, well, friendly-like. Many a time I heard you playing the piano in that room...'

'I don't understand,' I heard myself saying, 'she was strong and healthy. A woman with all that wealth and the best physic available. Surely something could have been done...'

'Ah, that's just it, Mr Will. We all know it can happen to anyone, but when it happens at the top it always seems more unusual, though we all know it can happen to queens and beggars alike. But, in this case, well, I won't deny there haven't been rumours...'

'Rumours? What rumours?'

'About that there Sir Andrew, Will. Turns out for all his money and property, he's a bit of a wrong'un. Now, I'm not one for gossip – I leave that to the missus – but we did hear from some of the servants up at the Hall that, well, that the way he treated that poor young woman was, well, inhuman, to put it bluntly, Will.'

I lifted my head slowly.

'Inhuman?'

'That's right, Will. The tales we heard were something terrible, and not a thing anyone could do about it. A man's wife is his to do as he pleases and that's the law, but when a man treats a woman like that – well, it's not right, not in the sight of God, Will, that's what I'm thinking. Not in the sight of God, law or no law.'

'Tell me, Sam.'

'Well, sir, we heard that he used to beat her regular like – with a leather strap. His drinking was to blame. He'd be off all hours of the night, gambling and drinking at some place at Clayford and then come home, and if anything was amiss in his eyes, why he'd beat the wife. As if that's what she was there for. And it's not surprising that she lost two children after the first was born – and one of those after a fall down the stairs. Of course, it was given as an accident, but the rumours were that she was pushed on purpose. Well, it may be all rumour, but there's no smoke where there's no fire, Will, and it's common knowledge that the man has lost a lot of money through gambling, and God knows what else, as well as the fact of his regular drunkenness. So it's a no wonder the poor girl couldn't make it through that final ordeal – she must have been sore tired and weakened – and not a friend to help or give comfort...'

'Please, Sam – no more. Is... is she buried here?'

'That she is, Will. And it was the master and mistress who paid for the headstone. That scoundrel did not even attend the funeral – though I say that's a good thing, all things considered. No, he was out drinking, just as he was the night that poor, motherless child was born. Will you be all right, Will? You look terrible pale. I know it was a terrible shock – it was to us all, and the master is still in mourning after all this time.'

I spoke with difficulty.

'I'll be all right. Thank you Sam. My regards to your wife. You'd best get back to work.'

He tipped his cap.

'Right you are, Will. God be with you.'

I stumbled into the churchyard, my legs and arms feeling as if they were made of lead, and I found myself in front of her headstone, staring at it as if by staring I could turn back time. But the stone and the words on it stared back at me with their bleak reality.

I don't know how long I stood there, but I became aware eventually that I was cold and the light was beginning to fade. I dropped the flowers that had been intended for my parents on Grace's grave and without thinking of what I was going to do next I walked slowly towards the stile that Grace and I had once so carefreely jumped over, and I thought of myself as I had been then; a foolish, naïve young man, believing that love could conquer any obstacle. I tried to laugh at myself, but what came out was a broken sob. I thought I had lost her before, but this final loss was beyond anything, and it was not just the pain of grief, it was the guilt. I had deserted her when I had promised to stay. I had assumed that she no longer needed me, that she was happy. No – worse. I had pretended to myself that she no longer needed me, because I was angry with her and did not want to admit it. I was angry because she had left me for money and status, and because she no longer acknowledged my existence. So I had broken my promise and betrayed our friendship by disappearing from the village without a word or message. And now I had returned too late to save her.

I walked blindly across the fields, not thinking of where I was going or what I should do next, until I saw in the distance the back of Alderton Hall, and then, moving slowly towards it from the west, a man on horseback.

I knew it was him immediately, and I stood still for a while as he slowly neared where I stood.

There was no mistaking him close up. He was drunk, slouched in his seat, a day's growth on his chin, his cravat untied and loose around his neck, his coat buttons undone. This was the man that Grace had chosen instead of me. The man who had given her nothing but pain, sorrow and death through his cruelty and neglect.

A surge of rage swept through me. I heard nothing except a ringing in my ears. I saw nothing except a kind of red-hued image of the man I hated.

I found myself in front of his horse, my hands on its bridle, bringing it to a halt and staring up at the eyes of my adversary.

'What the devil...!' he murmured, aroused out of his drunken stupor. I could smell the stench of stale brandy on his breath. 'Take your filthy hands off my mare, sir, and say who you are!'

I did not move, but I gave my name in a voice that I could barely keep steady.

'My name is William Days.'

'Days? Don't know an'one called Days. Now, step back before I horse-whip you.'

I held the horse steady, though she was obviously feeling nervous and was beginning to stamp and snort.

'I know you, sir,' I said, 'I know you and I know what you are. You killed your wife. You may as well have taken a knife and plunged it into her heart. It would have been an easier death than the one you gave her.'

He laughed. He threw back his head and laughed.

'Why, that little strumpet! She got no more than she deserved, sir! I knew as soon as I bedded the bitch, she had no heart for me.'

He leaned towards me, leaning against the mare's neck precariously, breathing his foul breath in my face.

'She was a whore, sir – or might's well've been. She was unfaithful; an adult'ress... well, in her mind at least. It was clear she thought of another when she lay with me. And an unfaithful wife is no better than a common whore...'

I grabbed his coat with my free hand. I wanted to kill him, but my intention was to drag him off his horse so we could stand equally, man to man, and have it out. I did not really care in that moment if he was armed. If he killed me, it did not matter; I would have welcomed it. In that moment, I cared nothing more than to get the chance to crush his skull with my fist.

But he came down too easily. He was already over-balanced due to his drunken state, and as I grabbed his sleeve, he just toppled further and slid forwards head first.

I heard his neck break as he hit the ground, and I knew he was dead. He lay at my feet and did not move again.

As my rage drained away and I realised what had happened, I instinctively looked around to see if there were any witnesses. I could be hanged for what I had just done, and despite my lack of concern for my own life moments earlier, the urge to survive took over. No-one was there. I was completely alone.

I looked towards the Hall and thought of Grace's two children, now orphans, and wondered what would become of them.

I wondered whether I should go to the Hall and tell them I had seen Sir Andrew fall off his horse. But I knew there might be questions raised. There might be an inquest. As the only witness I would be called upon.

The only person who knew I had been in the village that day was Sam the gardener, and I doubted that he would say anything that would raise suspicion.

It was best that I just left then and there. I would not go back into the village. I would take the road back to Clayford and back to the theatre, where no-one knew where I came from.

So that's what I did. And I did not return again for many years. And for two hundred years I have lived, knowing that I have blood on my hands, I am, in deed, a murderer, and this is the first time I have told anyone.

Chapter 19

Apart from the crackling of the fire and the gentle snoring of Charlie asleep in front of it, there was a long silence. The room was dark except for one small table lamp and the glow from the fire.

'I killed your ancestor,' he said, 'your great-great-great grandfather. Maybe not in cold blood, but with intent – in that moment I wanted him dead more than anything in the world. What do you think of me now?'

I watched the light of the fire dance on his skin, animating his face despite its stillness.

'You are not a murderer,' I said, 'what happened was more accident than design – and mostly his own fault. Besides, it just shows that you're human – despite the longevity. Very few of us can truly deny having murderous thoughts. I was a teacher for years, I should know.'

'Not everyone takes action, though. Not the civilized and the humane.'

'No – and if he hadn't been already drunk and off-balance, you wouldn't have killed him anyway. It may well have turned out the other way around.'

He stared into the fire.

'Perhaps.'

'Anyway,' I said, 'you were only protecting my memory and reputation.'

There was another silence. I wasn't sure whether he had noticed the pronoun, until his head moved slightly – quizzically – to one side.

'*Your* memory? You mean Grace's... hers.'

'Yes. I mean that. I also mean mine too.'

He looked straight at me then, as if he was wondering whether I had completely gone off the rails.

'What are you talking about?'

I put my empty glass down and uncurled myself so I could sit upright.

'I told you there was something I needed to tell you,' I said, 'it was earlier today that I realised. Something Maureen said, only it wasn't quite what she'd intended, but something clicked. It was like turning the focus on a camera. Everything had seemed blurred and fuzzy and then suddenly I could see everything clearly; it all made sense, in a way I would not have believed if I'd read it in a book, objectively. But everything that has happened just fits, completely, and once I saw that, I knew it was true.

'Ever since I came here, Will, I have had strange feelings about this village – but in particular, the manor house, this house and Alderton Hall. And I've had this strange thing about the front gate. I keep thinking it's locked and I'm shut out. Then there have been the dreams; horrible, stifling nightmares that wake me up terrified and sweating.

'I thought I was going mad. I've really been quite worried about my sanity.'

I looked at him. His expression gave nothing away, but he just continued to look at me with his calm, candid gaze.

'And then you came along, and even though everything you have said should be completely nutty and just confirm my insanity, instead it's the other way around. When I'm with you I feel completely one hundred percent sane and real, and all the fear and anxiety just goes away.

'Then, this afternoon, just when I thought you'd gone for good, I got it. I understood everything.'

I took a deep breath. My heart was pounding loudly in my ears. I did not know whether he was going to believe me.

'What I've realised is that everything that I've felt about these three places is a memory. These are places I have known before.'

Will said nothing, but I heard a slight catch in his breath.

'Let me tell you something about Grace,' I continued, 'something that you did not know.

'There was a reason why Grace did not look at you in church. She was afraid. Afraid of betraying you, and herself. Sir Andrew was a fiercely possessive man, and Grace was his possession. He already knew she did not love him, and suspected that her heart belonged to someone else, and he could not bear it. Not because he loved her but because he could not bear any man to already have what he could not possess. Just one look or glance at another man and he would – well, that man's life would not be safe, and she would also be in danger. By refusing to meet your eyes, she was protecting you.

'She had long since realised the mistake she had made. She had expected to have the same feelings as she had had with you when Sir Andrew kissed her for the first time; but instead his approaches left her cold. He was not gentle. He did not care about how she felt. His love-making was selfish, cruel and heartless, and on that first night she knew she had thrown away something rare that could never be repeated.

'When she was pregnant for the third time – the second having been lost early in its term – she realised that there was only one hope for her and her unborn child. You had promised to be there for her if she needed you...'

'Wait,' said Will, getting up from the armchair and pacing the floor. Charlie woke up and watched him, surprised by the sudden movement.

'How do you know all this?'

'Let me finish,' I said, 'what I'm about to tell you you might find difficult to hear, but I have to tell you, and then we'll talk about it.'

I could see he was already uncomfortable, but he perched back on the edge of the chair and prepared himself to listen. Charlie put his head down, sighed, and returned to his sleep.

'She decided to leave. She knew if she stayed with Sir Andrew he would destroy her, physically and mentally, and she feared for her unborn child. She also knew that by leaving she would ruin herself and her reputation, and she would be deserting her young son, but poverty and ruin, and the grief of leaving her living child seemed preferable to the loveless, empty life of slavery she was living.

'So one night when Sir Andrew was out gambling in Clayford, she threw on a cloak and crept out by a back door so no servants would see her, and walked across the fields to Little Dipping. It began to rain, but she did not care. She was free of Sir Andrew and of Alderton Hall. She only had to reach her destination and her life could begin again.

She arrived at the gates of your house in pouring rain. It was pitch black and there were no lights burning inside. The gate was shut and when she tried to open them she found them locked. She knew that you had gone. Despair overcame her and she collapsed, knowing that her life was over. All she could do was return to Alderton Hall. No-one else would take her in. She was married to Sir Andrew. She could not even return to the Manor House, bringing shame and dishonour on her parents, and there would be nothing they could do to stop him taking her back. She was his, legally.

So she went back. She covered her tracks as much as she could, but Sir Andrew discovered her sodden clothes and it was that very night that she fell downstairs and lost the third child.'

Will sat very still for a very long time. Then, in a very low voice, he said,

'And how do you know all this?'

'It's what I remember.'

'Remember? I'm not sure that I understand...'

'I've been having these dreams – as I told you – at least, they started off like dreams, but they became more real, like flashbacks of memory: a room at the end of a corridor; his room; a flight of stairs; rooms full of people I dare not look at. I didn't know what it all meant, but it all ties in with what you've said – and it is like a memory – not a dream. Like finding yourself in a place you've known before. That's how I felt the first time I saw the Manor House. I knew it, like something very familiar – as familiar as a childhood home – and yet I knew I'd never been there before. At least, not in this lifetime.'

He kept looking at me and then looking away. He was afraid to catch my eye. He rubbed his face with his hands.

'So... what exactly are you saying?'

'Well,' I said, speaking quite slowly, for I was not completely sure that I fully believed it myself, 'I think that somehow – and this is going to sound completely off the wall – somehow,

I seem to have Grace's memories. I think she found a way to return.'

Charlie sighed and stretched in his sleep. A log on the fire shifted, sending sparks up into the chimney. I sat very still, waiting for his response.

Will drew a long breath. Finally, he turned to meet my eyes.

'Who are you?' he asked.

I smiled.

'I am Catherine Burns. The person I've always been. But the person who was Grace Bailey is a part of me – just as she has been a part of every one of her descendants. But I think, this time, she is more present. In a way, she and I are more or less one person.'

Slowly, he got up and came to sit beside me. He took my hand and turned it over to look at my palm.

'The same hands,' he said, 'I saw it before.'

'Forgive me,' he said.

'What for?'

'I deserted you, when you needed me. I broke my promise.'

'I believe,' I replied, 'that it was Grace – I – who deserted you first. And it was an unfair promise I made you keep. There is nothing to forgive. I blame you for nothing. It was all my own doing. It is I who should be asking forgiveness.'

He shook his head.

'No. We were both young and foolish. We played the parts we had to play. And now you have returned.'

'That is what seems to have happened. I'm not quite sure how. I don't remember everything – and I don't particularly want to, but there's no doubt in my mind that she is somehow me and I am her. Funny feeling – like being two people at once, and yet knowing I am just one. The person I've always been.'

He stroked my hair with his other hand.

'Catherine Grace Bailey Burns,' he said, 'whoever you are, I do love you.'

Then he kissed me, and this time he did not hold his passion back. It was the kiss of one who has been starved of love for nearly two hundred years, forcefully yet lovingly giving, not taking, his arms around me, pressing me close.

When we finally moved apart, I was breathless, filled with an uncontrollable desire. Immediately I kissed him again, this time doing the giving, willing him to take my love, my hands in his hair, caressing his shoulders, inside his shirt.

I stopped, breathing heavily, and without speaking I stood up, took his hand and led him up the stairs to the room where he had been born, leaving Charlie sleeping unaware by the fire.

I awoke from a dreamless sleep to the smell of toast, bacon and coffee, and the sounds of Will moving about in the kitchen.

I got up, my limbs pleasantly aching from the love-making of the night before. I went downstairs and found him feeding the dog, a pile of toast on the table and eggs and bacon frying in a pan.

'Wow,' I said, 'you really are a star.'

'Good morning,' he said, 'I thought you might be hungry.'

'You thought correctly,' I replied, giving him a kiss. He returned it, but there was something distant and distracted about him. He did not meet my eyes. I felt a cold shiver of fear.

'What's the matter?'

He transferred the eggs and bacon onto plates and brought them to the table.

'Sit down,' he said.

I did, but my appetite was fading. I looked at him, my eyes

repeating my question.

'I've been thinking...'

'Bad idea.'

'No... wait.' He reached across the table and took my hand. 'I do love you.'

'There's a "but" coming isn't there?'

He continued to hold my hand, rubbing my fingers, concentrating on what he was going to say.

'Last night was probably – no, was – the best night of my entire life...'

I have to say I was impressed, given the number of nights he'd been on this planet.

'...but...'

I braced myself.

'...what we've discovered – about you and Grace – does it resolve anything?'

'What do you mean?'

'I'm still – likely to stay the way I am aren't I? I will continue to stay like this, while you...'

'Grow old. Die. Leave you behind. Is that what you mean?'

'Yes.'

I withdrew my hand and started buttering some toast. Men can be incredibly tiresome, I thought.

'You're not going to disappear again, are you Will?'

He didn't answer, but he looked like he was thinking about it.

'Oh, for goodness sake!' I said. I picked up my knife and fork. My appetite had suddenly returned. I felt calm and in control. I cut off a piece of crispy bacon and dipped it in the perfectly cooked egg.

'Do you think,' I said through a mouthful of food, 'do you

think I would really let you go again when you cook breakfast like this? I'd be quite mad.'

'Seriously, Catherine...'

'Seriously, Will, are you completely off your rocker? Here we are, after all this time, after all that suffering and loneliness and two hundred years of waiting – after all that, we've both been given a second chance. I don't know why, and I don't know how – perhaps there is a God after all, or perhaps Grace's spirit arranged it all, or perhaps it's just some power we don't understand, but for some reason, you have been given the chance to stay alive, to stay in touch with my ancestors – even to look after them and make sure the line continues – until we should meet again and Grace – or her essence or whatever – could return to that line with all of her genes and memories, so we could meet and continue where we left off. And you are now seriously considering whether we should go for it or not? Are you out of your mind? And am I going to let you out of my life again when you make coffee in a pot, and perfect fried eggs? I don't think so. So you can just jolly well stay put and pass me the marmalade.'

When I looked at him again as he handed me the jar, I saw he had tears in his eyes.

'You really are Grace, aren't you?'

'You'd better believe it.'

I bit into a golden brown slice of toast and grinned at him.

'I don't want to lose you,' he said.

'Then don't.'

'It might be difficult for you – in years to come.'

'Then let it. Bring it on. I'm ready for whatever happens.'

I took his hand.

'Will, we can talk ourselves out of anything if we want to.

Isn't that what we did before? Because of convention, because it didn't fit. Isn't that the kind of attitude you've been fighting all your life? The way people give up their abilities and beliefs? People give up on themselves, their careers, because of social niceties, rules or external events. Didn't my mother? Didn't Lizzie? Even Hannah, to an extent. But you've always said to me that all that external stuff is just an illusion – what's real is what's inside us. Isn't it the same with love? You have to stick with it, despite what might or might not happen. You have to go with what's true, and trust in it – otherwise, what's the point? Would you give up your music because one day you might not be able to play any more?'

'No, of course not.'

'Of course not. So don't give up on me, Will.'

It was there, in that moment, eye to eye, holding hands across the breakfast table, that he got it. He made the commitment and chose to trust. He nodded. There were no words, but we sat like that for some time, and I knew we were safe.

'More coffee?' he said eventually.

'I thought you'd never ask.'

Will stayed with me after that first night. He had taken his things out of storage – there wasn't much – and installed it in the cottage, and the Les Paul guitar now stood proudly in one corner of the living room.

He had even met my parents – a rather daunting experience for Will, but we kept up the pretence that he was the late Billy Days' son. All the same, my mother made the most classic double-take I have ever seen the first time she saw him.

'Billy...? But – my God – I'm sorry – Will – but you are the spitting image of your father, isn't he Jim?'

'Great Scott!' said my father, 'if I hadn't known it to be impossible – I'd have said it was Billy. Quite uncanny. Pleased to meet you, son. Very pleased indeed.'

It was Christmas morning when we noticed the change.

I awoke to a white light shining through the window. I got up and looked out onto frost-covered rooftops and trees. It looked exactly like a Christmas card.

I turned to look at Will, still asleep, lying on his back, his head slightly to one side. The clear, cold light made everything look crisp and sharp.

At first I thought I still had frost in my eyesight, but then it dawned on me.

'Will.'

He stirred, his eyes flickering open, then squinting against the light.

'Mmmmm? Hey you – Happy Christmas.'

'Happy Christmas to you, Will. You have a grey hair.'

It took just a second to enter his consciousness. Then he was up, struggling into his dressing gown and in front of my dressing table mirror in moments.

We sat together on the stool while he turned his head and touched the hair at his temples.

Our eyes met in the reflected image.

'You know what this means?' he said.

'Yes. It means you've been unfrozen. De-frosted – with a little light frosting.' I giggled. I felt slightly drunk.

'I must be the only person in the world who is overjoyed at finding my first grey hair.'

'So – you are mortal, after all.'

'I guess so.'

'You'll get wrinkles now.'

'I don't care.'

'Creaky knees. Stiff back. It's all downhill from here you know.'

'As long as it's not all in one go.'

'Ugh – I hadn't thought of that. You're not going to suddenly age 200 years are you? That I don't think I could handle...'

He laughed and put his arm round my shoulders.

'No – I think I'd know by now. Anyway, as long as you still love me when I'm old and wrinkled and creaky, I'll be happy for ever.'

'OK. It's a deal.'

EPILOGUE

Will continues to write and play music, and I continue to write novels. My first novel was not published. It was too raw, too un-disciplined. But I did not let that discourage me. I realised that all failures are learning exercises, the building blocks to success. I was going to be a published writer – for Hannah, for Anne, but most of all, for myself.

Fortunately, because Will now started to earn some serious money from his music, we were able to keep the house. Without fear of future questions, he was able to put his music on the market and he had a good success with a song he'd written which topped the charts with one of the UK's most popular singers.

On the day they demolished Alderton Hall, we went and watched, holding hands as the great edifice crumbled to the ground.

We celebrated by buying a piano, and Will taught me to play - a role reversal we both enjoyed. I'd like to say that I picked it up really quickly – but I guess I was out of practice.

Maureen and Peter became our closest friends, despite our age differences, and Will and I attended Maureen's first exhibition of drawings and bought one that she had made of the village with the church and Manor House.

So we write, play music and go for long walks with Charlie, and sit by the fire and eat good food. I suppose it sounds too good to be true – but we've waited a long time for this, and we deserve it. That goes for Charlie too – after his bad start in life, he'd found happiness with us.

We'd all of us finally come home.

About the Author

Rosamunde Bott is the author of several historical and semi-historical novels, often with the theme of family history, and including an element of mystery or fantasy. She has also written a children's fantasy adventure novel. You can find out more about Rosamunde and her writing at her website below. You can also contact her at info@rosamundebott.com.

Rosamunde is also a professional genealogist, and has provided ancestry tracing services for many years. Her genealogy website is also below.

You can connect with me on:

- http://www.rosamundebott.com
- http://www.tracingancestors-uk.com

Also by Rosamunde Bott

Isobel Brite

(Historical Novel)

When the travelling theatre company comes to town, young shoemaker's daughter, Isobel Brite, is entranced by the idea of a life on the stage, and also by the very handsome and charming lead actor, Frank Douglas. Life as an actress in the 1840s brings freedom and independence, but it is also full of challenges, and she will find that the line between fame and obscurity is a fragile one.

Legacies

(Semi-historical Novel)

(Out in 2019 - Please check my website for details)

Out of work actress, Sarah Turvey, is mystified when her uncle leaves her the family tree and an old box as an inheritance. Inside the box are some papers and an old key, which will take her on a journey through her ancestry, with the help of her friends, and some very odd dreams. But why is her cousin David so interested, and how far will he go to benefit from the family legacy?

The Light of Drombar

(Children's Novel)

Transported by a magic stone to the land of Drombar, four children find themselves on a quest to save its people from the darkness that is creeping over the land. They must travel to the most dangerous place of all - the source of the darkness and the evil Lord Saedor - and restore the light.

Tracing Your Ancestors in the UK

(Non-fiction)

Would you like to trace your UK ancestors, but have no idea how or where to start? My step-by-step process will enable you to trace your ancestors using professional techniques and the most important sources in genealogy. It will also help you to avoid many of the pitfalls that the amateur genealogist often falls into.

Printed in Great Britain
by Amazon

32867496R00158